Dashiell Hammett (1894–1961) was born in St Mary's County, Maryland. After spells at various menial jobs, he became an operative for Pinkerton's National Detective Agency. The First World War, in which he served stateside, interrupted his sleuthing and injured his health, but his experiences as a private detective had laid the foundation for his writing career. In the late 1920s he became the unquestioned master of detective fiction in America, with work including *Red Harvest* (1929), *The Glass Key* (1930), *The Thin Man* (1934) and some eighty short stories, mostly published in *Black Mask* magazine. He died in 1961.

By Dashiell Hammett

NOVELS

Red Harvest
The Glass Key
The Thin Man
The Dain Curse
The Maltese Falcon

SHORT STORIES

The Big Knockover
The Continental Op
Nightmare Town

THE GLASS KEY
DASHIELL HAMMETT

An Orion paperback

First published in Great Britain in 1931
by Alfred A. Knopf, Inc.
This paperback edition published in 2002
by Orion Books Ltd,
Orion House, 5 Upper St Martin's Lane,
London WC2H 9EA

An Hachette UK company

3 5 7 9 10 8 6 4 2

Reissued 2012

A CIP catalogue record for this book
is available from the British Library.

ISBN 978-1-4091-3804-4

Typeset at The Spartan Press Ltd,
Lymington, Hants

Printed and bound in Great Britain
by Clays Ltd, St Ives plc

The Orion Publishing Group's policy is to use papers
that are natural, renewable and recyclable products and
made from wood grown in sustainable forests. The logging
and manufacturing processes are expected to conform to
the environmental regulations of the country of origin.

www.orionbooks.co.uk

To Nell Martin

The Glass Key

1 The Body in China Street

Green dice rolled across the green table, struck the rim together, and bounced back. One stopped short holding six white spots in two equal rows uppermost. The other tumbled out to the center of the table and came to rest with a single spot on top.

Ned Beaumont grunted softly – 'Uhn!' – and the winners cleared the table of money.

Harry Sloss picked up the dice and rattled them in a pale broad hairy hand. 'Shoot two bits.' He dropped a twenty-dollar bill and a five-dollar bill on the table.

Ned Beaumont stepped back saying: 'Get on him, gamblers, I've got to refuel!' He crossed the billiard-room to the door. There he met Walter Ivans coming in. He said, ' 'Lo, Walt,' and would have gone on, but Ivans caught his elbow as he passed and turned to face him.

'D-d-did you t-talk to P-p-paul?' When Ivans said 'P-p-paul' a fine spray flew out between his lips.

'I'm going up to see him now.' Ivans's china-blue eyes brightened in his round fair face until Ned Beaumont, narrow of eye, added: 'Don't expect much. If you could wait awhile.'

Ivans's chin twitched. 'B-b-but she's going to have the b-b-baby next month.'

A startled look came into Ned Beaumont's dark eyes. He took his arm out of the shorter man's hand and stepped back. Then a corner of his mouth twitched under his dark mustache and he said: 'It's a bad time, Walt, and – well – you'll save yourself disappointment by not looking for much before November.' His eyes were narrow again and watchful.

'B-b-but if you t-tell him—'

'I'll put it to him as hot as I can and you ought to know he'll go the limit, but he's in a tough spot right now.' He moved his shoulders and his face became gloomy except for the watchful brightness of his eye.

Ivans wet his lips and blinked his eyes many times. He drew in a long breath and patted Ned Beaumont's chest with both hands. 'G-g-go up now,' he said in an urgent pleading voice. 'I-I'll wait here f-for you.'

II

Ned Beaumont went upstairs lighting a thin green-dappled cigar. At the second-floor landing, where the Governor's portrait hung, he turned towards the front of the building and knocked on the broad oaken door that shut off the corridor at that end.

When he heard Paul Madvig's 'All right' he opened the door and went in.

Paul Madvig was alone in the room, standing at the window, with his hands in his trousers-pockets, his back to the door, looking through the screen down into dark China Street.

He turned around slowly and said: 'Oh, here you are.' He was a man of forty-five, tall as Ned Beaumont, but forty pounds heavier without softness. His hair was light, parted in the middle, and brushed flat to his head. His face was handsome in a ruddy stout-featured way. His clothes were saved from flashiness by their quality and by his manner of wearing them.

Ned Beaumont shut the door and said: 'Lend me some money.'

From his inner coat-pocket Madvig took a large brown wallet. 'What do you want?'

'Couple of hundred.'

Madvig gave him a hundred-dollar bill and five twenties, asking: 'Craps?'

'Thanks.' Ned Beaumont pocketed the money. 'Yes.'

'It's a long time since you've done any winning, isn't it?' Madvig asked as he returned his hands to his trousers-pockets.

'Not so long – a month or six weeks.'

Madvig smiled. 'That's a long time to be losing.'

'Not for me.' There was a faint note of irritation in Ned Beaumont's voice.

Madvig rattled coins in his pocket. 'Much of a game tonight?' He sat on a corner of the table and looked down at his glistening brown shoes.

Ned Beaumont looked curiously at the blond man, then shook his head and said: 'Peewee.' He walked to the window. Above the buildings on the opposite side of the street the sky was black and heavy. He went behind Madvig to the telephone and called a number. 'Hello, Bernie. This is Ned. What's the price on Peggy O'Toole? Is that all? . . . Well, give me five hundred of each . . . Sure . . . I'm betting it's going to rain and if it does she'll beat Incinerator . . . All right, give me a better price then . . . Right.' He put the receiver on its prong and came around in front of Madvig again.

Madvig asked: 'Why don't you try laying off awhile when you hit one of these sour streaks?'

Ned Beaumont scowled. 'That's no good, only spreads it out. I ought to've put that fifteen hundred on the nose instead of spreading it across the board. Might as well take your punishment and get it over with.'

Madvig chuckled and raised his head to say: 'If you can stand the gaff.'

Ned Beaumont drew down the ends of his mouth, the ends of his mustache following them down. 'I can stand anything I've got to stand,' he said as he moved towards the door.

He had his hand on the door-knob when Madvig said, earnestly: 'I guess you can, at that, Ned.'

Ned Beaumont turned around and asked, 'Can what?' fretfully.

Madvig transferred his gaze to the window. 'Can stand anything,' he said.

Ned Beaumont studied Madvig's averted face. The blond man stirred uncomfortably and moved coins in his pockets again. Ned Beaumont made his eyes blank and asked in an utterly puzzled tone: 'Who?'

Madvig's face flushed. He rose from the table and took a step towards Ned Beaumont. 'You go to hell,' he said.

Ned Beaumont laughed.

Madvig grinned sheepishly and wiped his face with a green-bordered handkerchief. 'Why haven't you been out to the house?' he asked. 'Mom was saying last night she hadn't seen you for a month.'

'Maybe I'll drop in some night this week.'

'You ought to. You know how Mom likes you. Come for supper.' Madvig put his handkerchief away.

Ned Beaumont moved towards the door again, slowly, watching the blond man from the ends of his eyes. With his hand on the knob he asked: 'Was that what you wanted to see me about?'

Madvig frowned. 'Yes, that is—' He cleared his throat. 'Uh – oh – there's something else.' Suddenly his diffidence was gone, leaving him apparently tranquil and self-possessed. 'You know more about this stuff than I do. Miss Henry's birthday's Thursday. What do you think I ought to give her?'

Ned Beaumont took his hand from the door-knob. His eyes, by the time he was facing Madvig squarely again, had lost their shocked look. He blew cigar-smoke out and asked: 'They're having some kind of birthday doings, aren't they?'

'Yes.'

'You invited?'

Madvig shook his head. 'But I'm going there to dinner tomorrow night.'

Ned Beaumont looked down at his cigar, then up at Madvig's face again, and asked: 'Are you going to back the Senator, Paul?'

'I think we will.'

Ned Beaumont's smile was mild as his voice when he put his next question: 'Why?'

Madvig smiled. 'Because with us behind him he'll snow Roan under and with his help we can put over the whole ticket just like nobody was running against us.'

Ned Beaumont put his cigar in his mouth. He asked, still mildly: 'Without you' – he stressed the pronoun – 'behind him could the Senator make the grade this time?'

Madvig was calmly positive. 'Not a chance.'

Ned Beaumont, after a little pause, asked: 'Does he know that?'

'He ought to know it better than anybody else. And if he didn't know it— What the hell's the matter with you?'

Ned Beaumont's laugh was a sneer. 'If he didn't know it,' he suggested, 'you wouldn't be going there to dinner tomorrow night?'

Madvig, frowning, asked again: 'What the hell's the matter with you?'

Ned Beaumont took the cigar from his mouth. His teeth had bitten the end of it into shredded ruin. He said: 'There's nothing the matter with me.' He put thoughtfulness on his face: 'You don't think the rest of the ticket needs his support?'

5

'Support's something no ticket can get too much of,' Madvig replied carelessly, 'but without his help we could manage to hold up our end all right.'

'Have you promised him anything yet?'

Madvig pursed his lips. 'It's pretty well settled.'

Ned Beaumont lowered his head until he was looking up under his brows at the blond man. His face had become pale. 'Throw him down, Paul,' he said in a low husky voice. 'Sink him.'

Madvig put his fists on his hips and exclaimed softly and incredulously: 'Well, I'll be damned!'

Ned Beaumont walked past Madvig and with unsteady thin fingers mashed the burning end of his cigar in the hammered copper basin on the table.

Madvig stared at the younger man's back until he straightened and turned. Then the blond man grinned at him with affection and exasperation. 'What gets into you, Ned?' he complained. 'You go along fine for just so long and then for no reason at all you throw an ing-bing. I'll be a dirty so-and-so if I can make you out!'

Ned Beaumont made a grimace of distaste. He said, 'All right, forget it,' and immediately returned to the attack with a skeptical question: 'Do you think he'll play ball with you after he's re-elected?'

Madvig was not worried. 'I can handle him.'

'Maybe, but don't forget he's never been licked at anything in his life.'

Madvig nodded in complete agreement. 'Sure, and that's one of the best reasons I know for throwing in with him.'

'No, it isn't, Paul,' Ned Beaumont said earnestly. 'It's the very worst. Think that over even if it hurts your head. How far has this dizzy blond daughter of his got her hooks into you?'

Madvig said: 'I'm going to marry Miss Henry.'

Ned Beaumont made a whistling mouth, though he did not whistle. He made his eyes smaller and asked: 'Is that part of the bargain?'

Madvig grinned boyishly. 'Nobody knows it yet,' he replied, 'except you and me.'

Spots of color appeared in Ned Beaumont's lean cheeks. He smiled his nicest smile and said: 'You can trust me not to go around bragging about it and here's a piece of advice. If that's what you want, make them put it in writing and swear to it before a notary and post a cash bond, or, better still, insist on the wedding before election-day. Then you'll at least be sure of your pound of flesh, or she'll weigh around a hundred and ten, won't she?'

Madvig shifted his feet. He avoided Ned Beaumont's gaze while saying: 'I don't know why you keep talking about the Senator like he was a yegg. He's a gentleman and—'

'Absolutely. Read about it in the *Post* – one of the few aristocrats left in American politics. And his daughter's an aristocrat. That's why I'm warning you to sew your shirt on when you go to see them, or you'll come away without it, because to them you're a lower form of animal life and none of the rules apply.'

Madvig sighed and began: 'Aw, Ned, don't be so damned—'

But Ned Beaumont had remembered something. His eyes were shiny with malice. He said: 'And we oughtn't to forget that young Taylor Henry's an aristocrat too, which is probably why you made Opal stop playing around with him. How's that going to work out when you marry his sister and he's your daughter's uncle-in-law or something? Will that entitle him to begin playing around with her again?'

Madvig yawned. 'You didn't understand me right, Ned,' he said. 'I didn't ask for all this. I just asked you what kind of present I ought to give Miss Henry.'

Ned Beaumont's face lost its animation, became a slightly sullen mask. 'How far have you got with her?' he asked in a voice that expressed nothing of what he might have been thinking.

'Nowhere. I've been there maybe half a dozen times to talk to the Senator. Sometimes I see her and sometimes I don't, but only to say "How do you do" or something with other people around. You know, I haven't had a chance to say anything to her yet.'

Amusement glinted for a moment in Ned Beaumont's eyes and vanished. He brushed back one side of his mustache with a thumb-nail and asked: 'Tomorrow's your first dinner there?'

'Yes, though I don't expect it to be the last.'

'And you didn't get a bid to the birthday party?'

'No.' Madvig hesitated. 'Not yet.'

'Then the answer's one you won't like.'

Madvig's face was impassive. 'Such as?' he asked.

'Don't give her anything.'

'Oh, hell, Ned!'

Ned Beaumont shrugged. 'Do whatever you like. You asked me.'

'But why?'

'You're not supposed to give people things unless you're sure they'd like to get them from you.'

'But everybody likes to—'

'Maybe, but it goes deeper than that. When you give somebody something, you're saying out loud that you know they'd like to have you give—'

'I got you,' Madvig said. He rubbed his chin with fingers of his right hand. He frowned and said: 'I guess you're right.' His face cleared. He said: 'But I'll be damned if I'll pass up the chance.'

Ned Beaumont said quickly: 'Well, flowers then, or something like that, might be all right.'

'Flowers? Jesus! I wanted—'

'Sure, you wanted to give her a roadster or a couple of yards of pearls. You'll get your chance at that later. Start little and grow.'

Madvig made a wry face. 'I guess you're right, Ned. You know more about this kind of stuff than I do. Flowers it is.'

'And not too many of them.' Then, in the same breath: 'Walt Ivans's telling the world you ought to spring his brother.'

Madvig pulled the bottom of his vest down. 'The world can tell him Tim's going to stay indoors till after election.'

'You're going to let him stand trial?'

'I am,' Madvig replied, and added with more heat: 'You know damned well I can't help it, Ned. With everybody up for re-election and the women's clubs on the warpath it would be jumping in the lake to have Tim's case squared now.'

Ned Beaumont grinned crookedly at the blond man and made his voice drawl. 'We didn't have to do much worrying about women's clubs before we joined the aristocracy.'

'We do now.' Madvig's eyes were opaque.

'Tim's wife's going to have a baby next month,' Ned Beaumont said.

Madvig blew breath out in an impatient gust. 'Anything to make it tougher,' he complained. 'Why don't they think of those things before they get in trouble? They've got no brains, none of them.'

'They've got votes.'

'That's the hell of it,' Madvig growled. He glowered at the floor for a moment, then raised his head. 'We'll take care of him as soon as the votes are counted, but nothing doing till then.'

'That's not going over big with the boys,' Ned Beaumont said, looking obliquely at the blond man. 'Brains or no brains, they're used to being taken care of.'

Madvig thrust his chin out a little. His eyes, round and opaquely blue, were fixed on Ned Beaumont's. In a soft voice he asked: 'Well?'

Ned Beaumont smiled and kept his voice matter-of-fact. 'You know it won't take a lot of this to start them saying it was different in the old days before you put in with the Senator.'

'Yes?'

Ned Beaumont stood his ground with no change in voice or smile. 'You know how little of this can start them saying Shad O'Rory still takes care of his boys.'

Madvig, who had listened with an air of complete attentiveness, now said in a very deliberately quiet voice: 'I know you won't start them talking like that, Ned, and I know I can count on you to do your best to stop any of that kind of talk you happen to hear.'

For a moment after that they stood silent, looking eye into eye, and there was no change in the face of either. Ned Beaumont ended the silence. He said: 'It might help some if we took care of Tim's wife and the kid.'

'That's the idea.' Madvig drew his chin back and his eyes lost their opaqueness. 'Look after it, will you? Give them everything.'

III

Walter Ivans was waiting for Ned Beaumont at the foot of the stairs, bright-eyed and hopeful. 'Wh-what did he s-say?'

'It's what I told you: no can do. After election Tim's to have anything he needs to get out, but nothing stirring till then.'

Walter Ivans hung his head and made a low growling noise in his chest.

Ned Beaumont put a hand on the shorter man's shoulder and said: 'It's a tough break and nobody knows it better than Paul, but he can't help himself. He wants you to tell her not to pay any bills. Send them to him – rent, grocer, doctor, and hospital.'

Walter Ivans jerked his head up and caught Ned Beaumont's hand in both of his. 'B-by G-god that's white of him!' The china-blue eyes were wet. 'B-b-but I wish he could g-get Tim out.'

Ned Beaumont said, 'Well, there's always a chance that something will come up to let him,' freed his hand, said, 'I'll be seeing you,' and went around Ivans to the billiard-room door.

The billiard-room was deserted.

He got his hat and coat and went to the front door. Long oyster-colored lines of rain slanted down into China Street. He smiled and addressed the rain under his breath: 'Come down, you little darlings, thirty-two hundred and fifty dollars' worth of you.'

He went back and called a taxicab.

IV

Ned Beaumont took his hands away from the dead man and stood up. The dead man's head rolled a little to the left, away from the kerb, so that his face lay fully in the light from the corner street-lamp. It was a young face and its expression of anger was increased by the dark ridge that ran diagonally across the forehead from the edge of the curly fair hair to an eyebrow.

Ned Beaumont looked up and down China Street. As far up the street as the eye could see no person was there. Two blocks down the street, in front of the Log Cabin Club, two men were getting out of an automobile. They left the automobile standing in front of the Club, facing Ned Beaumont, and went into the Club.

Ned Beaumont, after staring down at the automobile for several seconds, suddenly twisted his head around to look up the street again and then, with a swiftness that made both movements one continuous movement, whirled and sprang upon the sidewalk in the shadow of the nearest tree. He was breathing through his mouth and though tiny points of sweat had glistened on his hands in the light he shivered now and turned up the collar of his overcoat.

He remained in the tree's shadow with one hand on the tree for perhaps half a minute. Then he straightened abruptly and began to walk towards the Log Cabin Club. He walked with increasing swiftness, leaning forward, and was moving at some-thing more than a half-trot when he spied a man coming up the other side of the street. He immediately slackened his pace and made himself walk erect. The man entered a house before he came opposite Ned Beaumont.

By the time Ned Beaumont reached the Club he had stopped breathing through his mouth. His lips were still somewhat faded. He looked at the empty automobile without pausing, climbed the Club's steps between the two lanterns, and went indoors.

Harry Sloss and another man were crossing the foyer from the cloak-room. They halted and said together: 'Hello, Ned.' Sloss added: 'I hear you had Peggy O'Toole today.'

'Yes.'

'For much?'

'Thirty-two hundred.'

Sloss ran his tongue over his lower lip. 'That's nice. You ought to be set for a game tonight.'

'Later, maybe. Paul in?'

'I don't know. We just got in. Don't make it too late: I promised the girl I'd be home early.'

Ned Beaumont said, 'Right,' and went over to the cloak-room. 'Paul in?' he asked the attendant.

'Yes, about ten minutes ago.'

Ned Beaumont looked at his wrist-watch. It was half past ten. He went up to the front second-story room. Madvig in dinner clothes was sitting at the table with a hand stretched out towards the telephone when Ned Beaumont came in.

Madvig withdrew his hand and said: 'How are you, Ned?' His large handsome face was ruddy and placid.

Ned Beaumont said, 'I've been worse,' while shutting the door behind him. He sat on a chair not far from Madvig's. 'How'd the Henry dinner go?'

The skin at the corners of Madvig's eyes crinkled. 'I've been at worse,' he said.

Ned Beaumont was clipping the end of a pale spotted cigar. The shakiness of his hands was incongruous with the steadiness of his voice asking: 'Was Taylor there?' He looked up at Madvig without raising his head.

'Not for dinner. Why?'

Ned Beaumont stretched out crossed legs, leaned back in his chair, moved the hand holding his cigar in a careless arc, and said: 'He's dead in a gutter up the street.'

Madvig, unruffled, asked: 'Is that so?'

Ned Beaumont leaned forward. Muscles tightened in his lean face. The wrapper of his cigar broke between his fingers with a thin crackling sound. He asked irritably: 'Did you understood what I said?'

Madvig nodded slowly.

'Well?'

'Well what?'

'He was killed.'

'All right,' Madvig said. 'Do you want me to get hysterical about it?'

Ned Beaumont sat up straight in his chair and asked: 'Shall I call the police?'

Madvig raised his eyebrows a little. 'Don't they know it?'

Ned Beaumont was looking steadily at the blond man. He replied: 'There was nobody around when I saw him. I wanted to see you before I did anything. Is it all right for me to say I found him?'

Madvig's eyebrows came down. 'Why not?' he asked blankly.

Ned Beaumont rose, took two steps towards the telephone, halted, and faced the blond man again. He spoke with slow emphasis: 'His hat wasn't there.'

'He won't need it now.' Then Madvig scowled and said: 'You're a God-damned fool, Ned.'

Ned Beaumont said, 'One of us is,' and went to the telephone.

TAYLOR HENRY MURDERED
BODY OF SENATOR'S SON FOUND
IN CHINA STREET

Believed to have been the victim of a hold-up, Taylor Henry, 26, son of Senator Ralph Bancroft Henry, was found dead in China Street near the corner of Pamela Avenue at a few minutes after 10 o'clock last night.

Coroner William J. Hoops stated that young Henry's death was due to a fracture of the skull and concussion of the brain caused by hitting the back of his head against the edge of the kerb after having been knocked down by a blow from a blackjack or other blunt instrument on his forehead.

The body is believed to have been first discovered by Ned Beaumont, 914 Randall Avenue, who went to the Log Cabin Club, two blocks away, to telephone the police; but before he had succeeded in getting Police Headquarters on the wire, the body had been found and reported by patrolman Michael Smitt.

Chief of Police Frederick M. Rainey immediately ordered a wholesale round-up of all suspicious characters in the city and issued a statement to the effect that no stone will be left unturned in his effort to apprehend the murderer or murderers at once.

Members of Taylor Henry's family stated that he left his home on Charles Street at about half past nine o'clock to . . .

Ned Beaumont put the newspaper aside, swallowed the coffee that remained in his cup, put cup and saucer on the table beside his bed, and leaned back against the pillows. His face was tired and sallow. He pulled the covers up to his neck, clasped his hands together behind his head, and stared with dissatisfied eyes at the etching that hung between his bedroom-windows.

For half an hour he lay there with only his eyelids moving.

Then he picked up the newspaper and reread the story. As he read, dissatisfaction spread from his eyes to all his face. He put the paper aside again, got out of bed, slowly, wearily, wrapped his lean white-pajamaed body in a small-figured brown and black kimono, thrust his feet into brown slippers, and, coughing a little, went into his living-room.

It was a large room in the old manner, high of ceiling and wide of window, with a tremendous mirror over the fireplace and much red plush on the furnishings. He took a cigar from a box on the table and sat in a wide red chair. His feet rested in a parallelogram of late morning sun and the smoke he blew out became suddenly full-bodied as it drifted into the sunlight. He frowned now and chewed a finger-nail when the cigar was not in his mouth.

Knocking sounded on his door. He sat up straight, keen of eye and alert. 'Come in.'

A white-jacketed waiter came in.

Ned Beaumont said, 'Oh, all right,' in a disappointed tone and relaxed again against the red plush of his chair.

The waiter passed through to the bedroom, came out with a tray of dishes, and went away. Ned Beaumont threw what was left of his cigar into the fireplace and went into his bathroom. By the time he had shaved, bathed, and dressed, his face had lost its sallowness, his carriage most of its weariness.

VI

It was not quite noon when Ned Beaumont left his rooms and walked eight blocks to a pale grey apartment-building in Link Street. He pressed a button in the vestibule, entered the building when the door-lock clicked, and rode to the sixth floor in a small automatic elevator.

He pressed the bell-button set in the frame of a door marked

611. The door was opened immediately by a diminutive girl who could have been only a few months out of her teens. Her eyes were dark and angry, her face white, except around her eyes, and angry. She said, 'Oh, hello,' and with a smile and a vaguely placatory motion of one hand apologized for her anger. Her voice had a metallic thinness. She wore a brown fur coat, but not a hat. Her short-cut hair – it was nearly black – lay smooth and shiny as enamel on her round head. The gold-set stones pendent from her ear-lobes were carnelian. She stepped back pulling the door back with her.

Ned Beaumont advanced through the doorway asking: 'Bernie up yet?'

Anger burned in her face again. She said in a shrill voice: 'The crummy bastard!'

Ned Beaumont shut the door behind him without turning around.

The girl came close to him, grasped his arms above the elbows, and tried to shake him. 'You know what I did for that bum?' she demanded. 'I left the best home any girl ever had and a mother and father that thought I was the original Miss Jesus. They told me he was no good. Everybody told me that and they were right and I was too dumb to know it. Well, I hope to tell you I know it now, the . . .' The rest was shrill obscenity.

Ned Beaumont, motionless, listened gravely. His eyes were not a well man's now. He asked, when breathlessness had stopped her words for the moment: 'What's he done?'

'Done? He's taken a run-out on me, the . . .' The rest of that sentence was obscenity.

Ned Beaumont flinched. The smile into which he pushed his lips was watery. He asked: 'I don't suppose he left anything for me?'

The girl clicked her teeth together and pushed her face nearer his. Her eyes widened. 'Does he owe you anything?'

'I won—' He coughed. 'I'm supposed to have won thirty-two hundred and fifty bucks on the fourth race yesterday.'

She took her hands from his arms and laughed scornfully. 'Try and get it. Look.' She held out her hands. A carnelian ring was on the little finger of her left hand. She raised her hands and touched her carnelian ear-rings. 'That's every stinking piece of my jewelry he left me and he wouldn't've left me that if I hadn't had them on.'

Ned Beaumont asked, in a queer detached voice: 'When did this happen?'

'Last night, though I didn't find it out till this morning, but don't think I'm not going to make Mr Son-of-a-bitch wish to God he'd never seen me.' She put a hand inside her dress and brought it out a fist. She held the fist up close to Ned Beaumont's face and opened it. Three small crumpled pieces of paper lay in her hand. When he reached for them she closed her fingers over them again, stepping back and snatching her hand away.

He moved the corners of his mouth impatiently and let his hand fall down at his side.

She said excitedly: 'Did you see the paper this morning about Taylor Henry?'

Ned Beaumont's reply, 'Yes,' was calm enough, but his chest moved out and in with a quick breath.

'Do you know what these are?' She held the three crumpled bits of paper out in her open hand once more.

Ned Beaumont shook his head. His eyes were narrow, shiny.

'They're Taylor Henry's I O Us,' she said triumphantly, 'twelve hundred dollars' worth of them.'

Ned Beaumont started to say something, checked himself, and when he spoke his voice was lifeless. 'They're not worth a nickel now he's dead.'

She thrust them inside her dress again and came close to Ned Beaumont. 'Listen,' she said: 'they never were worth a nickel and that's why he's dead.'

'Is that a guess?'

'It's any damned thing you want to call it,' she told him. 'But let me tell you something: Bernie called Taylor up last Friday and told him he'd give him just three days to come across.'

Ned Beaumont brushed a side of his mustache with a thumb-nail. 'You're not just being mad, are you?' he asked cautiously.

She made an angry face. 'Of course I'm mad,' she said 'I'm just mad enough to take them to the police and that's what I'm going to do. But if you think it didn't happen you're just a plain damned fool.'

He seemed still unconvinced. 'Where'd you get them?'

'Out of the safe.' She gestured with her sleek head towards the interior of the apartment.

He asked: 'What time last night did he blow?'

'I don't know. I got home at half past nine and sat around most of the night expecting him. It wasn't till morning that I began to suspect something and looked around and saw he'd cleaned house of every nickel in money and every piece of my jewelry that I wasn't wearing.'

He brushed his mustache with his thumb-nail again and asked: 'Where do you think he'd go?'

She stamped her foot and, shaking both fists up and down, began to curse the missing Bernie again in a shrill enraged voice.

Ned Beaumont said: 'Stop it.' He caught her wrists and held them still. He said: 'If you're not going to do anything about it but yell, give me those markers and I'll do something about it.'

She tore her wrists out of his hands, crying: 'I'll give you nothing. I'll give them to the police and not to another damned soul.'

'All right, then do it. Where do you think he'd go, Lee?'

Lee said bitterly that she didn't know where he would go, but she knew where she would like to have him go.

Ned Beaumont said wearily: 'That's the stuff. Wise-cracking is going to do us a lot of good. Think he'd go back to New York?'

'How do I know?' Her eyes had suddenly become wary.

Annoyance brought spots of color into Ned Beaumont's cheeks. 'What are you up to now?' he asked suspiciously.

Her face was an innocent mask. 'Nothing. What do you mean?'

He leaned down towards her. He spoke with considerable earnestness, shaking his head slowly from side to side with his words. 'Don't think you're not going to the police with them, Lee, because you are.'

She said: 'Of course I am.'

VII

In the drug-store that occupied part of the ground-floor of the apartment-building Ned Beaumont used a telephone. He called the Police Department's number, asked for Lieutenant Doolan, and said: 'Hello. Lieutenant Doolan? . . . I'm speaking for Miss Lee Wilshire. She's in Bernie Despain's apartment at 1666 Link Street. He seems to have suddenly disappeared last night, leaving some of Taylor Henry's I O Us behind him . . . That's right, and she says she heard him threaten him a couple of days ago . . . Yes, and she wants to see you as soon as possible . . . No, you'd better come up or send and as soon as you can . . . Yes . . . That doesn't make any difference. You don't know me. I'm just speaking for her because she didn't want to phone from his apartment . . .' He listened a moment longer, then, without having said anything else, put the receiver on its prong and went out of the drug-store.

VIII

Ned Beaumont went to a neat red-brick house in a row of neat red-brick houses in upper Thames Street. The door was opened to his ring by a young Negress who smiled with her whole brown face, said, 'How do you do, Mr Beaumont?' and made the opening of the door a hearty invitation.

Ned Beaumont said: ''Lo, June. Anybody home?'

'Yes, sir, they still at the dinner-table.'

He walked back to the dining-room where Paul Madvig and his mother sat facing one another across a red-and-white-clothed table. There was a third chair at the table, but it was not occupied and the plate and silver in front of it had not been used.

Paul Madvig's mother was a tall gaunt woman whose blondness had been faded not quite white by her seventy-some years. Her eyes were as blue and clear and young as her son's – younger than her son's when she looked up at Ned Beaumont entering the room. She deepened the lines in her forehead, however, and said: 'So here you are at last. You're a worthless boy to neglect an old woman like this.'

Ned Beaumont grinned impudently at her and said: 'Aw, Mom, I'm a big boy now and I've got my work to look after.' He flirted a hand at Madvig. ''Lo, Paul.'

Madvig said: 'Sit down and June'll scrape you up something to eat.'

Ned Beaumont was bending to kiss the scrawny hand Mrs Madvig had held out to him. She jerked it away and scolded him: 'Wherever did you learn such tricks?'

'I told you I was getting to be a big boy now.' He addressed Madvig: 'Thanks, I'm only a few minutes past breakfast.' He looked at the vacant chair. 'Where's Opal?'

Mrs Madvig replied: 'She's laying down. She's not feeling good.'

Ned Beaumont nodded, waited a moment, and asked politely: 'Nothing serious?' He was looking at Madvig.

Madvig shook his head. 'Headache or something. I think the kid dances too much.'

Mrs Madvig said: 'You certainly are a fine father not to know when your daughter has headaches.'

Skin crinkled around Madvig's eyes. 'Now, Mom, don't be

indecent,' he said and turned to Ned Beaumont. 'What's the good word?'

Ned Beaumont went around Mrs Madvig to the vacant chair. He sat down and said: 'Bernie Despain blew town last night with my winnings on Peggy O' Toole.'

The blond man opened his eyes.

Ned Beaumont said: 'He left behind him twelve hundred dollars' worth of Taylor Henry's I O Us.'

The blond man's eyes jerked narrow.

Ned Beaumont said: 'Lee says he called Taylor Friday and gave him three days to make good.'

Madvig touched his chin with the back of a hand. 'Who's Lee?'

'Bernie's girl.'

'Oh.' Then, when Ned Beaumont said nothing, Madvig asked: 'What'd he say he was going to do about it if Taylor didn't come across?'

'I didn't hear.' Ned Beaumont put a forearm on the table and leaned over it towards the blond man. 'Have me made a deputy sheriff or something, Paul.'

'For Christ's sake!' Madvig exclaimed, blinking. 'What do you want anything like that for?'

'It'll make it easier for me. I'm going after this guy and having a buzzer may keep me from getting in a jam.'

Madvig looked through worried eyes at the younger man. 'What's got you all steamed up?' he asked slowly.

'Thirty-two hundred and fifty dollars.'

'That's all right,' Madvig said, still speaking slowly, 'but something was itching you last night before you knew you'd been welshed on.'

Ned Beaumont moved an impatient arm. 'Do you expect me to stumble over corpses without batting an eye?' he asked. 'But forget that. That doesn't count now. This does. I've got to get this guy. I've got to.' His face was pale, set hard, and his voice was desperately earnest. 'Listen, Paul: it's not only the money, though thirty-two hundred is a lot, but it would be the same if it was five bucks. I go two months without winning a bet and that gets me down. What good am I if my luck's gone? Then I cop, or think I do, and I'm all right again. I can take my tail out from between my legs and feel that I'm a person again and not just something that's being kicked around. The money's important enough, but it's not the real thing. It's what losing and losing and losing does to me. Can you get that? It's getting me licked. And then, when I think I've worn out the jinx, this guy takes a Mickey Finn on me. I can't stand for it. If I stand for it I'm licked, my nerve's gone. I'm not going to stand for it. I'm going after him. I'm going regardless, but you can smooth the way a lot by fixing me up.'

Madvig put out a big open hand and roughly pushed Ned Beaumont's drawn face. 'Oh, hell, Ned!' he said, 'sure I'll fix you up. The only thing is I don't like you getting mixed up in things, but – hell! – if it's like that – I guess the best shot would be to make you a special investigator in the District Attorney's office. That way you'll be under Farr and he won't be poking his nose in.'

Mrs Madvig stood up with a plate in each bony hand. 'If I didn't make a rule of not ever meddling in men's affairs,' she said severely, 'I certainly would have something to say to the pair of you, running around with the good Lord only knows what kind of monkey-business afoot that's likely as not to get you into the Lord only knows what kind of trouble.'

Ned Beaumont grinned until she had left the room with the plates. Then he stopped grinning and said: 'Will you fix it up now so everything'll be ready this afternoon?'

'Sure,' Madvig agreed, rising. 'I'll phone Farr. And if there's anything else I can do, you know.'

Ned Beaumont said, 'Sure,' and Madvig went out.

Brown June came in and began to clear the table.

'Is Miss Opal sleeping now, do you think?' Ned Beaumont asked.

'No, sir, I just now took her up some tea and toast.'

'Run up and ask her if I can pop in for a minute?'

'Yes, sir, I sure will.'

After the Negress had gone out, Ned Beaumont got up from the table and began to walk up and down the room. Spots of color made his lean cheeks warm just beneath his cheek-bones. He stopped walking when Madvig came in.

'Oke,' Madvig said. 'If Farr's not in see Barbero. He'll fix you up and you don't have to tell him anything.'

Ned Beaumont said, 'Thanks,' and looked at the brown girl in the doorway.

She said: 'She says to come right up.'

IX

Opal Madvig's room was chiefly blue. She, in a blue and silver wrapper, was propped up on pillows in her bed when Ned Beaumont came in. She was blue-eyed as her father and grandmother, long-boned as they and firm-featured, with fair pink skin still childish in texture. Her eyes were reddened now.

She dropped a piece of toast on the tray in her lap, held her hand out to Ned Beaumont, showed him strong white teeth in a smile, and said: 'Hello, Ned.' Her voice was not steady.

He did not take her hand. He slapped the back of it lightly, said, ''Lo, snip,' and sat at the foot of her bed. He crossed his long legs and took a cigar from his pocket. 'Smoke hurt the head?'

'Oh, no,' she said.

He nodded as if to himself, returned the cigar to his pocket, and dropped his careless air. He twisted himself around on the bed to look more directly at her. His eyes were humid with sympathy. His voice was husky. 'I know, youngster, it's tough.'

She stared baby-eyed at him. 'No, really, most of the headache's gone and it wasn't so awfully wretched anyway.' Her voice was no longer unsteady.

He smiled at her with thinned lips and asked: 'So I'm an outsider now?'

She put a small frown between her brows. 'I don't know what you mean, Ned.'

Hard of mouth and eye, he replied: 'I mean Taylor.'

Though the tray moved a little on her knees, nothing in her face changed. She said: 'Yes, but – you know – I hadn't seen him for months, since Dad made—'

Ned Beaumont stood up abruptly. He said: 'All right,' over his shoulder as he moved towards the door.

The girl in the bed did not say anything.

He went out of the room and down the stairs.

Paul Madvig, putting on his coat in the lower hall, said: 'I've got to go down to the office to see about those sewer-contracts. I'll drop you at Farr's office if you want.'

Ned Beaumont had said, 'Fine,' when Opal's voice came to them from upstairs. 'Ned, oh, Ned!'

'Righto,' he called back and then to Madvig: 'Don't wait if you're in a hurry.'

Madvig looked at his watch. 'I ought to run along. See you at the Club tonight?'

Ned Beaumont said, 'Uh-huh,' and went upstairs again.

Opal had pushed the tray down to the foot of the bed. She said: 'Close the door.' When he had shut the door she moved over in bed to make a place for him to sit beside her. Then she asked: 'What makes you act like that?'

'You oughtn't to lie to me,' he said gravely as he sat down.

'But, Ned!' Her blue eyes tried to probe his brown ones.

He asked: 'How long since you saw Taylor?'

'You mean to talk to?' Her face and voice were candid. 'It's been weeks and—'

He stood up abruptly. He said, 'All right,' over his shoulder while walking towards the door.

She let him get within a step of the door before she called: 'Oh, Ned, don't make it so hard for me.'

He turned around slowly, his face blank.

'Aren't we friends?' she asked.

'Sure,' he replied readily without eagerness, 'but it's hard to remember it when we're lying to each other.'

She turned sidewise in bed, laying her cheek against the topmost pillow, and began to cry. She made no sound. Her tears fell down on the pillow and made a greyish spot there.

He returned to the bed, sat down beside her again, and moved her head from the pillow to his shoulder.

She cried there silently for several minutes. Then muffled words came from where her mouth was pressed against his coat: 'Did-did you know I had been meeting him?'

'Yes.'

She sat up straight, alarmed. 'Did Dad know it?'

'I don't think so. I don't know.'

She lowered her head to his shoulder so that her next words were muffled. 'Oh, Ned, I was with him only yesterday afternoon, all afternoon!'

He tightened his arm around her, but did not say anything.

After another pause she asked: 'Who – who do you think could have done it to him?'

He winced.

She raised her head suddenly. There was no weakness in her now. 'Do you know, Ned?'

He hesitated, wet his lips, mumbled: 'I think I do.'

'Who?' she asked fiercely.

He hesitated again, evading her eyes, then put a slow question to her: 'Will you promise to keep it to yourself till the time comes?'

'Yes,' she replied quickly, but when he would have spoken she stopped him by grabbing his nearer shoulder with both hands. 'Wait. I won't promise unless you'll promise me that they won't get off, that they'll be caught and punished.'

'I can't promise that. Nobody can.'

She stared at him, biting her lip, then said: 'All right, then, I'll promise anyway. Who?'

'Did he ever tell you that he owed a gambler named Bernie Despain more money then he could pay?'

'Did – did this Despain—?'

'I think so, but did he ever say anything to you about owing—?'

'I knew he was in trouble. He told me that, but he didn't say what it was except that he and his father had had a row about some money and that he was – "desperate" is what he said.'

'Didn't mention Despain?'

'No. What was it? Why do you think this Despain did it?'

'He had over a thousand dollars' worth of Taylor's I O Us and couldn't collect. He left town last night in a hurry. The police are looking for him now.' He lowered his voice, looking a little sidewise at her. 'Would you do something to help them catch and convict him?'

'Yes. What?'

'I mean something a bit off-color. You see, it's going to be hard to convict him, but, if he's guilty, would you do something that might be a little bit – well, off-color to make sure of nailing him?'

'Anything,' she replied.

He sighed and rubbed his lips together.

'What is it you want done?' she asked eagerly.

'I want you to get me one of his hats.'

'What?'

'I want one of Taylor's hats,' Ned Beaumont said. His face had flushed. 'Can you get me one?'

She was bewildered. 'But what for, Ned?'

'To make sure of nailing Despain. That's all I can tell you now. Can you get it for me or can't you?'

'I – I think I can, but I wish you'd—'

'How soon?'

'This afternoon, I think,' she said, 'but I wish—'

He interrupted her again. 'You don't want to know anything about it. The fewer know about it the better, and the same thing goes for your getting the hat.' He put his arm around her and drew her to him 'Did you really love him, snip, or was it just because your father—'

'I did really love him,' she sobbed. 'I'm pretty sure – I'm sure I did.'

2 The Hat Trick

I

Ned Beaumont, wearing a hat that did not quite fit him,
followed the porter carrying his bags through Grand
Central Terminal to a Forty-second Street exit, and
thence to a maroon taxicab. He tipped the porter, climbed into
the taxicab, gave its driver the name of a hotel off Broadway in
the Forties, and settled back lighting a cigar. He chewed the cigar
more than he smoked it as the taxicab crawled through theater-
bound traffic towards Broadway.

At Madison Avenue a green taxicab, turning against the light,
ran full tilt into Ned Beaumont's maroon one, driving it over
against a car that was parked by the kerb, hurling him into a
corner in a shower of broken glass.

He pulled himself upright and climbed out into the gathering
crowd. He was not hurt, he said. He answered a policeman's
questions. He found the hat that did not quite fit him and put it
on his head. He had his bags transferred to another taxicab, gave
the hotel's name to the second driver, and huddled back in a
corner, white-faced and shivering, while the ride lasted.

When he had registered at the hotel he asked for his mail and was given two telephone-memorandum-slips and two sealed envelopes without postage stamps.

He asked the bellboy who took him to his room to get him a pint of rye whisky. When the boy had gone he turned the key in the door and read the telephone-memoranda. Both slips were dated that day, one marked 4:50 P.M., the other 8:05 P.M. He looked at his wrist-watch. It was 8:45 P.M.

The earlier slip read: *At The Gargoyle.* The later read: *At Tom & Jerry's. Will phone later.* Both were sighed: *Jack.*

He opened one of the envelopes. It contained two sheets of paper covered by bold masculine handwriting, dated the previous day.

She is staying at the Matin, room 1211, registered as Eileen Dale, Chicago. She did some phoning from the depot and connected with a man and girl who live E. 30th. They went to a lot of places, mostly speakies, probably hunting him, but don't seem to have much luck. My room is 734. Man and girl named Brook.

The sheet of paper in the other envelope, covered by the same handwriting, was dated that day.

I saw Deward this morning, but he says he did not know Bernie was in town. Will phone later.

Both of these messages were signed: *Jack.*

Ned Beaumont washed, put on fresh linen from his bags, and was lighting a cigar when the bellboy brought him his pint of whisky. He paid the boy, got a tumbler from the bathroom, and drew a chair up to the bedroom-window. He sat there smoking, drinking, and staring down at the other side of the street until his telephone-bell rang.

'Hello,' he said into the telephone. 'Yes, Jack . . . Just now . . . Where? . . . Sure . . . Sure, on my way.'

He took another drink of whisky, put on the hat that did not quite fit him, picked up the overcoat he had dropped across a chair-back, put it on, patted one of its pockets, switched off the lights, and went out.

It was then ten minutes past nine o'clock.

II

Through double swinging glazed doors under an electric sign that said *Tom & Jerry's* down the front of a building within sight of Broadway, Ned Beaumont passed into a narrow corridor. A single swinging door in the corridor's left wall let him into a small restaurant.

A man at a corner-table stood up and raised a forefinger at him. The man was of medium height, young and dapper, with a sleek dark rather good-looking face.

Ned Beaumont went over to him. ''Lo, Jack,' he said as they shook hands.

'They're upstairs, the girl and those Brook people,' Jack told him. 'You ought to be all right sitting here with your back to the stairs. I can spot them if they go out, or him coming in, and there's enough people in the way to keep him from making you.'

Ned Beaumont sat down at Jack's table. 'They waiting for him?'

Jack moved his shoulders. 'I don't know, but they're doing some stalling about something. Want something to eat? You can't get anything to drink downstairs here.'

Ned Beaumont said: 'I want a drink. Can't we find a place upstairs where they won't see us?'

'It's not a very big joint,' Jack protested. 'There's a couple of booths up there where we might be hidden from them, but if he comes in he's likely to spot us.'

'Let's risk it. I want a drink and I might as well talk to him right here if he does show up.'

Jack looked curiously at Ned Beaumont, then turned his eyes away and said: 'You're the boss. I'll see if one of the booths is empty.' He hesitated, moved his shoulders again, and left the table.

Ned Beaumont twisted himself around in his chair to watch the dapper young man go back to the stairs and mount them. He watched the foot of the stairs until the young man came down again. From the second step Jack beckoned. He said, when Ned Beaumont had joined him there: 'The best of them's empty and her back's this way, so you can get a slant at the Brooks as you go over.'

They went upstairs. The booths – tables and benches set within breast-high wooden stalls – were to the right of the stair-head. They had to turn and look through a wide arch and down past the bar to see into the second-floor dining-room.

Ned Beaumont's eyes focused on the back of Lee Wilshire in sleeveless fawn gown and brown hat. Her brown fur coat was hanging over the back of her chair. He looked at her companions. At her left was a hawk-nosed long-chinned pale man, a predatory animal of forty or so. Facing her sat a softly fleshed red-haired girl with eyes set far apart. She was laughing.

Ned Beaumont followed Jack to their stall. They sat down with the table between them. Ned Beaumont sat with his back to the dining-room, close to the end of his bench to take full advantage of the wooden wing's shelter. He took off his hat, but not his overcoat.

A waiter came. Ned Beaumont said: 'Rye.' Jack said: 'Rickey.'

Jack opened a package of cigarettes, took one out, and, staring at it, said: 'It's your game and I'm working for you, but this isn't a hell of a good spot to go up against him if he's got friends here.'

'Has he?'

Jack put the cigarette in a corner of his mouth so it moved batonwise with his words. 'If they're waiting here for him, it might be one of his hang-outs.'

The waiter came with their drinks. Ned Beaumont drained his glass immediately and complained: 'Cut to nothing.'

'Yes, I guess it is,' Jack said and took a sip from his glass. He set fire to the end of his cigarette and took another sip.

'Well,' Ned Beaumont said, 'I'm going up against him as soon as he shows.'

'Fair enough.' Jack's good-looking dark face was inscrutable. 'What do I do?'

Ned Beaumont said, 'Leave it to me,' and caught their waiter's attention.

He ordered a double Scotch, Jack another rickey. Ned Beaumont emptied his glass as soon as it arrived. Jack let his first drink be carried away no more than half consumed and sipped at his second. Presently Ned Beaumont had another double Scotch and another while Jack had time to finish none of his drinks.

Then Bernie Despain came upstairs.

Jack, watching the head of the stairs, saw the gambler and put a foot on Ned Beaumont's under the table. Ned Beaumont, looking up from his empty glass, became suddenly hard and cold of eye. He put his hands flat on the table and stood up. He stepped out of the stall and faced Despain. He said: 'I want my money, Bernie.'

The man who had come upstairs behind Despain now walked around him and struck Ned Beaumont very hard in the body with his left fist. He was not a tall man, but his shoulders were heavy and his fists were large globes.

Ned Beaumont was knocked back against a stall-partition. He bent forward and his knees gave, but he did not fall. He hung there for a moment. His eyes were glassy and his skin had taken on a greenish tinge. He said something nobody could have understood and went to the head of the stairs.

He went down the stairs, loose-jointed, pallid, and bare-headed. He went through the downstairs dining-room to the street and out to the kerb, where he vomited. When he had vomited, he went to a taxicab that stood a dozen feet away, climbed into it, and gave the driver an address in Greenwich Village.

III

Ned Beaumont left the taxicab in front of a house whose open basement-door, under brown stone steps, let noise and light out into a dark street. He went through the basement-doorway into a narrow room where two white-coated bar-tenders served a dozen men and women at a twenty-foot bar and two waiters moved among tables at which other people sat.

The balder bar-tender said, 'For Christ's sake, Ned!' put down the pink mixture he was shaking in a tall glass, and stuck a wet hand out across the bar.

Ned Beaumont said, ''Lo, Mack,' and shook the wet hand.

One of the waiters came up to shake Ned Beaumont's hand and then a round and florid Italian whom Ned Beaumont called Tony. When these greetings were over Ned Beaumont said he would buy a drink.

'Like hell you will,' Tony said. He turned to the bar and rapped on it with an empty cocktail-glass. 'This guy can't buy so much as a glass of water tonight,' he said when he had the bar-tenders' attention. 'What he wants is on the house.'

Ned Beaumont said: 'That's all right for me, so I get it. Double Scotch.'

Two girls at a table in the other end of the room stood up and called together: 'Yoo-hoo, Ned!'

He told Tony, 'Be back in a minute,' and went to the girls' table. They embraced him, asked him questions, introduced him to the men with them, and made a place for him at their table.

He sat down and replied to their questions that he was back in

New York only for a short visit and not to stay and that his was double Scotch.

At a little before three o'clock they rose from their table, left Tony's establishment, and went to another almost exactly like it three blocks away, where they sat at a table that could hardly have been told from the first and drank the same sort of liquor they had been drinking.

One of the men went away at half past three. He did not say good-by to the others, nor they to him. Ten minutes later Ned Beaumont, the other man, and the two girls left. They got into a taxicab at the corner and went to a hotel near Washington Square, where the other man and one of the girls got out.

The remaining girl took Ned Beaumont, who called her Fedink, to an apartment on Seventy-third Street. The apartment was very warm. When she opened the door warm air came out to meet them. When she was three steps inside the living-room she sighed and fell down on the floor.

Ned Beaumont shut the door and tried to awaken her, but she would not wake. He carried and dragged her difficultly into the next room and put her on a chintz-covered day-bed. He took off part of her clothing, found some blankets to spread over her, and opened a window. Then he went into the bathroom and was sick. After that he returned to the living-room, lay down on the sofa in all his clothes, and went to sleep.

IV

A telephone-bell, ringing close to Ned Beaumont's head, awakened him. He opened his eyes, put his feet down on the floor, turned on his side, and looked around the room. When he saw the telephone he shut his eyes and relaxed.

The bell continued to ring. He groaned, opened his eyes again, and squirmed until he had freed his left arm from beneath his body. He put his wrist close to his eyes and looked at his watch, squinting. The watch's crystal was gone and its hands had stopped at twelve minutes to twelve.

Ned Beaumont squirmed again on the sofa until he was leaning on his left elbow, holding his head up on his left hand. The telephone-bell was still ringing. He looked around the room with miserably dull eyes. The lights were burning. Through an open doorway he could see Fedink's blanket-covered feet on an end of the day-bed.

He groaned again and sat up, running fingers through his tousled dark hair, squeezing his temples between the heels of his palms. His lips were dry and brownly encrusted. He ran his tongue over them and made a distasteful face. Then he rose, coughing a little, took off his gloves and overcoat, dropped them on the sofa, and went into the bathroom.

When he came out he went to the day-bed and looked down at Fedink. She was sleeping heavily, face down, one blue-sleeved arm crooked above her head. The telephone-bell had stopped ringing. He pulled his tie straight and returned to the living-room.

Three Murad cigarettes were in an open box on the table between two chairs. He picked up one of the cigarettes, muttered, 'Nonchalant,' without humor, found a paper of matches, lit the cigarette, and went into the kitchen. He squeezed the juice of four oranges into a tall glass and drank it. He made and drank two cups of coffee.

As he came out of the kitchen Fedink asked in a woefully flat voice: 'Where's Ted?' Her one visible eye was partially open.

Ned Beaumont went over to her. 'Who's Ted?' he asked.

'That fellow I was with.'

'Were you with somebody? How do I know?'

She opened her mouth and made an unpleasant clucking sound shutting it. 'What time is it?'

'I don't know that either. Somewhere around daylight.'

She rubbed her face into the chintz cushion under it and said: 'A swell guy I turned out to be, promising to marry him yesterday and then leaving him to take the first tramp I run into home with me.' She opened and shut the hand that was above her head. 'Or am I home?'

'You had a key to the place, anyway,' Ned Beaumont told her. 'Want some orange-juice and coffee?'

'I don't want a damned thing except to die. Will you go away, Ned, and not ever come back?'

'It's going to be hard on me,' he said ill-naturedly, 'but I'll try.'

He put on his overcoat and gloves, took a dark wrinkled cap from one overcoat-pocket, put the cap on, and left the house.

V

Half an hour later Ned Beaumont was knocking on the door of room 734 at his hotel. Presently Jack's voice, drowsy, came through the door: 'Who's that?'

'Beaumont.'

'Oh,' without enthusiasm, 'all right.'

Jack opened the door and turned on the lights. He was in green-spotted pajamas. His feet were bare. His eyes were dull, his face flushed, with sleepiness. He yawned, nodded, and went back to bed, where he stretched himself out on his back and stared at the ceiling. Then he asked, with not much interest: 'How are you this morning?'

Ned Beaumont had shut the door. He stood between door and bed looking sullenly at the man in the bed. He asked: 'What happened after I left?'

'Nothing happened.' Jack yawned again. 'Or do you mean what did I do?' He did not wait for a reply. 'I went out and took a plant across the street till they came out. Despain and the girl and the guy that slugged you came out. They went to the Buckman, Forty-eighth Street. That's where Despain's holing up – apartment 938 – name of Barton Dewey. I hung around there till after three and then knocked off. They were all still in there unless they were fooling me.' He jerked his head slightly in the direction of a corner of the room. 'Your hat's on the chair there. I thought I might as well save it for you.'

Ned Beaumont went over to the chair and picked up the hat that did not quite fit him. He stuffed the wrinkled dark cap in his overcoat-pocket and put the hat on his head.

Jack said: 'There's some gin on the table if you want a shot.'

Ned Beaumont said: 'No, thanks. Have you got a gun?'

Jack stopped staring at the ceiling. He sat up in bed, stretched his arms out wide, yawned for the third time, and asked: 'What are you figuring on doing?' His voice held nothing beyond polite curiosity.

'I'm going to see Despain.'

Jack had drawn his knees up, had clasped his hands around them, and was sitting hunched forward a little staring at the foot of the bed. He said slowly: 'I don't think you ought to, not right now.'

'I've got to, right now,' Ned Beaumont said.

His voice made Jack look at him. Ned Beaumont's face was an unhealthy yellowish grey. His eyes were muddy, red-rimmed, not sufficiently open to show any of the whites. His lips were dry and somewhat thicker than usual.

'Been up all night?' Jack asked.

'I got some sleep.'

'Unkdray?'

'Yes, but how about the gun?'

Jack swung his legs out from beneath the covers and down over the side of the bed. 'Why don't you get some sleep first? Then we can go after them. You're in no shape now.'

Ned Beaumont said: 'I'm going now.'

Jack said: 'All right, but you're wrong. You know they're no babies to go up against shaky. They mean it.'

'Where's the gun?' Ned Beaumont asked.

Jack stood up and began to unbutton his pajama-coat.

Ned Beaumont said: 'Give me the gun and get back in bed. I'm going.'

Jack fastened the button he had just unfastened and got into bed. 'The gun's in the top bureau-drawer,' he said. 'There are extra cartridges in there too if you want them.' He turned over on his side and shut his eyes.

Ned Beaumont found the pistol, put it in a hip-pocket, said, 'See you later,' switched off the lights, and went out.

VI

The Buckman was a square-built yellow apartment-building that filled most of the block it stood in. Inside, Ned Beaumont said he wanted to see Mr Dewey. When asked for his name he said: 'Ned Beaumont.'

Five minutes later he was walking away from an elevator down a long corridor towards an open door where Bernie Despain stood.

Despain was a small man, short and stringy, with a head too large for his body. The size of his head was exaggerated until it seemed a deformity by long thick fluffy waved hair. His face was swarthy, large-featured except for the eyes, and strongly lined across the forehead and down from nostrils past the mouth. He had a faintly reddish scar on one cheek. His blue suit was carefully pressed and he wore no jewelry.

He stood in the doorway, smiling sardonically, and said: 'Good morning, Ned.'

Ned Beaumont said: 'I want to talk to you, Bernie.'

'I guessed you did. As soon as they phoned your name up I said to myself: "I bet you he wants to talk to me."'

Ned Beaumont said nothing. His yellow face was tight-lipped.

Despain's smile became looser. He said: 'Well, my boy, you don't have to stand here. Come on in.' He stepped aside.

The door opened into a small vestibule. Through an opposite door that stood open Lee Wilshire and the man who had struck Ned Beaumont could be seen. They had stopped packing two traveling-bags to look at Ned Beaumont.

He went into the vestibule.

Despain followed him in, shut the corridor-door, and said: 'The Kid's kind of hasty and when you come up to me like that he thought maybe you were looking for trouble, see? I give him hell about it and maybe if you ask him he'll apologize.'

The Kid said something in an undertone to Lee Wilshire, who was glaring at Ned Beaumont. She laughed a vicious little laugh and replied: 'Yes, a sportsman to the last.'

Bernie Despain said: 'Go right in, Mr Beaumont. You've already met the folks, haven't you?'

Ned Beaumont advanced into the room where Lee and the Kid were.

The Kid asked: 'How's the belly?'

Ned Beaumont did not say anything.

Bernie Despain exclaimed: 'Jesus! For a guy that says he came up here to talk you've done less of it than anybody I ever heard of.'

'I want to talk to you,' Ned Beaumont said. 'Do we have to have all these people around?'

'I do,' Despain replied. 'You don't. You can get away from them just by walking out and going about your own business.'

'I've got business here.'

'That's right, there was something about money.' Despain grinned at the Kid. 'Wasn't there something about money, Kid?'

The Kid had moved to stand in the doorway through which Ned Beaumont had come into the room. 'Something,' he said in a rasping voice, 'but I forget what.'

Ned Beaumont took off his overcoat and hung it on the back of a brown easy-chair. He sat down in the chair and put his hat behind him. He said: 'That's not my business this time. I'm – let's see.' He took a paper from his inner coat-pocket, unfolded it,

39

glanced at it, and said: 'I'm here as special investigator for the District Attorney's office.'

For a small fraction of a second the twinkle in Despain's eyes was blurred, but he said immediately: 'Ain't you getting up in the world! The last time I saw you you were just punking around for Paul.'

Ned Beaumont refolded the paper and returned it to his pocket.

Despain said: 'Well, go ahead, investigate something for us – anything – just to show us how it's done.' He sat down facing Ned Beaumont, wagging his too-large head. 'You ain't going to tell me you came all the way to New York to ask me about killing Taylor Henry?'

'Yes.'

'That's too bad. I could've saved you the trip.' He flourished a hand at the traveling-bags on the floor. 'As soon as Lee told me what it was all about I started packing up to go back and laugh at your frame-up.'

Ned Beaumont lounged back comfortably in his chair. One of his hands was behind him. He said: 'If it's a frame-up it's Lee's. The police got their dope from her.'

'Yes,' she said angrily, 'when I had to because you sent them there, you bastard.'

Despain said: 'Uh-huh, Lee's a dumb cluck, all right, but those markers don't mean anything. They—'

'I'm a dumb cluck, am I?' Lee cried indignantly. 'Didn't I come all the way here to warn you after you'd run off with every stinking piece of—'

'Yes,' Despain agreed pleasantly, 'and coming here shows just what a dumb cluck you are, because you led this guy right to me.'

'If that's the way you feel about it I'm damned glad I did give the police those I O Us, and what do you think of that?'

Despain said: 'I'll tell you just exactly what I think of it after our company's gone.' He turned to Ned Beaumont. 'So honest Paul Madvig's letting you drop the shuck on me, huh?'

Ned Beaumont smiled. 'You're not being framed, Bernie, and you know it. Lee gave us the lead-in and the rest that we got clicked with it.'

'There's some more besides what she gave you?'

'Plenty.'

'What?'

Ned Beaumont smiled again. 'There are lots of things I could say to you, Bernie, that I wouldn't want to say in front of a crowd.'

Despain said: 'Nuts!'

The Kid spoke from the doorway to Despain in his rasping voice: 'Let's chuck this sap out on his can and get going.'

'Wait,' Despain said. Then he frowned and put a question to Ned Beaumont: 'Is there a warrant out for me?'

' Well, I don't—'

'Yes or no?' Despain's bantering humor was gone.

Ned Beaumont said slowly: 'Not that I know of.'

Despain stood up and pushed his chair back. 'Then get the hell out of here and make it quick, or I'll let the Kid take another poke at you.'

Ned Beaumont stood up. He picked up his overcoat. He took his cap out of his overcoat-pocket and, holding it in one hand, his overcoat over the other arm, said seriously: 'You'll be sorry.' Then he walked out in a dignified manner. The Kid's rasping laughter and Lee's shriller hooting followed him out.

VII

Outside the Buckman Ned Beaumont started briskly down the street. His eyes were glowing in his tired face and his dark mustache twitched above a flickering smile.

At the first corner he came face to face with Jack. He asked: 'What are you doing here?'

Jack said: 'I'm still working for you, far as I know, so I came along to see if I could find anything to do.'

'Swell. Find us a taxi quick. They're sliding out.'

Jack said, 'Ay, ay,' and went down the street.

Ned Beaumont remained on the corner. The front and side entrances of the Buckman could be seen from there.

In a little while Jack returned in a taxicab. Ned Beaumont got into it and they told the driver where to park it.

'What did you do to them?' Jack asked when they were sitting still.

'Things.'

'Oh.'

Ten minutes passed and Jack, saying, 'Look,' was pointing a forefinger at a taxicab drawing up to the Buckman's side door.

The Kid, carrying two traveling-bags, left the building first, then, when he was in the taxicab, Despain and the girl ran out to join him. The taxicab ran away.

Jack leaned forward and told his driver what to do. They ran along in the other cab's wake. They wound through streets that were bright with morning sunlight, going by a devious route finally to a battered brownstone house on West Forty-ninth Street.

Despain's cab stopped in front of the house and, once more, the Kid was the first of the trio out on the sidewalk. He looked up and down the street. He went up to the front door of the house and unlocked it. Then he returned to the taxicab. Despain and the girl jumped out and went indoors hurriedly. The Kid followed with the bags.

'Stick here with the cab,' Ned Beaumont told Jack.

'What are you going to do?'

'Try my luck.'

Jack shook his head. 'This is another wrong neighborhood to look for trouble in,' he said.

Ned Beaumont said: 'If I come out with Despain, you beat it. Get another taxi and go back to watch the Buckman. If I don't come out, use your own judgment.'

He opened the cab-door and stepped out. He was shivering. His eyes were shiny. He ignored something that Jack leaned out to say and hurried across the street to the house into which the two men and the girl had gone.

He went straight up the front steps and put a hand on the door-knob. The knob turned in his hand. The door was not locked. He pushed it open and, after peering into the dim hallway, went in.

The door slammed shut behind him and one of the Kid's fists struck his head a glancing blow that carried his cap away and sent him crashing into the wall. He sank down a little, giddily, almost to one knee, and the Kid's other fist struck the wall over his head.

He pulled his lips back over his teeth and drove a fist into the Kid's groin, a short sharp blow that brought a snarl from the Kid and made him fall back so that Ned Beaumont could pull himself up straight before the Kid was upon him again.

Up the hallway a little, Bernie Despain was leaning against the wall, his mouth stretched wide and thin, his eyes narrowed to dark points, saying over and over in a low voice: 'Sock him, Kid, sock him . . .' Lee Wilshire was not in sight.

The Kid's next two blows landed on Ned Beaumont's chest, mashing him against the wall, making him cough. The third, aimed at his face, he avoided. Then he pushed the Kid away from him with a forearm against his throat and kicked the kid in the belly. The Kid roared angrily and came in with both fists going, but forearm and foot had carried him away from Ned Beaumont and had given Ned Beaumont time to get his right hand to his hip-pocket to get Jack's revolver out of his pocket. He had no time to level the revolver, but, holding it at a downward angle, he pulled the trigger and managed to shoot the Kid in the right thigh. The Kid yelped and fell down on the hallway floor. He lay there looking up at Ned Beaumont with frightened bloodshot eyes.

Ned Beaumont stepped back from him, put his left hand in his trousers-pocket, and addressed Bernie Despain: 'Come on out with me. I want to talk to you.' His face was sullenly determined.

Footsteps ran overhead, somewhere back in the building a door opened, and down the hallway excited voices were audible, but nobody came into sight.

Despain stared for a long moment at Ned Beaumont as if horribly fascinated. Then, without a word, he stepped over the man on the floor and went out of the building ahead of Ned Beaumont. Ned Beaumont put the revolver in his jacket-pocket before he went down the street-steps, but he kept his hand on it.

'Up to that taxi,' he told Despain, indicating the car out of which Jack was getting. When they reached the taxicab he told the chauffeur to drive them anywhere, 'just around till I tell you where to go.'

They were in motion when Despain found his voice. He said: 'This is a hold-up. I'll give you anything you want because I don't want to be killed, but it's just a hold-up.'

Ned Beaumont laughed disagreeably and shook his head. 'Don't forget I've risen in the world to be something or other in the District Attorney's office.'

'But there's no charge against me. I'm not wanted. You said—'

'I was spoofing you, Bernie, for reasons. You're wanted.'

'For what?'

'Killing Taylor Henry.'

'That? Hell, I'll go back and face that. What've you got against me? I had some of his markers, sure. And I left the night he was killed, sure. And I gave him hell because he wouldn't make them good, sure. What kind of a case is that for a first-class lawyer to beat? Jesus, if I left the markers behind in my safe at some time before nine-thirty – to go by Lee's story – don't that show I wasn't trying to collect that night?'

'No, and that isn't all the stuff we've got on you.'

'That's all there could be,' Despain said earnestly.

Ned Beaumont sneered. 'Wrong, Bernie. Remember I had a hat on when I came to see you this morning?'

'Maybe. I think you did.'

'Remember I took a cap out of my coat-pocket and put it on when I left?'

Bewilderment, fear, began to come into the swarthy man's small eyes. 'By Jesus! Well? What are you getting at?'

'I'm getting at the evidence. Do you remember the hat didn't fit me very well?'

Bernie Despain's voice was hoarse: 'I don't know, Ned. For Christ's sake, what do you mean?'

'I mean it didn't fit me because it wasn't my hat. Do you remember that the hat Taylor was wearing when he was murdered wasn't found?'

'I don't know. I don't know anything about him.'

'Well, I'm trying to tell you the hat I had this morning was Taylor's hat and it's now planted down between the cushion-seat and the back of that brown easy-chair in the apartment you had at the Buckman. Do you think that, with the rest, would be enough to sit you on the hot seat?'

Despain would have screamed in terror if Ned Beaumont had not clapped a hand over his mouth and growled, 'Shut up,' in his ear.

Sweat ran down the swarthy face. Despain fell over on Ned Beaumont, seizing the lapels of his coat with both hands, babbling: 'Listen, don't you do that to me, Ned. You can have every cent I owe you, every cent with interest, if you won't do that. I never meant to rob you, Ned, honest to God. It was just that I was caught short and thought I'd treat it like a loan. Honest to God, Ned. I ain't got much now, but I'm fixed to get the money for Lee's rocks that I'm selling today and I'll give you your dough, every nickel of it, out of that. How much was it, Ned? I'll give you all of it right away, this morning.

Ned Beaumont pushed the swarthy man over to his own side of the taxicab and said: 'It was thirty-two hundred and fifty dollars.'

'Thirty-two hundred and fifty dollars. You'll get it, every cent of it, this morning, right away.' Despain looked at his watch.

'Yes, sir, right this minute as soon as we can get there. Old Stein will be at his place before this. Only say you'll let me go, Ned, for old times' sake.'

Ned Beaumont rubbed his hands together thoughtfully. 'I can't exactly let you go. Not right now, I mean. I've got to remember the District Attorney connection and that you're wanted for questioning. So all we can dicker about is the hat. Here's the proposition: give me my money and I'll see that I'm alone when I turn up the hat and nobody else will ever know about it. Otherwise I'll see that half the New York police are with me and— There you are. Take it or leave it.'

'Oh, God!' Bernie Despain groaned. 'Tell him to drive us to old Stein's place. It's on . . .'

3 The Cyclone Shot

Ned Beaumont leaving the train that had brought him back from New York was a clear-eyed erect tall man. Only the flatness of his chest hinted at any constitutional weakness. In color and line his face was hale. His stride was long and elastic. He went nimbly up the concrete stairs that connected train-shed with street-level, crossed the waiting-room, waved a hand at an acquaintance behind the information counter, and passed out of the station through one of the street-doors.

While waiting on the sidewalk for the porter with his bags to come he bought a newspaper. He opened it when he was in a taxicab riding towards Randall Avenue with his luggage. He read a half-column on the front page:

SECOND BROTHER KILLER
FRANCIS F. WEST MURDERED
CLOSE TO SPOT WHERE
BROTHER MET DEATH

For the second time within two weeks tragedy came to the West family of 1342 N. Achland Avenue last night when Francis W. West,

31, was shot to death in the street less than a block from the corner where he had seen his brother Norman run down and killed by an alleged bootleg car last month.

Francis West, who was employed as waiter at the Rockaway Café, was returning from work at a little after midnight, when, according to those who witnessed the tragedy, he was overtaken by a black touring car that came down Achland Avenue at high speed. The car swung in to the kerb as it reached West, and more than a score of shots are said to have been fired from it. West fell with eight bullets in his body, dying before anybody could reach him. The death car, which is said not to have stopped, immediately picked up speed again and vanished around the corner of Bowman Street. The police are hampered in their attempt to find the car by conflicting descriptions given by witnesses, none of whom claims to have seen any of the men in the automobile.

Boyd West, the surviving brother, who also witnessed Norman's death last month, could ascribe no reason for Francis's murder. He said he knew of no enemies his brother had made. Miss Marie Shepperd, 1917 Baker Avenue, to whom Francis West was to have been married next week, was likewise unable to name anyone who might have desired her fiancé's death.

Timothy Ivans, alleged driver of the car that accidentally ran down and killed Norman West last month, refused to talk to reporters in his cell at the City Prison, where he is held without bail, awaiting trial for manslaughter.

Ned Beaumont folded the newspaper with careful slowness and put it in one of his overcoat-pockets. His lips were drawn a little together and his eyes were bright with thinking. Otherwise his face was composed. He leaned back in a corner of the taxicab and played with an unlighted cigar.

In his rooms he went, without pausing to remove hat or coat, to the telephone and called four numbers, asking each time whether Paul Madvig was there and whether it was known where he could be found. After the fourth call he gave up trying to find Madvig.

He put the telephone down, picked his cigar up from where he had laid it on the table, lighted the cigar, laid it on the edge of the table again, picked up the telephone, and called the City Hall's number. He asked for the District Attorney's office. While he waited he dragged a chair, by means of a foot hooked under one of its rounds, over to the telephone, sat down, and put the cigar in his mouth.

Then he said into the telephone: 'Hello. Is Mr Farr in . . . Ned Beaumont . . . Yes, thanks.' He inhaled and exhaled smoke slowly. 'Hello, Farr? . . . Just got in a couple of minutes ago . . . Yes. Can I see you now? . . . That's right. Has Paul said anything to you about the West killing? . . . Don't know where he is, do you? Well, there's an angle I'd like to talk to you about . . . Yes, say half an hour . . . Right.'

He put the telephone aside and went across the room to look at the mail on a table by the door. There were some magazines and nine letters. He looked rapidly at the envelopes, dropped them on the table again without having opened any, and went into his bedroom to undress, then into his bathroom to shave and bathe.

II

District Attorney Michael Joseph Farr was a stout man of forty. His hair was a florid stubble above a florid pugnacious face. His walnut desk-top was empty except for a telephone and a large desk-set of green onyx whereon a nude metal figure holding aloft an airplane stood on one foot between two black and white fountain-pens that slanted off to either side at rakish angles.

He shook Ned Beaumont's hand in both of his and pressed him down into a leather-covered chair before returning to his own seat. He rocked back in his chair and asked: 'Have a nice trip?' Inquisitiveness gleamed through the friendliness in his eyes.

'It was all right,' Ned Beaumont replied. 'About this Francis

West: with him out of the way how does the case against Tim Ivans stand?'

Farr started, then made that startled motion part of a deliberate squirming into a more comfortable position in his chair.

'Well, it won't make such a lot of difference there,' he said, 'that is, not a whole lot, since there's still the other brother to testify against Ivans.' He very noticeably did not watch Ned Beaumont's face, but looked at a corner of the walnut desk. 'Why? What'd you have on your mind?'

Ned Beaumont was looking gravely at the man who was not looking at him. 'I was just wondering. I suppose it's all right, though, if the other brother can and will identify Tim.'

Farr, still not looking up, said: 'Sure.' He rocked his chair back and forth gently, an inch or two each way half a dozen times. His fleshy cheeks moved in little ripples where they covered his jaw-muscles. He cleared his throat and stood up. He looked at Ned Beaumont now with friendly eyes. 'Wait a minute,' he said. 'I've got to go see about something. They forget everything if I don't keep right on their tails. Don't go. I want to talk to you about Despain.'

Ned Beaumont murmured, 'Don't hurry,' as the District Attorney left the office, and sat and smoked placidly all the fifteen minutes he was gone.

Farr returned frowning. 'Sorry to leave you like that,' he said as he sat down, 'but we're fairly smothered under work. If it keeps up like this—' He completed the sentence by making a gesture of hopelessness with his hands.

'That's all right. Anything new on the Taylor Henry killing?'

'Nothing here. That's what I wanted to ask you about – Despain.' Again Farr was definitely not watching Ned Beaumont's face.

A thin mocking smile that the other man could not see twitched for an instant the corners of Ned Beaumont's mouth. He said: 'There's not much of a case against him when you come to look at it closely.'

Farr nodded slowly at the corner of his desk. 'Maybe, but his blowing town that same night don't look so damned good.'

'He had another reason for that,' Ned Beaumont said, 'a pretty good one.' The shadowy smile came and went.

Farr nodded again in the manner of one willing to be convinced. 'You don't think there's a chance that he really killed him?'

Ned Beaumont's reply was given carelessly: 'I don't think he did it, but there's always a chance and you've got plenty to hold him awhile on if you want to.'

The District Attorney raised his head and looked at Ned Beaumont. He smiled with a mixture of diffidence and good-fellowship and said: 'Tell me to go to hell if it's none of my business, but why in the name of God did Paul send you to New York after Bernie Despain?'

Ned Beaumont withheld his reply for a thoughtful moment. Then he moved his shoulders a little and said: 'He didn't send me. He let me go.'

Farr did not say anything.

Ned Beaumont filled his lungs with cigar-smoke, emptied them, and said: 'Bernie welshed on a bet with me. That's why he took the run-out. It just happened that Taylor Henry was killed the night of the day Peggy O' Toole came in in front with fifteen hundred of my dollars on her.'

The District Attorney said hastily: 'That's all right, Ned. It's none of my business what you and Paul do. I'm – you see, it's just that I'm not so damned sure that maybe Despain didn't happen to run into young Henry on the street by luck and take a crack at him. I think maybe I'll hold him awhile to be safe.' His blunt undershot mouth curved in a smile that was somewhat ingratiating. 'Don't think I'm pushing my snoot into Paul's affairs, or yours, but—' His florid face was turgid and shiny. He suddenly bent over and yanked a desk-drawer open. Paper rattled under his fingers. His hand came out of the drawer and went across the desk towards Ned Beaumont. In his hand was a small white envelope with a slit edge. 'Here.' His voice was thick. 'Look at this and see what you think of it, or is it only damned foolishness?'

Ned Beaumont took the envelope, but did not immediately look at it. He kept his eyes, now cold and bright, focused on the District Attorney's red face.

Farr's face became a darker red under the other man's stare and he raised a beefy hand in a placatory gesture. His voice was placatory: 'I don't attach any importance to it, Ned, but – I mean we always get a lot of junk like that on every case that comes up and – well, read it and see.'

After another considerable moment Ned Beaumont shifted his gaze from Farr to the envelope. The address was typewritten:

M. J. Farr, Esq.
District Attorney
City Hall
City
Personal

The postmark was dated the previous Saturday. Inside was a single sheet of white paper on which three sentences with neither salutation nor signature were typewritten:

Why did Paul Madvig steal one of Taylor Henry's hats after he was murdered?

What became of the hat that Taylor Henry was wearing when he was murdered?

Why was the man who claimed to have first found Taylor Henry's body made a member of your staff?

Ned Beaumont folded this communication, returned it to its envelope, dropped it down on the desk, and brushed his mustache with a thumb-nail from center to left and from center to right, looking at the District Attorney with level eyes, addressing him in a level tone: 'Well?'

Farr's cheeks rippled again where they covered his jaw-muscles. He frowned over pleading eyes. 'For God's sake, Ned,' he said earnestly, 'don't think I'm taking that seriously. We get bales of that kind of crap every time anything happens. I only wanted to show it to you.'

Ned Beaumont said: 'That's all right as long as you keep on feeling that way about it.' He was still level of eye and voice. 'Have you said anything to Paul about it?'

'About the letter? No. I haven't seen him since it came this morning.'

Ned Beaumont picked the envelope up from the desk and put it in his inner coat-pocket. The District Attorney, watching the letter go into the pocket, seemed uncomfortable, but he did not say anything.

Ned Beaumont said, when he had stowed the letter away and had brought a thin dappled cigar out of another pocket: 'I don't think I'd say anything to him about it if I were you. He's got enough on his mind.'

Farr was saying, 'Sure, whatever you say, Ned,' before Ned Beaumont had finished his speech.

After that neither of them said anything for a while during which Farr resumed his staring at the desk-corner and Ned Beaumont stared thoughtfully at Farr. This period of silence was ended by a soft buzzing that came from under the District Attorney's desk.

Farr picked up his telephone and said: 'Yes . . . Yes.' His undershot lip crept out over the edge of the upper lip and his florid face became mottled. 'The hell he's not!' he snarled. 'Bring the bastard in and put him up against him and then if he don't we'll do some work on him . . . Yes . . . Do it.' He slammed the receiver on its prong and glared at Ned Beaumont.

Ned Beaumont had paused in the act of lighting his cigar. It was in one hand. His lighter, alight, was in the other. His face was thrust forward a little between them. His eyes glittered. He put the tip of his tongue between his lips, withdrew it, and moved his lips in a smile that had nothing to do with pleasure. 'News?' he asked in a low persuasive voice.

The District Attorney's voice was savage: 'Boyd West, the other brother that identified Ivans. I got to thinking about it when we were talking and sent out to see if he could still identify him. He says he's not sure, the bastard.'

Ned Beaumont nodded as if this news was not unexpected. 'How'll that fix things?'

'He can't get away with it,' Farr snarled. 'He identified him once and he'll stick to it when he gets in front of a jury. I'm having him brought in now and by the time I get through with him he'll be a good boy.'

Ned Beaumont said: 'Yes? And suppose he doesn't?'

The District Attorney's desk trembled under a blow from the District Attorney's fist. 'He will.'

Apparently Ned Beaumont was unimpressed. He lighted his cigar, extinguished and pocketed his lighter, blew smoke out, and asked in a mildly amused tone: 'Sure he will, but suppose he doesn't? Suppose he looks at Tim and says: "I'm not sure that's him"?'

Farr smote his desk again. 'He won't – not when I'm through with him – he won't do anything but get up in front of the jury and say: "That's him."'

Amusement went out of Ned Beaumont's face and he spoke a bit wearily: 'He's going to back down on the identification and you know he is. Well, what can you do about it? There's nothing you can do about it, is there? It means your case against Tim Ivans goes blooey. You found the carload of booze where he left it, but the only proof you've got that he was driving it when it ran down Norman West was the eyewitness testimony of his two brothers. Well, if Francis is dead and Boyd's afraid to talk you've got no case and you know it.'

In a loud enraged voice Farr began: 'If you think I'm going to sit on my—'

But with an impatient motion of the hand holding his cigar Ned Beaumont interrupted him. 'Sitting, standing, or riding a bicycle,' he said, 'you're licked and you know it.'

'Do I? I'm District Attorney of this city and county and I—' Abruptly Farr stopped blustering. He cleared his throat and swallowed. Belligerence went out of his eyes, to be replaced first by confusion and then by something akin to fear. He leaned across the desk, too worried to keep worry from showing in his florid face. He said: 'Of course you know if you – if Paul – I mean if there's any reason why I shouldn't – you know – we can let it go at that.'

The smile that had nothing to do with pleasure was lifting the ends of Ned Beaumont's lips again and his eyes glittered through cigar-smoke. He shook his head slowly and spoke slowly in an unpleasantly sweet tone: 'No, Farr, there isn't any reason, or none of that kind. Paul promised to spring Ivans after election, but, believe it or not, Paul never had anybody killed and, even if he did, Ivans wasn't important enough to have anybody killed for. No, Farr, there isn't any reason and I wouldn't like to think you were going around thinking there was.'

'For God's sake, Ned, get me right,' Farr protested. 'You know damned well there's nobody in the city any stronger for Paul and for you than me. You ought to know that. I didn't mean anything by what I said except that – well, that you can always count on me.'

Ned Beaumont said, 'That's fine,' without much enthusiasm and stood up.

Farr rose and came around the desk with a red hand out. 'What's your hurry?' he said. 'Why don't you stick around and see how this West acts when they bring him in? Or' – he looked at his watch – 'what are you doing tonight? How about going to dinner with me?'

'Sorry, I can't,' Ned Beaumont replied. 'I've got to run along.'

He let Farr pump his hand up and down, murmured a 'Yes,

I will' in response to the District Attorney's insistence that he drop in often and that they get together some night, and went out.

III

Walter Ivans was standing beside one of a row of men operating nailing-machines in the box-factory where he was employed as foreman, when Ned Beaumont came in. He saw Ned Beaumont at once and, hailing him with an uplifted hand, came down the center aisle, but in Ivans's china-blue eyes and round fair face there was somewhat less pleasure than he seemed to be trying to put there.

Ned Beaumont said, ''Lo, Walt,' and by turning slightly towards the door escaped the necessity of either taking or pointedly ignoring the shorter man's proffered hand. 'Let's get out of this racket.'

Ivans said something that was blurred by the din of metal driving metal into wood and they went to the open door by which Ned Beaumont had entered. Outside was a wide platform of solid timber. A flight of wooden steps ran down twenty feet to the ground.

They stood on the wooden platform and Ned Beaumont asked: 'You know one of the witnesses against your brother was knocked off last night?'

'Y-yes, I saw it in the p-p-paper.'

Ned Beaumont asked: 'You know the other one's not sure now he can identify Tim?'

'N-no, I didn't know that, N-ned.'

Ned Beaumont said: 'You know if he doesn't Tim'll get off.'

'Y-yes.'

Ned Beaumont said: 'You don't look as happy about it as you ought to.'

Ivans wiped his forehead with his shirt-sleeve. 'B-b-but I am, N-ned, b-by God I am!'

'Did you know West? The one that was killed.'

'N-no, except that I went to s-see him once, t-to ask him to g-go kind of easy on T-tim.'

'What'd he say?'

'He wouldn't.'

'When was that?'

Ivans shifted his feet and wiped his face with his sleeve again. 'T-t-two or three d-days ago.'

Ned Beaumont asked softly: 'Any idea who could have killed him, Walt?'

Ivans shook his head violently from side to side.

'Any idea who could've had him killed, Walt?'

Ivans shook his head.

For a moment Ned Beaumont stared reflectively over Ivans's shoulder. The clatter of the nailing-machines came through the door ten feet away and from another story came the whirr of saws. Ivans drew in and expelled a long breath.

Ned Beaumont's mien had become sympathetic when he transferred his gaze to the shorter man's china-blue eyes again. He leaned down a little and asked: 'Are you all right, Walt? I mean there are going to be people who'll think maybe you might have shot West to save your brother. Have you got—?'

'I-I-I was at the C-club all last night, from eight o'clock t-t-till after t-two this morning,' Walter Ivans replied as rapidly as the impediment in his speech permitted. 'Harry Sloss and B-ben Ferris and Brager c-c-can tell you.'

Ned Beaumont laughed. 'That's a lucky break for you, Walt,' he said gaily.

He turned his back on Walter Ivans and went down the wooden steps to the street. He paid no attention to Walter Ivans's very friendly 'Good-by, Ned.'

IV

From the box-factory Ned Beaumont walked four blocks to a restaurant and used a telephone. He called the four numbers he had called earlier in the day, asking again for Paul Madvig and, not getting him on the wire, left instructions for Madvig to call him. Then he got a taxicab and went home.

Additional pieces of mail had been put with those already on the table by the door. He hung up his hat and overcoat, lighted a cigar, and sat down with his mail in the largest of the red-plush chairs. The fourth envelope he opened was similar to the one the District Attorney had shown him. It contained a single sheet of paper bearing three typewritten sentences without salutation or signature:

Did you find Taylor Henry's body after he was dead or were you present when he was murdered?

Why did you not report his death until after the police had found the body?

Do you think you can save the guilty by manufacturing evidence against the innocent?

Ned Beaumont screwed up his eyes and wrinkled his forehead over this message and drew much smoke from his cigar. He compared it with the one the District Attorney had received. Paper and typing were alike, as were the manner in which each paper's three sentences were arranged and the time of the postmarks.

Scowling, he returned each to its envelope and put them in his pocket, only to take them out again immediately to reread and re-examine them. Too rapid smoking made his cigar burn irregularly down one side. He put the cigar on the edge of the table beside him with a grimace of distaste and picked at his mustache with nervous fingers. He put the messages away once more and leaned back in his chair, staring at the ceiling and biting a finger-nail. He ran fingers through his hair. He put the end of a finger between his collar and his neck. He sat up and took the envelopes out of his pocket again, but put them back without having looked at them. He chewed his lower lip. Finally he shook himself impatiently and began to read the rest of his mail. He was reading it when the telephone-bell rang.

He went to the telephone. 'Hello . . . Oh, 'lo, Paul, where are you? . . . How long will you be there? . . . Yes, fine, drop in on your way . . . Right, I'll be here.'

He returned to his mail.

V

Paul Madvig arrived at Ned Beaumont's rooms as the bells in the grey church across the street were ringing the Angelus. He came in saying heartily: 'Howdy, Ned. When'd you get back?' His big body was clothed in grey tweeds.

'Late this morning,' Ned Beaumont replied as they shook hands.

'Make out all right?'

Ned Beaumont showed the edges of his teeth in a contented smile. 'I got what I went after – all of it.'

'That's great.' Madvig threw his hat on a chair and sat on another beside the fireplace.

Ned Beaumont returned to his chair. 'Anything happen while I was gone?' he asked as he picked up the half-filled cocktail-glass standing beside the silver shaker on the table at his elbow.

'We got the muddle on the sewer-contract straightened out.'

Ned Beaumont sipped his cocktail and asked: 'Have to make much of a cut?'

'Too much. There won't be anything like the profit there ought to be, but that's better than taking a chance on stirring things up this close to election. We'll make it up on the street-work next year when the Salem and Chestnut extensions go through.'

Ned Beaumont nodded. He was looking at the blond man's outstretched crossed ankles. He said: 'You oughtn't to wear silk socks with tweeds.'

Madvig raised a leg straight out to look at the ankle. 'No? I like the feel of silk.'

'Then lay off tweeds. Taylor Henry buried?'

'Friday.'

'Go to the funeral?'

'Yes,' Madvig replied and added a little self-consciously: 'The Senator suggested it.'

Ned Beaumont put his glass on the table and touched his lips with a white handkerchief taken from the outer breast-pocket of his coat. 'How is the Senator?' He looked obliquely at the blond man and did not conceal the amusement in his eyes.

Madvig replied, still somewhat self-consciously: 'He's all right. I spent most of this afternoon up there with him.'

'At his house?'

'Uh-huh.'

'Was the blond menace there?'

Madvig did not quite frown. He said: 'Janet was there.'

Ned Beaumont, putting his handkerchief away, made a choked gurgling sound in his throat and said: 'M-m-m. It's Janet now. Getting anywhere with her?'

Composure came back to Madvig. He said evenly: 'I still think I'm going to marry her.'

'Does she know yet that – that your intentions are honorable?'

'For Christ's sake, Ned!' Madvig protested. 'How long are you going to keep me on the witness-stand?'

Ned Beaumont laughed, picked up the silver shaker, shook it, and poured himself another drink. 'How do you like the Francis West killing?' he asked when he was sitting back with the glass in his hand.

Madvig seemed puzzled for a moment. Then his face cleared

and he said: 'Oh, that's the fellow that got shot on Achland Avenue last night.'

'That's the fellow.'

A fainter shade of puzzlement returned to Madvig's blue eyes. He said: 'Well, I didn't know him.'

Ned Beaumont said: 'He was one of the witnesses against Walter Ivans's brother. Now the other witness, Boyd West, is afraid to testify, so the rap falls through.'

'That's swell,' Madvig said, but by the time the last word had issued from his mouth a doubtful look had come into his eyes. He drew his legs in and leaned forward. 'Afraid?' he asked.

'Yes, unless you like scared better.'

Madvig's face hardened into attentiveness and his eyes became stony blue disks. 'What are you getting at, Ned?' he asked in a crisp voice.

Ned Beaumont emptied his glass and set it on the table. 'After you told Walt Ivans you couldn't spring Tim till election was out of the way he took his troubles to Shad O'Rory,' he said in a deliberate monotone, as if reciting a lesson. 'Shad sent some of his gorillas around to scare the two Wests out of appearing against Tim. One of them wouldn't scare and they bumped him off.'

Madvig, scowling, objected: 'What the hell does Shad care about Tim Ivans's troubles?'

Ned Beaumont, reaching for the cocktail-shaker, said irritably: 'All right, I'm just guessing. Forget it.'

'Cut it out, Ned. You know your guesses are good enough for me. If you've got anything on your mind, spill it.'

Ned Beaumont set the shaker down without having poured a drink and said: 'It might be just a guess, at that, Paul, but this is the way it looks to me. Everybody knows Walt Ivans's been working for you down in the Third Ward and is a member of the Club and everything and that you'd do anything you could to get his brother out of a jam if he asked you. Well, everybody, or a lot of them, is going to start wondering whether you didn't have the witnesses against his brother shot and frightened into silence.

That goes for the outsiders, the women's clubs you're getting so afraid of these days, and the respectable citizens. The insiders – the ones that mostly wouldn't care if you had done that – are going to get something like the real news. They're going to know that one of your boys had to go to Shad to get fixed up and that Shad fixed him up. Well, that's the hole Shad's put you in – or don't you think he'd go that far to put you in a hole?'

Madvig growled through his teeth: 'I know damned well he would, the louse.' He was lowering down at a green leaf worked in the rug at his feet.

Ned Beaumont, after looking intently at the blond man, went on: 'And there's another angle to look for. Maybe it won't happen, but you're open to it if Shad wants to work it.'

Madvig looked up to ask: 'What?'

'Walt Ivans was at the Club all last night, till two this morning. That's about three hours later than he ever stayed there before except on election- or banquet-nights. Understand? He was making himself an alibi – in our Club. Suppose' – Ned Beaumont's voice sank to a lower key and his dark eyes were round and grave – 'Shad jobs Walt by planting evidence that he killed West? Your women's clubs and all the people who like to squawk about things like that are going to think that Walt's alibi is phony – that we fixed it up to shield him.'

Madvig said: 'The louse.' He stood up and thrust his hands into his trousers-pockets. 'I wish to Christ the election was either over or further away.'

'None of this would've happened then.'

Madvig took two steps into the center of the room. He muttered, 'God damn him,' and stood frowning at the telephone on the stand beside the bedroom-door. His huge chest moved with his breathing. He said from the side of his mouth, without looking at Ned Beaumont: 'Figure out a way of blocking that angle.' He took a step towards the telephone and halted. 'Never mind,' he said and turned to face Ned Beaumont. 'I think I'll knock Shad loose from our little city. I'm tired of having him around. I think I'll knock him loose right away, starting tonight.'

Ned Beaumont asked: 'For instance?'

Madvig grinned. 'For instance,' he replied, 'I think I'll have Rainey close up the Dog House and Paradise Gardens and every dive that we know Shad or any of his friends are interested in. I think I'll have Rainey smack them over in one long row, one after the other, this very same night.'

Ned Beaumont spoke hesitantly: 'You're putting Rainey in a tough spot. Our coppers aren't used to bothering with Prohibition-enforcement. They're not going to like it very much.'

'They can do it once for me,' Madvig said, 'without feeling that they've paid all their debts.'

'Maybe.' Ned Beaumont's face and voice were dubious still. 'But this wholesale stuff is too much like using a cyclone shot to blow off a safe-door when you could get it off without any fuss by using a come-along.'

'Have you got something up your sleeve, Ned?'

Ned Beaumont shook his head. 'No,' he said. 'Nothing I'm sure of, but it wouldn't hurt to wait a couple of days until—'

Now Madvig shook his head. 'No,' he said. 'I want action. I don't know a damned thing about opening safes, Ned, but I do know fighting – my kind – going in with both hands working. I never could learn to box and the only times I ever tried I got licked. We'll give Mr O'Rory the cyclone shot.'

VI

The stringy man in horn-rimmed spectacles said: 'So you don't have to worry none about that.' He sat complacently back in his chair.

The man on his left – a raw-boned man with a bushy brown mustache and not much hair on his head – said to the man on his left: 'It don't sound so God-damned swell to me.'

'No?' The stringy man turned to glare through his spectacles at the raw-boned man. 'Well, Paul don't never have to come down to my ward hisself to—'

The raw-boned man said: 'Aw, nurts!'

Madvig addressed the raw-boned man: 'Did you see Parker, Breen?'

Breen said: 'Yes, I saw him and he says five, but I think we can get a couple more out of him.'

The bespectacled man said contemptuously: 'My God, I'd think so!'

Breen sneered sidewise at him. 'Yes? And who'd you ever get that much out of?'

Three knocks sounded on the broad oaken door.

Ned Beaumont rose from the chair he was straddling and went to the door. He opened it less than a foot.

The man who had knocked was a small-browed dark man in blue clothes that needed pressing. He did not try to enter the room and he tried to speak in an undertone, but excitement made his words audible to everyone in the room. 'Shad O'Rory's downstairs. He wants to see Paul.'

Ned Beaumont shut the door and turned with his back against it to look at Paul Madvig. Only those two of the ten men in the room seemed undisturbed by the small-browed man's announcement. All the others did not show their excitement frankly – in some it could be seen in their suddenly acquired stoniness – but there was none whose respiration was exactly as it had been before.

Ned Beaumont, pretending he did not know repetition was unnecessary, said, in a tone that expressed suitable interest in his words: 'O'Rory wants to see you. He's downstairs.'

Madvig looked at his watch. 'Tell him I'm tied up right now, but if he'll wait a little while I'll see him.'

Ned Beaumont nodded and opened the door. 'Tell him Paul's busy now,' he instructed the man who had knocked, 'but if he'll stick around awhile Paul'll see him.' He shut the door.

Madvig was questioning a square-faced yellowish man about their chances of getting more votes on the other side of Chestnut Street. The square-faced man replied that he thought they would get more than last time 'by a hell of a sight,' but still not enough to make much of a dent in the opposition. While he talked his eyes kept crawling sidewise to the door.

Ned Beaumont sat astride his chair by the window again smoking a cigar.

Madvig addressed to another man a question having to do with the size of the campaign-contribution to be expected from a man named Hartwick. This other man kept his eyes from the door, but his reply lacked coherence.

Neither Madvig's and Ned Beaumont's calmness of mien nor their business-like concentration on campaign-problems could check the growth of tension in the room.

After fifteen minutes Madvig rose and said: 'Well, we're not on Easy Street yet, but she's shaping up. Keep hard at it and we'll make the grade.' He went to the door and shook each man's hand as they went out. They went out somewhat hurriedly.

Ned Beaumont, who had not left his chair, asked, when he and Madvig were the only ones in the room: 'Do I stick around or beat it?'

'Stick around.' Madvig crossed to the window and looked down into the sunny China Street.

'Both hands working?' Ned Beaumont asked after a little pause.

Madvig turned from the window nodding. 'I don't know anything else' – he grinned boyishly at the man straddling the chair – 'except maybe the feet too.'

Ned Beaumont started to say something, but was interrupted by the noise the turning door-knob made.

A man opened the door and came in. He was a man of little more than medium height, trimly built with a trimness that gave him a deceptively frail appearance. Though his hair was a sheer sleek white he was probably not much past his thirty-fifth year. His eyes were a notable clear grey-blue set in a rather long and narrow, but very finely sculptured, face. He wore a dark blue overcoat over a dark blue suit and carried a black derby hat in a black-gloved hand.

The man who came in behind him was a bow-legged ruffian of the same height, a swarthy man with something apish in the slope of his big shoulders, the length of his thick arms, and the flatness of his face. This one's hat – a grey fedora – was on his head. He shut the door and leaned against it, putting his hands in the pockets of his plaid overcoat.

The first man, having advanced by then some four or five steps into the room, put his hat on a chair and began to take off his gloves.

Madvig, hands in trousers-pockets, smiled amiably and said: 'How are you, Shad?'

The white-haired man said: 'Fine, Paul. How's yourself?' His voice was a strong musical baritone. The faintest of brogues colored his words.

Madvig indicated with a small jerk of his head the man on the chair and asked: 'You know Beaumont?'

O'Rory said: 'Yes.'

Ned Beaumont said: 'Yes.'

Neither nodded to the other and Ned Beaumont did not get up from his chair.

Shad O'Rory had finished taking off his gloves. He put them in an overcoat-pocket and said: 'Politics is politics and business is business. I've been paying my way and I'm willing to go on paying my way, but I want what I'm paying for.' His modulated voice was no more than pleasantly earnest.

'What do you mean by that?' Madvig asked as if he did not greatly care.

'I mean that half the coppers in town are buying their cakes and ale with dough they're getting from me and some of my friends.'

Madvig sat down by the table. 'Well?' he asked, carelessly as before.

'I want what I'm paying for. I'm paying to be let alone. I want to be let alone.'

Madvig chuckled. 'You don't mean, Shad, that you're complaining to me because your coppers won't stay bought?'

'I mean that Doolan told me last night that the orders to shut up my places came straight from you.'

Madvig chuckled again and turned his head to address Ned Beaumont: 'What do you think of that, Ned?'

Ned Beaumont smiled thinly, but said nothing.

Madvig said: 'You know what I think of it? I think Captain Doolan's been working too hard. I think somebody ought to give Captain Doolan a nice long leave of absence. Don't let me forget it.'

O'Rory said: 'I bought protection, Paul, and I want it. Business is business and politics is politics. Let's keep them apart.'

Madvig said: 'No.'

Shad O'Rory's blue eyes looked dreamily at some distant thing. He smiled a little sadly and there was a note of sadness in his musical slightly Irish voice when he spoke. He said: 'It's going to mean killing.'

Madvig's blue eyes were opaque and his voice was as difficultly read as his eyes. He said: 'If you make it mean killing.'

The white-haired man nodded. 'It'll have to mean killing,' he said, still sadly. 'I'm too big to take the boot from you now.'

Madvig leaned back in his chair and crossed his legs. His tone attached little importance to his words. He said: 'Maybe you're too big to take it laying down, but you'll take it.' He pursed his lips and added as an afterthought: 'You are taking it.'

Dreaminess and sadness went swiftly out of Shad O'Rory's eyes. He put his black hat on his head. He adjusted his coat-collar to his neck. He pointed a long white finger at Madvig and said: 'I'm opening the Dog House again tonight. I don't want to be bothered. Bother me and I'll bother you.'

Madvig uncrossed his legs and reached for the telephone on the table. He called the Police Department's number, asked for the

Chief, and said to him: 'Hello, Rainey . . . Yes, fine. How are the folks? . . . That's good. Say, Rainey, I hear Shad's thinking of opening up again tonight . . . Yes . . . Yes, slam it down so hard it bounces . . . Right . . . Sure. Good-by.' He pushed the telephone back and addressed O'Rory: 'Now do you understand how you stand? You're through, Shad. You're through here for good.'

O'Rory said softly, 'I understand,' turned, opened the door, and went out.

The bow-legged ruffian paused to spit – deliberately – on the rug in front of him and to stare with bold challenging eyes at Madvig and Ned Beaumont. Then he went out.

Ned Beaumont wiped the palms of his hands with a handkerchief. He said nothing to Madvig, who was looking at him with questioning eyes. Ned Beaumont's eyes were gloomy.

After a moment Madvig asked: 'Well?'

Ned Beaumont said: 'Wrong, Paul.'

Madvig rose and went to the window. 'Jesus Christ!' he complained over his shoulder, 'don't anything ever suit you?'

Ned Beaumont got up from his chair and walked towards the door.

Madvig, turning from the window, asked angrily: 'Some more of your God-damned foolishness?'

Ned Beaumont said, 'Yes,' and went out of the room. He went downstairs, got his hat, and left the Log Cabin Club. He walked seven blocks to the railroad station, bought a ticket for New York, and made reservations on a night train. Then he took a taxicab to his rooms.

VII

A stout shapeless woman in grey clothes and a chubby half-grown boy were packing Ned Beaumont's trunk and three leather bags under his supervision when the door-bell rang.

The woman rose grunting from her knees and went to the door. She opened it wide. 'My goodness, Mr Madvig,' she said. 'Come right on in.'

Madvig came in saying: 'How are you, Mrs Duveen? You get younger-looking every day.' His gaze passed over the trunk and bags to the boy. 'Hello, Charley. Ready for the job running the cement-mixer yet?'

The boy grinned bashfully and said: 'How do you do, Mr Madvig?'

Madvig's smile came around to Ned Beaumont 'Going places?'

Ned Beaumont smiled politely. 'Yes,' he said.

The blond man looked around the room, at the bags and trunk again, at the clothes piled on chairs and the drawers standing open. The woman and the boy went back to their work. Ned Beaumont found two somewhat faded shirts in a pile on a chair and put them aside.

Madvig asked: 'Got half an hour to spare, Ned?'

'I've got plenty of time.'

Madvig said: 'Get your hat.'

Ned Beaumont got his hat and overcoat. 'Get as much of it in as you can,' he told the woman as he and Madvig moved towards the door, 'and what's left over can be sent on with the other stuff.'

He and Madvig went downstairs to the street. They walked south a block. Then Madvig asked: 'Where're you going, Ned?'

'New York.'

They turned into an alley.

Madvig asked: 'For good?'

Ned Beaumont shrugged. 'I'm leaving here for good.'

They opened a green wooden door set in the red-brick rear wall of a building and went down a passageway and through another door into a bar-room where half a dozen men were drinking. They exchanged greetings with the bar-tender and three of the drinkers as they passed through to a small room where there were four tables. Nobody else was there. They sat at one of the tables.

The bar-tender put his head in and asked: 'Beer as per usual, gents?'

Madvig said, 'Yes,' and then, when the bar-tender had drawn: 'Why?'

Ned Beaumont said: 'I'm tired of hick-town stuff.'

'Meaning me?'

Ned Beaumont did not say anything.

Madvig did not say anything for a while. Then he sighed and said: 'This is a hell of a time to be throwing me down.'

The bar-tender came in with two seidels of pale beer and a bowl of pretzels. When he had gone out again, shutting the door behind him, Madvig exclaimed: 'Christ, you're hard to get along with, Ned!'

Ned Beaumont moved his shoulders. 'I never said I wasn't.' He lifted his seidel and drank.

Madvig was breaking a pretzel into small bits. 'Do you really want to go, Ned?' he asked.

'I'm going.'

Madvig dropped the fragments of pretzel on the table and took a check-book from his pocket. He tore out a check, took a fountain-pen from another pocket, and filled in the check. Then he fanned it dry and dropped it on the table in front of Ned Beaumont.

Ned Beaumont, looking down at the check, shook his head and said: 'I don't need money and you don't owe me anything.'

'I do. I owe you more than that, Ned. I wish you'd take it.'

Ned Beaumont said, 'All right, thanks,' and put the check in his pocket.

Madvig drank beer, ate a pretzel, started to drink again, set his seidel down on the table, and asked: 'Was there anything on your mind – any kick – besides that back in the Club this afternoon?'

Ned Beaumont shook his head. 'You don't talk to me like that. Nobody does.'

'Hell, Ned, I didn't say anything.'

Ned Beaumont did not say anything.

Madvig drank again. 'Mind telling me why you think I handled O'Rory wrong?'

'It wouldn't do any good.'

'Try.'

Ned Beaumont said: 'All right, but it won't do any good.' He tilted his chair back, holding his seidel in one hand, some pretzels in the other. 'Shad'll fight. He's got to. You've got him in a corner. You've told him he's through here for good. There's nothing he can do now but play the long shot. If he can upset you this election he'll be fixed to square anything he has to do to win. If you win the election he's got to drift anyhow. You're using the police on him. He'll have to fight back at the police and he will. That means you're going to have something that can be made to look like a crime-wave. You're trying to re-elect the whole city administration. Well, giving them a crime-wave and one it's an even bet they're not going to be able to handle – just before election – isn't going to make them look any too efficient. They—'

'You think I ought to've laid down to him?' Madvig demanded scowling.

'I don't think that. I think you should have left him an out, a line of retreat. You shouldn't have got him with his back to the wall.'

Madvig's scowl deepened. 'I don't know anything about your kind of fighting. He started it. All I know is when you got somebody cornered you go in and finish them. That system's worked all right for me so far.' He blushed a little. 'I don't mean I think I'm Napoleon or something, Ned, but I came up from running errands for Packy Flood in the old Fifth to where I'm sitting kind of pretty today.'

Ned Beaumont emptied his seidel and let the front legs of his chair come down on the floor. 'I told you it wouldn't do any good,' he said. 'Have it your own way. Keep on thinking that what was good enough for the old Fifth is good enough anywhere.'

In Madvig's voice there was something of resentment and something of humility when he asked: 'You don't think much of me as a big-time politician, do you, Ned?'

Now Ned Beaumont's face flushed. He said: 'I didn't say that, Paul.'

'But that's what it amounts to, isn't it?' Madvig insisted.

'No, but I do think you've let yourself be outsmarted this time. First you let the Henrys wheedle you into backing the Senator. There was your chance to go in and finish an enemy who was cornered, but that enemy happened to have a daughter and social position and what not, so you—'

'Cut it out, Ned,' Madvig grumbled.

Ned Beaumont's face became empty of expression. He stood up saying, 'Well, I must be running along,' and turned to the door.

Madvig was up behind him immediately, with a hand on his shoulder, saying: 'Wait, Ned.'

Ned Beaumont said: 'Take your hand off me.' He did not look around.

Madvig put his other hand on Ned Beaumont's arm and turned him around. 'Look here, Ned,' he began.

Ned Beaumont said: 'Let go.' His lips were pale and stiff.

Madvig shook him. He said: 'Don't be a God-damned fool. You and I—'

Ned Beaumont struck Madvig's mouth with his left fist.

Madvig took his hands away from Ned Beaumont and fell back two steps. While his pulse had time to beat perhaps three times his mouth hung open and astonishment was in his face. Then his face darkened with anger and he shut his mouth tight, so his jaw was hard and lumpy. He made fists of his hands, hunched his shoulders, and swayed forward.

Ned Beaumont's hand swept out to the side to grasp one of the heavy glass seidels on the table, though he did not lift it from the table. His body leaned a little to that side as he had leaned to get the seidel. Otherwise he stood squarely confronting the blond man. His face was drawn thin and rigid, with white lines of strain around the mouth. His dark eyes glared fiercely into Madvig's blue ones.

They stood thus, less than a yard apart – one blond, tall and powerfully built, leaning far forward, big shoulders hunched, big fists ready; the other dark of hair and eye, tall and lean, body bent a little to one side with an arm slanting down from that side to hold a heavy glass seidel by its handle – and except for their breathing there was no sound in the room. No sound came in from the bar-room on the other side of the thin door, the rattling of glasses nor the hum of talk nor the splash of water.

When quite two minutes had passed Ned Beaumont took his hand away from the seidel and turned his back to Madvig. Nothing changed in Ned Beaumont's face except that his eyes, when no longer focused on Madvig's, became hard and cold instead of angrily glaring. He took an unhurried step towards the door.

Madvig spoke hoarsely from deep down in him. 'Ned.'

Ned Beaumont halted. His face became paler. He did not turn around.

Madvig said: 'You crazy son of a bitch.'

Then Ned Beaumont turned around, slowly.

Madvig put out an open hand and pushed Ned Beaumont's face sidewise, shoving him off balance so he had to put a foot out quickly to that side and put a hand on one of the chairs at the table.

Madvig said: 'I ought to knock hell out of you.'

Ned Beaumont grinned sheepishly and sat down on the chair he had staggered against. Madvig sat down facing him and knocked on the top of the table with his seidel.

The bar-tender opened the door and put his head in.

'More beer,' Madvig said.

From the bar-room, through the open door, came the sound of men talking and the sound of glasses rattling against glasses and against wood.

4 The Dog House

I

Ned Beaumont, at breakfast in bed, called, 'Come in,' and then, when the outer door had opened and closed: 'Yes?'

A low-pitched rasping voice in the living-room asked: 'Where are you, Ned?' Before Ned Beaumont could reply the rasping voice's owner had come to the bedroom-door and was saying: 'Pretty soft for you.' He was a sturdy young man with a square-cut sallow face, a wide thick-lipped mouth, from a corner of which a cigarette dangled, and merry dark squinting eyes.

''Lo , Whisky,' Ned Beaumont said to him. 'Treat yourself to a chair.'

Whisky looked around the room. 'Pretty good dump you've got here,' he said. He removed the cigarette from his lips and, without turning his head, used the cigarette to point over his shoulder at the living-room behind him. 'What's all the keysters for? Moving out?'

Ned Beaumont thoroughly chewed and swallowed the scrambled eggs in his mouth before replying: 'Thinking of it.'

Whisky said, 'Yes?' while moving towards a chair that faced the bed. He sat down. 'Where to?'

'New York maybe.'

'What do you mean maybe?'

Ned Beaumont said: 'Well, I've got a ducat that reads to there, anyway.'

Whisky knocked cigarette-ash on the floor and returned the cigarette to the left side of his mouth. He snuffled. 'How long you going to be gone?'

Ned Beaumont held a coffee-cup half-way between the tray and his mouth. He looked thoughtfully over it at the sallow young man. Finally he said, 'It's a one-way ticket,' and drank.

Whisky squinted at Ned Beaumont now until one of his dark eyes was entirely shut and the other was no more than a thin black gleam. He took the cigarette from his mouth and knocked more ash on the floor. His rasping voice held a persuasive note. 'Why don't you see Shad before you go?' he suggested.

Ned Beaumont put his cup down and smiled. He said: 'Shad and I aren't good enough friends that his feelings'll be hurt if I go away without saying good-by.'

Whisky said: 'That ain't the point.'

Ned Beaumont moved the tray from his lap to the bedside-table. He turned on his side, propping himself up on an elbow on the pillows. He pulled the bed-clothes higher up over his chest. Then he asked: 'What is the point?'

'The point is you and Shad ought to be able to do business together.'

Ned Beaumont shook his head. 'I don't think so.'

'Can't you be wrong?' Whisky demanded.

'Sure,' the man in bed confessed. 'Once back in 1912 I was. I forget what it was about.'

Whisky rose to mash his cigarette in one of the dishes on the tray. Standing beside the bed, close to the table, he said: 'Why don't you try it, Ned?'

Ned Beaumont frowned. 'Looks like a waste of time, Whisky. I don't think Shad and I could get along together.'

Whisky sucked a tooth noisily. The downward curve of his

thick lips gave the noise a scornful cast. 'Shad thinks you could,' he said.

Ned Beaumont opened his eyes. 'Yes?' he asked. 'He sent you here?'

'Hell, yes,' Whisky said. 'You don't think I'd be here talking like this if he hadn't.'

Ned Beaumont narrowed his eyes again and asked: 'Why?'

'Because he thought him and you could do business together.'

'I mean,' Ned Beaumont explained, 'why did he think I'd want to do business with him?'

Whisky made a disgusted face. 'Are you trying to kid me, Ned?' he asked.

'No.'

'Well, for the love of Christ, don't you think everybody in town knows about you and Paul having it out at Pip Carson's yesterday?'

Ned Beaumont nodded. 'So that's it,' he said softly, as if to himself.

'That's it,' the man with the rasping voice assured him, and 'Shad happens to know you fell out over thinking Paul hadn't ought to've had Shad's joints smeared. So you're sitting pretty with Shad now if you use your head.'

Ned Beaumont said thoughtfully: 'I don't know. I'd like to get out of here, get back to the big city.'

'Use your head,' Whisky rasped. 'The big city'll still be there after election. Stick around. You know Shad's dough-heavy and's putting it out in chunks to beat Madvig. Stick around and get yourself a slice of it.'

'Well,' Ned Beaumont said slowly, 'it wouldn't hurt to talk it over with him.'

'You're damned right it wouldn't,' Whisky said heartily. 'Pin your diapers on and we'll go now.'

Ned Beaumont said, 'Right,' and got out of bed.

Shad O'Rory rose and bowed. 'Glad to see you, Beaumont,' he said. 'Drop your hat and coat anywhere.' He did not offer to shake hands.

Ned Beaumont said, 'Good morning,' and began to take off his overcoat.

Whisky, in the doorway said: 'Well, I'll be seeing you guys later.'

O'Rory said, 'Yes, do,' and Whisky, drawing the door shut as he backed out, left them.

Ned Beaumont dropped his overcoat on the arm of a sofa, put his hat on the overcoat, and sat down beside them. He looked without curiosity at O'Rory.

O'Rory had returned to his chair, a deeply padded squat affair of dull wine and gold. He crossed his knees and put his hands together – tips of fingers and thumbs touching – atop his uppermost knee. He let his finely sculptured head sink down towards his chest so that his grey-blue eyes looked upward under his brows at Ned Beaumont. He said, in his pleasantly modulated Irish voice: 'I owe you something for trying to talk Paul out of—'

'You don't,' Ned Beaumont said.

O'Rory asked: 'I don't?'

'No. I was with him then. What I told him was for his own good. I thought he was making a bad play.'

O'Rory smiled gently. 'And he'll know it before he's through,' he said.

Silence was between them awhile then. O'Rory sat half-buried in his chair smiling at Ned Beaumont. Ned Beaumont sat on the sofa looking, with eyes that gave no indication of what he thought, at O'Rory.

The silence was broken by O'Rory asking: 'How much did Whisky tell you?'

'Nothing. He said you wanted to see me.'

'He was right enough as far as he went,' O'Rory said. He took his finger-tips apart and patted the back of one slender hand with the palm of the other. 'Is it so that you and Paul have broken for good and all?'

'I thought you knew it,' Ned Beaumont replied. 'I thought that's why you sent for me.'

'I heard it,' O'Rory said, 'but that's not always the same thing. What were you thinking you might do now?'

'There's a ticket for New York in my pocket and my clothes are packed.'

O'Rory raised a hand and smoothed his sleek white hair. 'You came here from New York, didn't you?'

'I never told anybody where I came from.'

O'Rory took his hand from his hair and made a small gesture of protestation. 'You don't think I'm one to give a damn where any man comes from, do you?' he asked.

Ned Beaumont did not say anything.

The white-haired man said: 'But I do care about where you go and if I have my way as much as I'd like you won't be going off to New York yet awhile. Did you never happen to think that maybe you could still do yourself a lot of good right here?'

'No,' Ned Beaumont said, 'that is, not till Whisky came.'

'And what do you think now?'

'I don't know anything about it. I'm waiting to hear what you've got to say.'

O'Rory put his hand to his hair again. His blue-grey eyes were friendly and shrewd. He asked: 'How long have you been here?'

'Fifteen months.'

'And you and Paul have been close as a couple of fingers how long?'

'Year.'

O'Rory nodded. 'And you ought to know a lot of things about him,' he said.

'I do.'

O'Rory said: 'You ought to know a lot of things I could use.'

Ned Beaumont said evenly: 'Make your proposition.'

O'Rory got up from the depths of his chair and went to a door opposite the one through which Ned Beaumont had come. When he opened the door a huge English bulldog waddled in. O'Rory went back to his chair. The dog lay on the rug in front of the wine and gold chair staring with morose eyes up at its master.

O'Rory said: 'One thing I can offer you is a chance to pay Paul back plenty.'

Ned Beaumont said: 'That's nothing to me.'

'It is not?'

'Far as I'm concerned we're quits.'

O'Rory raised his head. He asked softly: 'And you wouldn't want to do anything to hurt him?'

'I didn't say that,' Ned Beaumont replied a bit irritably. 'I don't mind hurting him, but I can do it any time I want to on my own account and I don't want you to think you're giving me anything when you give me a chance to.'

O'Rory wagged his head up and down, pleasantly. 'Suits me,' he said, 'so he's hurt. Why did he bump off young Henry?'

Ned Beaumont laughed. 'Take it easy,' he said. 'You haven't made your proposition yet. That's a nice pooch. How old is he?'

'Just about the limit, seven.' O'Rory put out a foot and rubbed the dog's nose with the tip of it. The dog moved its tail sluggishly. 'How does this hit you? After election I'll stake you to the finest gambling-house this state's ever seen and let you run it to suit yourself with all the protection you ever heard of.'

'That's an *if* offer,' Ned Beaumont said in a somewhat bored manner, '*if* you win. Anyhow, I'm not sure I want to stay here after election, or even that long.'

O'Rory stopped rubbing the dog's nose with his shoe-tip. He looked up at Ned Beaumont again, smiled dreamily, and asked: 'Don't you think we're going to win the election?'

Ned Beaumont smiled. 'You won't bet even money on it.'

O'Rory, still smiling dreamily, asked another question: 'You're not so God-damned hot for putting in with me, are you, Beaumont?'

'No.' Ned Beaumont rose and picked up his hat. 'It wasn't any idea of mine.' His voice was casual, his face politely expressionless. 'I told Whisky it'd just be wasting time.' He reached for his overcoat.

The white-haired man said: 'Sit down. We can still talk, can't we? And maybe we'll get somewhere before we're through.'

Ned Beaumont hesitated, moved his shoulders slightly, took off his hat, put it and his overcoat on the sofa, and sat down beside them.

O'Rory said: 'I'll give you ten grand in cash right now if you'll come in and ten more election-night if we beat Paul and I'll keep that house-offer open for you to take or leave.'

Ned Beaumont pursed his lips and stared gloomily at O'Rory under brows drawn together. 'You want me to rat on him, of course,' he said.

'I want you to go into the *Observer* with the lowdown on everything you know about him being mixed up in – the sewer-contracts, the how and why of killing Taylor Henry, that Shoemaker junk last winter, the dirt on how he's running the city.'

'There's nothing in the sewer-business now,' Ned Beaumont said, speaking as if his mind was more fully occupied with other thoughts. 'He let his profits go to keep from raising a stink.'

'All right,' O'Rory conceded, blandly confident, 'but there is something in the Taylor Henry business.'

'Yes, we'd have him there,' Ned Beaumont said, frowning, 'but I don't know whether we could use the Shoemaker stuff' – he hesitated – 'without making trouble for me.'

'Hell, we don't want that,' O'Rory said quickly. 'That's out. What else have we got?'

'Maybe we can do something with the street-car-franchise extension and with that trouble last year in the County Clerk's office. We'll have to do some digging first, though.'

'It'll be worth it for both of us,' O'Rory said. 'I'll have Hinkle –

he's the *Observer* guy – put the stuff in shape. You just give him the dope and let him write it. We can start off with the Taylor Henry thing. That's something that's right on tap.'

Ned Beaumont brushed his mustache with a thumb-nail and murmured: 'Maybe.'

Shad O'Rory laughed. 'You mean we ought to start off first with the ten thousand dollars?' he asked. 'There's something in that.' He got up and crossed the room to the door he had opened for the dog. He opened it and went out, shutting it behind him. The dog did not get up from in front of the wine and gold chair.

Ned Beaumont lit a cigar. The dog turned his head and watched him.

O'Rory came back with a thick sheaf of green hundred-dollar bills held together by a band of brown paper on which was written in blue ink: $10,000. He thumped the sheaf down on the hand not holding it and said: 'Hinkle's out there now. I told him to come in.'

Ned Beaumont frowned. 'I ought to have a little time to straighten it out in my mind.'

'Give it to Hinkle any way it comes to you. He'll put it in shape.'

Ned Beaumont nodded. He blew cigar-smoke out and said: 'Yes, I can do that.'

O'Rory held out the sheaf of paper money.

Saying, 'Thanks,' Ned Beaumont took it and put it in his inside coat-pocket. It made a bulge there in the breast of his coat over his flat chest.

Shad O'Rory said, 'The thanks go both ways,' and went back to his chair.

Ned Beaumont took the cigar out of his mouth. 'Here's something I want to tell you while I think of it,' he said. 'Framing Walt Ivans for the West killing won't bother Paul as much as leaving it as is.'

O'Rory looked curiously at Ned Beaumont for a moment before asking: 'Why?'

'Paul's not going to let him have the Club alibi.'

'You mean he's going to give the boys orders to forget Ivans was there?'

'Yes.'

O'Rory made a clucking noise with his tongue, asked: 'How'd he get the idea I was going to play tricks on Ivans?'

'Oh, we figured it out.'

O'Rory smiled. 'You mean you did,' he said. 'Paul's not that shifty.'

Ned Beaumont made a modest grimace and asked: 'What kind of job did you put up on him?'

O'Rory chuckled. 'We sent the clown over to Braywood to buy the guns that were used.' His grey-blue eyes suddenly became hard and sharp. Then amusement came back into them and he said: 'Oh, well, none of that's big stuff now, now that Paul's hell-bent on making a row of it. But that's what started him picking on me, isn't it?'

'Yes,' Ned Beaumont told him, 'though it was likely to come sooner or later anyhow. Paul thinks he gave you your start here and you ought to stay under his wing and not grow big enough to buck him.'

O'Rory smiled gently. 'And I'm the boy that'll make him sorry he ever gave me that start,' he promised. 'He can—'

A door opened and a man came in. He was a young man in baggy grey clothes. His ears and nose were very large. His indefinitely brown hair needed trimming and his rather grimy face was too deeply lined for his years.

'Come in, Hinkle,' O'Rory said. 'This is Beaumont. He'll give you the dope. Let me see it when you've shaped it up and we'll get the first shot in tomorrow's paper.'

Hinkle smiled with bad teeth and muttered something unintelligibly polite to Ned Beaumont.

Ned Beaumont stood up saying: 'Fine. We'll go over to my place now and get to work on it.'

O'Rory shook his head. 'It'll be better here,' he said.

Ned Beaumont, picking up hat and overcoat, smiled and said: 'Sorry, but I'm expecting some phone-calls and things. Get your hat, Hinkle.'

Hinkle, looking frightened, stood still and dumb.

O'Rory said: 'You'll have to stay here, Beaumont. We can't afford to have anything happen to you. Here you'll have plenty of protection.'

Ned Beaumont smiled his nicest smile. 'If it's the money you're worried about' – he put his hand inside his coat and brought it out holding the money – 'you can hang on to it till I've turned in the stuff.'

'I'm not worried about anything,' O'Rory said calmly. 'But you're in a tough spot if Paul gets the news you've come over to me and I don't want to take any chances on having you knocked off.'

'You'll have to take them,' Ned Beaumont said. 'I'm going.'

O'Rory said: 'No.'

Ned Beaumont said: 'Yes.'

Hinkle turned quickly and went out of the room.

Ned Beaumont turned around and started for the other door, the one through which he had come into the room, walking erectly without haste.

O'Rory spoke to the bulldog at his feet. The dog got up in cumbersome haste and waddled around Ned Beaumont to the door. He stood on wide-spread legs in front of the door and stared morosely at Ned Beaumont.

Ned Beaumont smiled with tight lips and turned to face O'Rory again. The package of hundred-dollar bills was in Ned Beaumont's hand. He raised the hand, said, 'You know where you can stick it,' and threw the package of bills at O'Rory.

As Ned Beaumont's arm came down the bulldog, leaping clumsily, came up to meet it. His jaws shut over Ned Beaumont's wrist. Ned Beaumont was spun to the left by the impact and he sank on one knee with his arm down close to the floor to take the dog's weight off his arm.

Shad O'Rory rose from his chair and went to the door through which Hinkle had retreated. He opened it and said: 'Come in a minute.' Then he approached Ned Beaumont who, still down on one knee, was trying to let his arm yield to the strain of the dog's pulling. The dog was almost flat on the floor, all four feet braced, holding the arm.

Whisky and two other men came into the room. One of the others was the apish bow-legged man who had accompanied Shad O'Rory to the Log Cabin Club. One was a sandy-haired boy of nineteen or twenty, stocky, rosy-cheeked, and sullen. The sullen boy went around behind Ned Beaumont, between him and the door. The bow-legged ruffian put his right hand on Ned Beaumont's left arm, the arm the dog was not holding. Whisky halted half-way between Ned Beaumont and the other door.

Then O'Rory said, 'Patty,' to the dog.

The dog released Ned Beaumont's wrist and waddled over to its master.

Ned Beaumont stood up. His face was pallid and damp with sweat. He looked at his torn coat-sleeve and wrist and at the blood running down his hand. His hand was trembling.

O'Rory said in his musical Irish voice: 'You would have it.'

Ned Beaumont looked up from his wrist at the white-haired man. 'Yes,' he said, 'and it'll take some more of it to keep me from going out of here.'

III

Ned Beaumont opened his eyes and groaned.

The rosy-cheeked boy with sandy hair turned his head over his shoulder to growl: 'Shut up, you bastard.'

The apish dark man said: 'Let him alone, Rusty. Maybe he'll try to get out again and we'll have some more fun.' He grinned down at his swollen knuckles. 'Deal the cards.'

Ned Beaumont mumbled something about Fedink and sat up. He was in a narrow bed without sheets or bedclothes of any sort. The bare mattress was blood-stained. His face was swollen and bruised and blood-smeared. Dried blood glued his shirt-sleeve to the wrist the dog had bitten and that hand was caked with drying blood. He was in a small yellow and white bedroom furnished with two chairs, a table, a chest of drawers, a wall-mirror, and three white-framed French prints, besides the bed. Facing the foot of the bed was a door that stood open to show part of the interior of a white-tiled bathroom. There was another door, shut. There were no windows.

The apish dark man and the rosy-cheeked boy with sandy hair sat on the chairs playing cards on the table. There was about twenty dollars in paper and silver on the table.

Ned Beaumont looked, with brown eyes wherein hate was a dull glow that came from far beneath the surface, at the card-players and began to get out of bed. Getting out of bed was a difficult task for him. His right arm hung useless. He had to push his legs over the side of the bed one at a time with his left hand and twice he fell over on his side and had to push himself upright again in bed with his left arm.

Once the apish man leered up at him from his cards to ask humorously: 'How're you making out, brother?' Otherwise the two at the table let him alone.

He stood finally, trembling, on his feet beside the bed. Steadying himself with his left hand on the bed he reached its end. There he drew himself erect and, staring fixedly at his goal, lurched towards the closed door. Near it he stumbled and went down on his knees, but his left hand, thrown desperately out, caught the knob and he pulled himself up on his feet again.

Then the apish man laid his cards carefully down on the table and said: 'Now.' His grin, showing remarkably beautiful white teeth, was wide enough to show that the teeth were not natural. He went over and stood beside Ned Beaumont.

Ned Beaumont was tugging at the door-knob.

The apish man said, 'Now there, Houdini,' and with all his weight behind the blow drove his right fist into Ned Beaumont's face.

Ned Beaumont was driven back against the wall. The back of his head struck the wall first, then his body crashed flat against the wall, and he slid down the wall to the floor.

Rosy-cheeked Rusty, still holding his cards at the table, said gloomily, but without emotion: 'Jesus, Jeff, you'll croak him.'

Jeff said: 'Him?' he indicated the man at his feet by kicking him not especially hard on the thigh. 'You can't croak him. He's tough. He's a tough baby. He likes this.' He bent down, grasped one of the unconscious man's lapels in each hand, and dragged him to his knees. 'Don't you like it, baby?' he asked and, holding Ned Beaumont up on his knees with one hand, struck his face with the other fist.

The door-knob was rattled from the outside.

Jeff called: 'Who's that?'

Shad O'Rory's pleasant voice: 'Me.'

Jeff dragged Ned Beaumont far enough from the door to let it open, dropped him there, and unlocked the door with a key taken from his pocket.

O'Rory and Whisky came in. O'Rory looked at the man on the floor, then at Jeff, and finally at Rusty. His blue-grey eyes were clouded. When he spoke it was to ask Rusty: 'Jeff been slapping him down for the fun of it?'

The rosy-cheeked boy shook his head. 'This Beaumont is a son of a bitch,' he said sullenly. 'Every time he comes to he gets up and starts something.'

'I don't want him killed, not yet,' O'Rory said. He looked down at Ned Beaumont. 'See if you can bring him around again. I want to talk to him.'

Rusty got up from the table. 'I don't know,' he said. 'He's pretty far gone.'

Jeff was more optimistic. 'Sure we can,' he said. 'I'll show you.

Take his feet, Rusty.' He put his hands under Ned Beaumont's armpits.

They carried the unconscious man into the bathroom and put him in the tub. Jeff put the stopper in and turned on cold water from both the faucet below and the shower above. 'That'll have him up and singing in no time,' he predicted.

Five minutes later, when they hauled him dripping from the tub and set him on his feet, Ned Beaumont could stand. They took him into the bedroom again. O'Rory was sitting on one of the chairs smoking a cigarette. Whisky had gone.

'Put him on the bed,' O'Rory ordered.

Jeff and Rusty led their charge to the bed, turned him around, and pushed him down on it. When they took their hands away from him he fell straight back on the bed. They pulled him into a sitting position again and Jeff slapped his battered face with an open hand, saying: 'Come on, Rip Van Winkle, come to life.'

'A swell chance of him coming to life,' the sullen Rusty grumbled.

'You think he won't?' Jeff asked cheerfully and slapped Ned Beaumont again.

Ned Beaumont opened the one eye not too swollen to be opened.

O'Rory said: 'Beaumont.'

Ned Beaumont raised his head and tried to look around the room, but there was nothing to show he could see Shad O'Rory.

O'Rory got up from his chair and stood in front of Ned Beaumont, bending down until his face was a few inches from the other man's. He asked: 'Can you hear me, Beaumont?'

Ned Beaumont's open eye looked dull hate into O'Rory's eyes.

O'Rory said: 'This is O'Rory, Beaumont. Can you hear what I say?'

Moving his swollen lips with difficulty, Ned Beaumont uttered a thick 'Yes.'

O'Rory said: 'Good. Now listen to what I tell you. You're going to give me the dope on Paul.' He spoke very distinctly without raising his voice, without his voice losing any of its musical quality. 'Maybe you think you won't, but you will. I'll have you worked on from now till you do. Do you understand me?'

Ned Beaumont smiled. The condition of his face made the smile horrible. He said: 'I won't.'

O'Rory stepped back and said: 'Work on him.'

While Rusty hesitated, the apish Jeff knocked aside Ned Beaumont's upraised hand and pushed him down on the bed. 'I got something to try.' He scooped up Ned Beaumont's legs and tumbled them on the bed. He leaned over Ned Beaumont, his hands busy on Ned Beaumont's body.

Ned Beaumont's body and arms and legs jerked convulsively and three times he groaned. After that he lay still.

Jeff straightened up and took his hands away from the man on the bed. He was breathing heavily through his ape's mouth. He growled, half in complaint, half in apology: 'It ain't no good now. He's throwed another joe.'

IV

When Ned Beaumont recovered consciousness he was alone in the room. The lights were on. As laboriously as before he got himself out of bed and across the room to the door. The door was locked. He was fumbling with the knob when the door was thrown open pushing him back against the wall.

Jeff in his underwear, barefoot, came in. 'Ain't you a pip?' he said. 'Always up to some kind of tricks. Don't you never get tired of being bounced off the floor?' He took Beaumont by the throat with his left hand and struck him in the face with his right fist, twice, but not so hard as he had hit him before. Then he pushed him backwards over to the bed and threw him on it. 'And stay put awhile this time,' he growled.

Ned Beaumont lay still with closed eyes.

Jeff went out, locking the door behind him.

Painfully Ned Beaumont climbed out of bed and made his way to the door. He tried it. Then he withdrew two steps and tried to hurl himself against it, succeeding only in lurching against it. He kept trying until the door was flung open again by Jeff.

Jeff said: 'I never seen a guy that liked being hit so much or that I liked hitting so much.' He leaned far over to one side and swung his fist up from below his knee.

Ned Beaumont stood blindly in the fist's path. It struck his cheek and knocked him the full length of the room. He lay still where he fell. He was lying there two hours later when Whisky came into the room.

Whisky awakened him with water from the bathroom and helped him to the bed. 'Use your head,' Whisky begged him. 'These mugs'll kill you. They've got no sense.'

Ned Beaumont looked dully at Whisky through a dull and bloody eye. 'Let 'em,' he managed to say.

He slept then until he was awakened by O'Rory, Jeff, and Rusty. He refused to tell O'Rory anything about Paul Madvig's affairs. He was dragged out of bed, beaten into unconsciousness, and flung into bed again.

This was repeated a few hours later. No food was brought to him.

Going on hands and knees into the bathroom when he had regained consciousness after the last of these beatings, he saw, on the floor behind the wash-stand's pedestal, a narrow safety-razor-blade red with the rust of months. Getting it out from behind the pedestal was a task that took him all of ten minutes and his nerveless fingers failed a dozen times before they succeeded in picking it up from the tile floor. He tried to cut his throat with it, but it fell out of his hand after he had no more than scratched his chin in three pieces. He lay down on the bathroom-floor and sobbed himself to sleep.

When he awakened again he could stand, and did. He doused

his head in cold water and drank four glasses of water. The water made him sick and after that he began to shake with a chill. He went into the bedroom and lay down on the bare blood-stained mattress, but got up almost immediately to go stumbling and staggering in haste back to the bathroom, where he got down on hands and knees and searched the floor until he had found the rusty razor-blade. He sat on the floor and put the razor-blade into his vest-pocket. Putting it in, his fingers touched his lighter. He took the lighter out and looked at it. A cunning gleam came into his one open eye as he looked at the lighter. The gleam was not sane.

Shaking so that his teeth rattled together, he got up from the bathroom-floor and went into the bedroom again. He laughed harshly when he saw the newspaper under the table where the apish dark man and the sullen rosy-cheeked boy had played cards. Tearing and rumpling and wadding the paper in his hands, he carried it to the door and put it on the floor there. In each of the drawers in the chest of drawers he found a piece of wrapping-paper folded to cover the bottom. He rumpled them and put them with the newspaper against the door. With the razor-blade he made along gash in the mattress, pulled out big handfulls of the coarse grey cotton with which the mattress was stuffed, and carried them to the door. He was not shaking now, nor stumbling, and he used both hands dexterously, but presently he tired of gutting the mattress and dragged what was left of it – tick and all – to the door.

He giggled then and, after the third attempt, got his lighter ignited. He set fire to the bottom of the heap against the door. At first he stood close to the heap, crouching over it, but as the smoke increased it drove him back step by step, reluctantly, coughing as he retreated. Presently he went into the bathroom, soaked a towel with water, and wrapped it around his head, covering eyes, nose, and mouth. He came stumbling back into the bedroom, a dim figure in the smoky room, fell against the bed, and sat down on the floor beside it.

Jeff found him there when he came in.

Jeff came in cursing and coughing through the rag he held against nose and mouth. In opening the door he had pushed most of the burning heap back a little. He kicked some more out of the way and stamped through the rest to reach Ned Beaumont. He took Ned Beaumont by the back of the collar and dragged him out of the room.

Outside, still holding Ned Beaumont by the back of the collar, Jeff kicked him to his feet and ran him down to the far end of the corridor. There he pushed him through an open doorway, bawled, 'I'm going to eat one of your ears when I come back, you bastard,' at him, kicked him again, stepped back into the corridor, slammed the door, and turned the key in its lock.

Ned Beaumont, kicked into the room, saved himself from a fall by catching hold of a table. He pushed himself up a little nearer straight and looked around. The towel had fallen down muffler-fashion around his neck and shoulders. The room had two windows. He went to the nearer window and tried to raise it. It was locked. He unfastened the lock and raised the window. Outside was night. He put a leg over the sill, then the other, turned so that he was lying belly-down across the sill, lowered himself until he was hanging by his hands, felt with his feet for some support, found none, and let himself drop.

5 The Hospital

I

A nurse was doing something to Ned Beaumont's face.

'Where am I?' he asked.

'St Luke's Hospital.' She was a small nurse with very large bright hazel eyes, a breathless sort of hushed voice, and an odor of mimosa.

'What day?'

'It's Monday.'

'What month and year?' he asked. When she frowned at him he said: 'Oh, never mind. How long have I been here?'

'This is the third day.'

'Where's the telephone?' He tried to sit up.

'Stop that,' she said. 'You can't use the telephone and you mustn't get yourself excited.'

'You use it, then. Call Hartford six one one six and tell Mr Madvig that I've got to see him right away.'

'Mr Madvig's here every afternoon,' she said, 'but I don't think Doctor Tait will let you talk to anybody yet. As a matter of fact you've done a whole lot more talking now than you ought to.'

'What is it now? Morning or afternoon?'

'Morning.'

'That's too long to wait,' he said. 'Call him now.'

'Doctor Tait will be in in a little while.'

'I don't want any Doctor Taits,' he said irritably. 'I want Paul Madvig.'

'You'll do what you're told,' she replied. 'You'll lie there and be quiet till Doctor Tait comes.'

He scowled at her. 'What a swell nurse you are. Didn't anybody ever tell you it's not good for patients to be quarreled with?'

She ignored his question.

He said: 'Besides, you're hurting my jaw.'

She said: 'If you'd keep it still it wouldn't get hurt.'

He was quiet for a moment. Then he asked: 'What's supposed to have happened to me? Or didn't you get far enough in your lessons to know?'

'Probably a drunken brawl,' she told him, but she could not keep her face straight after that. She laughed and said: 'But honestly you shouldn't talk so much and you can't see anybody till the doctor says so.'

II

Paul Madvig arrived early in the afternoon. 'Christ, I'm glad to see you alive again!' he said. He took the invalid's unbandaged left hand in both of his.

Ned Beaumont said: 'I'm all right. But here's what we've got to do: grab Walt Ivans and have him taken over to Braywood and shown to the gun-dealers there. He—'

'You told me all that,' Madvig said. 'That's done.'

Ned Beaumont frowned. 'I told you?'

'Sure – the morning you were picked up. They took you to the Emergency Hospital and you wouldn't let them do anything to you till you'd seen me and I came down there and you told me about Ivans and Braywood and passed out cold.'

'It's blank to me,' Ned Beaumont said. 'Did you nail them?'

'We got the Ivanses, all right, and Walt Ivans talked after he was identified in Braywood and the Grand Jury indicted Jeff Gardner and two John Does, but we're not going to be able to nail Shad on it. Gardner's the man Ivans dickered with and anybody knows he wouldn't do anything without Shad's say-so, but proving it's another thing.'

'Jeff's the monkey-looking guy, huh? Has he been picked up yet?'

'No. Shad took him into hiding with him after you got away, I guess. They had you, didn't they?'

'Uh-huh. In the Dog House, upstairs. I went there to lay a trap for the gent and he out-trapped me.' He scowled. 'I remember going there with Whisky Vassos and being bitten by the dog and knocked around by Jeff and a blond kid. Then there was something about a fire and – that's about all. Who found me? and where?'

'A copper found you crawling on all fours up the middle of Colman Street at three in the morning leaving a trail of blood behind you.'

'I think of funny things to do,' Ned Beaumont said.

III

The small nurse with large eyes opened the door cautiously and put her head in.

Ned Beaumont addressed her in a tired voice: 'All right – peekaboo! But don't you think you're a little old for that?'

The nurse opened the door wider and stood on the sill holding the edge of the door with one hand. 'No wonder people beat you up,' she said. 'I wanted to see if you were awake. Mr Madvig and'

– the breathless quality became more pronounced in her voice and her eyes became brighter – 'a lady are here.'

Ned Beaumont looked at her curiously and a bit mockingly. 'What kind of lady?'

'It's Miss Janet Henry,' she replied in the manner of one revealing some unexpected pleasant thing.

Ned Beaumont turned on his side, his face away from the nurse. He shut his eyes. A corner of his mouth twitched, but his voice was empty of expression: 'Tell them I'm still asleep.'

'You can't do that,' she said. 'They know you're not asleep – even if they haven't heard you talking – or I'd've been back before this.'

He groaned dramatically and propped himself up on his elbow. 'She'll only come back again some other time,' he grumbled. 'I might as well get it over with.'

The nurse, looking at him with contemptuous eyes, said sarcastically: 'We've had to keep policemen in front of the hospital to fight off all the women that've been trying to see you.'

'That's all right for you to say,' he told her. 'Maybe you're impressed by senators' daughters who are in the roto all the time, but you've never been hounded by them the way I have. I tell you they've made my life miserable, them and their brown roto-sections. Senators' daughters, always senators' daughters, never a representative's daughter or a cabinet minister's daughter or an alderman's daughter for the sake of variety – never anything but— Do you suppose senators are more prolific than—'

'You're not really funny,' the nurse said. 'It's the way you comb your hair. I'll bring them in.' She left the room.

Ned Beaumont took a long breath. His eyes were shiny. He moistened his lips and then pressed them together in a tight secretive smile, but when Janet Henry came into the room his face was a mask of casual politeness.

She came straight to his bed and said: 'Oh, Mr Beaumont, I was so glad to hear that you were recovering so nicely that I simply had to come.' She put a hand in his and smiled down at him. Though her eyes were not a dark brown her otherwise pure blondness made them seem dark. 'So if you didn't want me to come you're not to blame Paul. I made him bring me.'

Ned Beaumont smiled back at her and said: 'I'm awfully glad you did. It's terribly kind of you.'

Paul Madvig, following Janet Henry into the room, had gone around to the opposite side of the bed. He grinned affectionately from her to Ned Beaumont and said: 'I knew you'd be, Ned. I told her so. How's it go today?'

'Nobly. Pull some chairs up.'

'We can't stay,' the blond man replied. 'I've got to meet M'Laughlin at the Grandcourt.'

'But I don't,' Janet Henry said. She directed her smile at Ned Beaumont again. 'Mayn't I stay – a little while?'

'I'd love that,' Ned Beaumont assured her while Madvig, coming around the bed to place a chair for her, beamed delightedly upon each of them in turn and said: 'That's fine.' When the girl was sitting beside the bed and her black coat had been laid back over the back of the chair, Madvig looked at his watch and growled: 'I've got to run.' He shook Ned Beaumont's hand. 'Anything I can get for you?'

'No, thanks, Paul.'

'Well, be good.' The blond man turned towards Janet Henry, stopped, and addressed Ned Beaumont again: 'How far do you think I ought to go with M'Laughlin this first time?'

Ned Beaumont moved his shoulders a little. 'As far as you want, so long as you don't put anything in plain words. They scare him. But you could hire him to commit murders if you put it to him in a long-winded way, like: "If there was a man named Smith who lived in such and such a place and he got sick or something and didn't get well and you happened to drop in to see me some time and just by luck an envelope addressed to you had been sent there in care of me, how would I know it had five hundred dollars in it?"'

Madvig nodded. 'I don't want any murders,' he said, 'but we do need that railroad vote.' He frowned. 'I wish you were up, Ned.'

'I will be in a day or two. Did you see the *Observer* this morning?'

'No.'

Ned Beaumont looked around the room. 'Somebody's run off with it. The dirt was in an editorial in a box in the middle of the front page. *What are our city officials going to do about it?* A list of six weeks' crimes to show we're having a crime-wave. A lot smaller list of who's been caught to show the police aren't able to do much about it. Most of the squawking done about Taylor Henry's murder.'

When her brother was named, Janet Henry winced and her lips parted in a little silent gasp. Madvig looked at her and then quickly at Ned Beaumont to move his head in a brief warning gesture.

Ned Beaumont, ignoring the effect of his words on the others, continued: 'They were brutal about that. Accused the police of deliberately keeping their hands off the murder for a week so a gambler high in political circles could use it to square a grievance with another gambler – meaning my going after Despain to collect my money. Wondered what Senator Henry thought of his new political allies' use of his son's murder for this purpose.'

Madvig, red of face, fumbling for his watch, said hastily: 'I'll get a copy and read it. I've got to—'

'Also,' Ned Beaumont went on serenely, 'they accuse the police of raiding – after having protected them for years – those joints whose owners wouldn't come across with enormous campaign-contributions. That's what they make of your fight with Shad O'Rory. And they promise to print a list of the places that are still running because their owners did come across.'

Madvig said, 'Well, well,' uncomfortably, said, 'Good-by, have a nice visit,' to Janet Henry, 'See you later,' to Ned Beaumont, and went out.

Janet Henry leaned forward in her chair. 'Why don't you like me?' she asked Ned Beaumont.

'I think maybe I do,' he said.

She shook her head. 'You don't. I know it.'

'You can't go by my manners,' he told her. 'They're always pretty bad.'

'You don't like me,' she insisted, not answering his smile, 'and I want you to.'

He was modest. 'Why?'

'Because you are Paul's best friend,' she replied.

'Paul,' he said, looking obliquely at her, 'has a lot of friends: he's a politician.'

She moved her head impatiently. 'You're his best friend.' She paused, then added: 'He thinks so.'

'What do you think?' he asked with incomplete seriousness.

'I think you are,' she said gravely, 'or you would not be here now. You would not have gone through that for him.'

His mouth twitched in a meager smile. He did not say anything.

When it became manifest that he was not going to speak she said earnestly: 'I wish you would like me, if you can.'

He repeated: 'I think maybe I do.'

She shook her head. 'You don't.'

He smiled at her. His smile was very young and engaging, his eyes shy, his voice youthfully diffident and confiding, as he said: 'I'll tell you what makes you think that, Miss Henry. It's – you see, Paul picked me up out of the gutter, as you might say, just a year or so ago, and so I'm kind of awkward and clumsy when I'm around people like you who belong to another world altogether – society and roto-sections and all – and you mistake that – uh – *gaucherie* for enmity, which it isn't at all.'

She rose and said, 'You're ridiculing me,' without resentment.

When she had gone Ned Beaumont lay back on his pillows and stared at the ceiling with glittering eyes until the nurse came in.

The nurse came in and asked: 'What have you been up to now?'

Ned Beaumont raised his head to look sullenly at her, but he did not speak.

The nurse said: 'She went out of here as near crying as anybody could without crying.'

Ned Beaumont lowered his head to the pillow again. 'I must be losing my grip,' he said. 'I usually make senators' daughters cry.'

IV

A man of medium size, young and dapper, with a sleek, dark, rather good-looking face, came in.

Ned Beaumont sat up in bed and said: ' 'Lo, Jack.'

Jack said, 'You don't look as bad as I thought you would,' and advanced to the side of the bed.

'I'm still all in one piece. Grab a chair.'

Jack sat down and took out a package of cigarettes.

Ned Beaumont said: 'I've got another job for you.' He put a hand under his pillows and brought out an envelope.

Jack lit his cigarette before he took the envelope from Ned Beaumont's hand. It was a plain white envelope addressed to Ned Beaumont at St Luke's Hospital and bore the local postmark dated two days before. Inside was a single typewritten sheet of paper which Jack took out and read.

What do you know about Paul Madvig that Shad O'Rory was so anxious to learn?

Has it anything to do with the murder of Taylor Henry?

If not, why should you have gone to such lengths to keep it secret?

Jack refolded the sheet of paper and returned it to the envelope before he raised his head. Then he asked: 'Does it make sense?'

'Not that I know of. I want you to find out who wrote it.'

Jack nodded. 'Do I keep it?'

'Yes.'

Jack put the envelope in his pocket. 'Any ideas about who might have done it?'

'None at all.'

Jack studied the lighted end of his cigarette. 'It's a job, you know,' he said presently.

'I know it,' Ned Beaumont agreed, 'and all I can tell you is that there's been a lot of them – or several of them – in the past week. That's my third. I know Farr got at least one. I don't know who else has been getting them.'

'Can I see some of the others?'

Ned Beaumont said: 'That's the only one I kept. They're all pretty much alike, though – same paper, same typewriting, three questions in each, all on the same subject.'

Jack regarded Ned Beaumont with inquisitive eyes. 'But not exactly the same questions?' he asked.

'Not exactly, but all getting to the same point.'

Jack nodded and smoked his cigarette.

Ned Beaumont said: 'You understand this is to be strictly on the qt.'

'Sure.' Jack took the cigarette from his mouth. 'The "same point" you mentioned is Madvig's connection with the murder?'

'Yes,' Ned Beaumont replied, looking with level eyes at the sleek dark young man, 'and there isn't any connection.'

Jack's dark face was inscrutable. 'I don't see how there could be,' he said as he stood up.

V

The nurse came in carrying a large basket of fruit. 'Isn't it lovely?' she said as she set it down.

Ned Beaumont nodded cautiously.

The nurse took a small stiff envelope from the basket. 'I bet you it's from her,' she said, giving Ned Beaumont the envelope.

'What'll you bet?'

'Anything you want.'

Ned Beaumont nodded as if some dark suspicion had been confirmed. 'You looked,' he said.

'Why, you—' Her words stopped when he laughed, but indignation remained in her mien.

He took Janet Henry's card from the envelope. One word was written on it: *Please!* Frowning at the card, he told the nurse, 'You win,' and tapped the card on a thumb-nail. 'Help yourself to that gunk and take enough of it so it'll look as if I'd been eating it.'

Later that afternoon he wrote:

My Dear Miss Henry—

You've quite overwhelmed me with your kindness – first your coming to see me, and then the fruit. I don't at all know how to thank you, but I hope I shall some day be able to more clearly show my gratitude.

Sincerely yours,
Ned Beaumont

When he had finished he read what he had written, tore it up, and rewrote it on another sheet of paper, using the same words, but rearranging them to make the ending of the second sentence read: 'be able some day to show my gratitude more clearly.'

VI

Ned Beaumont, in bathrobe and slippers this morning, was reading a copy of the *Observer* over his breakfast at a table by the window of his hospital-room when Opal Madvig came in. He folded the newspaper, put it face-down on the table beside his tray, and rose saying, ' 'Lo, snip,' cordially. He was pale.

'Why didn't you call me up when you got back from New York?' she demanded in an accusing tone. She too was pale. Pallor accentuated the child-like texture of her skin, yet made her face seem less young. Her blue eyes were wide open and dark with emotion, but not to be read easily. She held herself tall without stiffness, in the manner of one more sure of his balance than of stability underfoot. Ignoring the chair he moved out from the wall for her, she repeated, imperatively as before: 'Why didn't you?'

He laughed at her, softly, indulgently, and said: 'I like you in that shade of brown.'

'Oh, Ned, please—'

'That's better,' he said. 'I intended coming out to the house, but – well – there were lots of things happening when I got back and a lot of loose ends of things that had happened while I was gone, and by the time I finished with those I ran into Shad O'Rory and got sent here.' He waved an arm to indicate the hospital.

Her gravity was not affected by the lightness of his tone.

'Are they going to hang this Despain?' she asked curtly.

He laughed again and said: 'We're not going to get very far talking like this.'

She frowned, but said, 'Are they, Ned?' with less haughtiness.

'I don't think so,' he told her, shaking his head a little. 'The chances are he didn't kill Taylor after all.'

She did not seem surprised. 'Did you know that when you asked me to – to help you get – or fix up – evidence against him?'

He smiled reproachfully. 'Of course not, snip. What do you think I am?'

'You did know it.' Her voice was cold and scornful as her blue eyes. 'You only wanted to get the money he owed you and you made me help you use Taylor's murder for that.'

'Have it your own way,' he replied indifferently.

She came a step closer to him. The faintest of quivers disturbed her chin for an instant, then her young face was firm and bold again. 'Do you know who killed him?' she asked, her eyes probing his.

He shook his head slowly from side to side.

'Did Dad?'

He blinked. 'You mean did Paul know who killed him?'

She stamped a foot. 'I mean did Dad kill him?' she cried.

He put a hand over her mouth. His eyes had jerked into focus on the closed door. 'Shut up,' he muttered.

She stepped back from his hand as one of her hands pushed it away from her face. 'Did he?' she insisted.

In a low angry voice he said: 'If you must be a nitwit at least don't go around with a megaphone. Nobody cares what kind of idiotic notions you have as long as you keep them to yourself, but you've got to keep them to yourself.'

Her eyes opened wide and dark. 'Then he did kill him,' she said in a small flat voice, but with utter certainty.

He thrust his face down towards hers. 'No, my dear,' he said in an enraged sugary voice, 'he didn't kill him.' He held his face near hers. A vicious smile distorted his features.

Firm of countenance and voice, not drawing back from him, she said: 'If he didn't I can't understand what difference it makes what I say or how loud.'

An end of his mouth twitched up in a sneer. 'You'd be surprised how many things there are you can't understand,' he said angrily, 'and never will if you keep on like this.' He stepped back from her, a long step, and put his fists in the pockets of his bathrobe. Both corners of his mouth were pulled down now and there were grooves in his forehead. His narrowed eyes stared at the floor in front of her feet. 'Where'd you get this crazy idea?' he growled.

'It's not a crazy idea. You know it's not.'

He moved his shoulders impatiently and demanded: 'Where'd you get it?'

She too moved her shoulders. 'I didn't get it anywhere. I – I suddenly saw it.'

'Nonsense,' he said sharply, looking up at her under his brows. 'Did you see the *Observer* this morning?'

'No.'

He stared at her with hard skeptical eyes.

Annoyance brought a little color into her face. 'I did not,' she said. 'Why do you ask?'

'No?' he asked in a tone that said he did not believe her, but the skeptical gleam had gone out of his eyes. They were dull and thoughtful. Suddenly they brightened. He took his right hand from his bathrobe-pocket. He held it out towards her, palm up, 'Let me see the letter,' he said.

She stared at him with round eyes. 'What?'

'The letter,' he said, 'the typewritten letter – three questions and no signature.'

She lowered her eyes to avoid his and embarrassment disturbed, very slightly, her features. After a moment of hesitation she asked, 'How did you know?' and opened her brown hand-bag.

'Everybody in town's had at least one,' he said carelessly. 'Is this your first?'

'Yes.' She gave him a crumpled sheet of paper.

He straightened it out and read:

Are you really too stupid to know that your father murdered your lover?

If you do not know it, why did you help him and Ned Beaumont in their attempt to fasten the crime on an innocent man?

Do you know that by helping your father escape justice you are making yourself an accomplice in his crime?

Ned Beaumont nodded and smiled lightly. 'They're all pretty much alike,' he said. He wadded the paper in a loose ball and tossed it at the waste-basket beside the table. 'You'll probably get some more of them now you're on the mailing-list.'

Opal Madvig drew her lower lip in between her teeth. Her blue eyes were bright without warmth. They studied Ned Beaumont's composed face.

He said: 'O'Rory's trying to make campaign-material out of it. You know about my trouble with him. That was because he thought I'd broken with your father and could be paid to help frame him for the murder – enough at least to beat him at the polls – and I wouldn't.'

Her eyes did not change. 'What did you and Dad fight about?' she asked.

'That's nobody's business but ours, snip,' he said gently, 'if we did fight.'

'You did,' she said, 'in Carson's speakeasy.' She put her teeth together with a click and said boldly: 'You quarreled when you found out that he really had – had killed Taylor.'

He laughed and asked in a mocking tone: 'Hadn't I known that all along?'

Her expression was not affected by his humor. 'Why did you ask if I had seen the *Observer*?' she demanded. 'What was in it?'

'Some more of the same sort of nonsense,' he told her evenly. 'It's there on the table if you want to see it. There'll be plenty of it before the campaign's over: this is going to be that kind. And you'll be giving your father a swell break by swallowing—' He broke off with an impatient gesture because she was no longer listening to him.

She had gone to the table and was picking up the newspaper he had put down when she came in.

He smiled pleasantly at her back and said: 'It's on the front page, *An Open Letter to the Mayor.*'

As she read she began to tremble – her knees, her hands, her mouth – so that Ned Beaumont frowned anxiously at her, but when she had finished and had dropped the newspaper on the table and had turned to face him directly her tall body and fair face were statue-like in their immobility. She addressed him in a low voice between lips that barely moved to let the words out: 'They wouldn't dare say such things if they were not true.'

'That's nothing to what'll be said before they're through,' he drawled lazily. He seemed amused, though there was a suggestion of anger difficultly restrained in the glitter of his eyes.

She looked at him for a long moment, then, saying nothing, turned towards the door.

He said: 'Wait.'

She halted and confronted him again. His smile was friendly now, ingratiating. Her face was a tinted statue's.

He said: 'Politics is a tough game, snip, the way it's being played here this time. The *Observer* is on the other side of the fence and they're not worrying much about the truth of anything that'll hurt Paul. They—'

'I don't believe that,' she said. 'I know Mr Mathews – his wife was only a few years ahead of me at school and we were friends – and I don't believe he'd say anything like that about Dad unless it was true, or unless he had good reason for thinking it true.'

Ned Beaumont chuckled. 'You know a lot about it. Mathews is up to his ears in debt. The State Central Trust Company holds both mortgages on his plant – one on his house too, for that matter. The State Central belongs to Bill Roan. Bill Roan is running for the Senate against Henry. Mathews does what he's told to do and prints what he's told to print.'

Opal Madvig did not say anything. There was nothing to indicate that she had been at all convinced by Ned Beaumont's argument.

He went on, speaking in an amiable, persuasive tone: 'This' – he flicked a finger at the paper on the table – 'is nothing to what'll come later. They're going to rattle Taylor Henry's bones till they think up something worse and we're going to have this sort of stuff to read till election's over. We might just as well get used to it now and you, of all people, oughtn't to let yourself be bothered by it. Paul doesn't mind it much. He's a politician and—'

'He's a murderer,' she said in a low distinct voice.

'And his daughter's a chump,' he exclaimed irritably.' Will you stop that foolishness?'

'My father is a murderer,' she said.

'You're crazy. Listen to me, snip. Your father had absolutely nothing to do with Taylor's murder. He—'

'I don't believe you,' she said gravely. 'I'll never believe you again.'

He scowled at her.

She turned and went to the door.

'Wait,' he said. 'Let me—'

She went out and shut the door behind her.

VII

Ned Beaumont's face, after a grimace of rage at the closed door, became heavily thoughtful. Lines came into his forehead. His dark eyes grew narrow and introspective. His lips puckered up under his mustache. Presently he put a finger to his mouth and bit its nail. He breathed regularly, but with more depth than usual.

Footsteps sounded outside the door. He dropped his appearance of thoughtfulness and walked idly towards the window, humming *Little Lost Lady*. The footsteps went on past his door. He stopped humming and bent to pick up the sheet of paper holding the three questions that had been addressed to Opal Madvig. He did not smooth the paper, but thrust it, crumpled in a loose ball as it was, into one of his bathrobe-pockets.

He found and lit a cigar then and, with it between his teeth burning, stood by the table and squinted down through smoke at the front page of the *Observer* lying there.

AN OPEN LETTER TO THE MAYOR

Sir:

The *Observer* has come into possession of certain information which it believes to be of paramount importance in clearing up the mystery surrounding the recent murder of Taylor Henry.

This information is incorporated in several affidavits now in the *Observer*'s safety-deposit box. The substance of these affidavits is as follows:

1. That Paul Madvig quarreled with Taylor Henry some months ago over the young man's attentions to his daughter and forbade his daughter to see Henry again.
2. That Paul Madvig's daughter nevertheless continued to meet Taylor Henry in a furnished room he had rented for that purpose.
3. That they were together in this furnished room the afternoon of the very day on which he was killed.
4. That Paul Madvig went to Taylor Henry's home that evening, supposedly to remonstrate with the young man, or his father, again.
5. That Paul Madvig appeared angry when he left the Henry residence a few minutes before Taylor Henry was murdered.
6. That Paul Madvig and Taylor Henry were seen within half a block of each other, less than a block from the spot where the young man's body was found, not more than fifteen minutes before his body was found.
7. That the Police Department has not at present a single detective engaged in trying to find Taylor Henry's murderer.

The *Observer* believes that you should know these things and that the voters and taxpayers should know them. The *Observer* has no ax to grind, no motive except the desire to see justice done. The *Observer* will welcome an opportunity to hand these affidavits, as well as all other information it has, to you or to any qualified city or state official and, if such a course can be shown an aid to justice, to refrain from publishing any or all of the details of these affidavits.

But the *Observer* will not permit the information incorporated in these affidavits to be ignored. If the officials elected and appointed to enforce law and order in this city and state do not consider these affidavits of sufficient importance to be acted upon, the *Observer* will carry the matter to that higher tribunal, the People of this City, by publishing them in full.

H. K. Mathews, Publisher

Ned Beaumont grunted derisively and blew cigar-smoke down at this declaration, but his eyes remained somber.

VIII

Early that afternoon Paul Madvig's mother came to see Ned Beaumont.

He put his arms around her and kissed her on both cheeks until she pushed him away with a mock-severe 'Do stop it. You're worse than the Airedale Paul used to have.'

'I'm part Airedale,' he said, 'on my father's side,' and went behind her to help her out of her sealskin coat.

Smoothing her black dress, she went to the bed and sat on it.

He hung the coat on the back of a chair and stood – legs apart, hands in bathrobe-pockets – before her.

She studied him critically. 'You don't look so bad,' she said presently, 'nor yet so good. How do you feel?'

'Swell. I'm only hanging around here on account of the nurses.'

'That wouldn't surprise me much, neither,' she told him. 'But don't stand there ogling me like a Cheshire cat. You make me nervous. Sit down.' She patted the bed beside her.

He sat down beside her.

She said: 'Paul seems to think you did something very grand and noble by doing whatever it was you did, but you can't tell me that if you had behaved yourself you would ever have got into whatever scrape you got into at all.'

'Aw, Mom,' he began.

She cut him off. The gaze of her blue eyes that were young as her son's bored into Ned Beaumont's brown ones. 'Look here, Ned, Paul didn't kill that whipper-snapper, did he?'

Surprise opened Ned Beaumont's eyes and mouth. 'No.'

'I didn't think so,' the old woman said. 'He's always been a good boy, but I've heard that there's some nasty hints going around and the Lord only knows what goes on in this politics. I'm sure I haven't any idea.'

Amazement tinged with humor was in the eyes with which Ned Beaumont looked at her bony face.

She said: 'Well, goggle at me, but I haven't got any way of knowing what you men are up to, or what you do without thinking anything of it. It was a long while before ever you were born that I gave up trying to find out.'

He patted her shoulder. 'You're a humdinger, Mom,' he said admiringly.

She drew away from his hand and fixed him with severe penetrant eyes again. 'Would you tell me if he had killed him?' she demanded.

He shook his head no.

'Then how do I know he didn't?'

He laughed. 'Because,' he explained, 'if he had I'd still say, "No," but then, if you asked me if I'd tell you the truth if he had, I'd say, "Yes."' Merriment went out of his eyes and voice. 'He didn't do it, Mom.' He smiled at her. He smiled with his lips only and they were thin against his teeth. 'It would be nice if somebody in town besides me thought he didn't do it and it would be especially nice if that other one was his mother.'

IX

An hour after Mrs Madvig's departure Ned Beaumont received a package containing four books and Janet Henry's card. He was writing her a note of thanks when Jack arrived.

Jack, letting cigarette-smoke come out with his words, said: 'I think I've got something, though I don't know how you're going to like it.'

Ned Beaumont looked thoughtfully at the sleek young man and smoothed the left side of his mustache with a forefinger. 'If it's what I hired you to get I'll like it well enough.' His voice was matter-of-fact as Jack's. 'Sit down and tell me about it.'

Jack sat down carefully, crossed his legs, put his hat on the floor, and looked from his cigarette to Ned Beaumont. He said: 'It looks like those things were written by Madvig's daughter.'

Ned Beaumont's eyes widened a little, but only for a moment. His face lost some of its color and his breathing became irregular. There was no change in his voice. 'What makes it look like that?'

From an inner pocket Jack brought two sheets of paper similar in size and make, folded alike. He gave them to Ned Beaumont who, when he had unfolded them, saw that on each were three typewritten questions, the same three questions on each sheet.

'One of them's the one you gave me yesterday,' Jack said. 'Could you tell which?'

Ned Beaumont shook his head slowly from side to side.

'There's no difference,' Jack said. 'I wrote the other one on Charter Street where Taylor Henry had a room that Madvig's daughter used to come to – with a Corona typewriter that was there and on paper that was there. So far as anybody seems to know there were only two keys to the place. He had one and she had one. She's been back there at least a couple of times since he was killed.'

Ned Beaumont, scowling now at the sheets of paper in his hands, nodded without looking up.

Jack lit a fresh cigarette from the one he had been smoking, rose and went to the table to mash the old cigarette in the ashtray there, and returned to his seat. There was nothing in his face or manner to show that he had any interest in Ned Beaumont's reaction to their discovery.

After another minute of silence Ned Beaumont raised his head a little and asked: 'How'd you get this?'

Jack put his cigarette in a corner of his mouth where it wagged with his words. 'The *Observer* tip on the place this morning gave me the lead. That's where the police got theirs too, but they got there first. I got a pretty good break, though: the copper left in charge was a friend of mine – Fred Hurley – and for a ten-spot he let me do all the poking around I wanted.'

Ned Beaumont rattled the papers in his hand. 'Do the police know this?' he asked.

Jack shrugged. 'I didn't tell them. I pumped Hurley, but he didn't know anything – just put there to watch things till they decide what they're going to do. Maybe they know, maybe they don't.' He shook cigarette-ash on the floor. 'I could find out.'

'Never mind that. What else did you turn up?'

'I didn't look for anything else.'

Ned Beaumont, after a quick glance at the dark young man's inscrutable face, looked down at the sheets of paper again. 'What kind of dump is it?'

'Thirteen twenty-four. They had a room and bath under the name of French. The woman that runs the place claims she didn't know who they really were till the police came today. Maybe she didn't. It's the kind of joint where not much is asked. She says they used to be there a lot, mostly in the afternoons, and that the girl's been back a couple of times in the last week or so that she knows of, though she could pop in and out without being seen easily enough.'

'Sure it's her?'

Jack made a noncommittal gesture with one hand. 'The description's right.' He paused, then added carelessly as he exhaled smoke: 'She's the only one the woman saw since he was killed.'

Ned Beaumont raised his head again. His eyes were hard. 'Taylor had others coming there?' he asked.

Jack made the noncommittal gesture once more. 'The woman

wouldn't say so. She said she didn't know, but from the way she said it I'd say it was a safe bet she was lying.'

'Couldn't tell by what's in the place?'

Jack shook his head. 'No. There's not much woman stuff there – just a kimono and toilet things and pajamas and stuff like that.'

'Much of his stuff there?'

'Oh, a suit and a pair of shoes and some underwear and pajamas and socks and so on.'

'Any hats?'

Jack smiled. 'No hats,' he said.

Ned Beaumont got up and went to the window. Outside darkness was almost complete. A dozen raindrops clung to the glass and as many more struck it lightly while Ned Beaumont stood there. He turned to face Jack again. 'Thanks a lot, Jack,' he said slowly. His eyes were focused on Jack's face in a dully absent-minded stare. 'I think maybe I'll have another job for you soon – maybe tonight. I'll give you a ring.'

Jack said, 'Right,' and rose and went out.

Ned Beaumont went to the closet for his clothes, carried them into the bathroom, and put them on. When he came out a nurse was in his room, a tall full-bodied woman with a shiny pale face.

'Why, you're dressed!' she exclaimed.

'Yes, I've got to go out.'

Alarm joined astonishment in her mien. 'But you can't, Mr Beaumont,' she protested. 'It's night and it's beginning to rain and Doctor Tait would—'

'I know, I know,' he said impatiently, and went around her to the door.

6 The Observer

I

Mrs Madvig opened her front door. 'Ned!' she cried, 'are you crazy? Running around on a night like this, and you just out of the hospital.'

'The taxi didn't leak,' he said, but his grin lacked virility. 'Paul in?'

'He went out no more than half an hour ago, I think to the Club. But come in, come in.'

'Opal home?' he asked as he shut the door and followed her down the hall.

'No. She's been off somewhere since morning.'

Ned Beaumont halted in the living-room doorway. 'I can't stay,' he said. 'I'll run on down to the Club and see Paul there.' His voice was not quite steady.

The old woman turned quickly towards him. 'You'll do no such thing,' she said in a scolding voice. 'Look at you, you're just about to have a chill. You'll sit right down there by the fire and let me get you something hot to drink.'

'Can't, Mom,' he told her. 'I've got to go places.'

Her blue eyes wherein age did not show became bright and keen. 'When did you leave the hospital?' she demanded.

'Just now.'

She put her lips together hard, then opened them a little to say accusingly: 'You walked out.' A shadow disturbed the clear blueness of her eyes. She came close to Ned Beaumont and held her face close to his: she was nearly as tall as he. Her voice was harsh now as if coming from a parched throat. 'Is it something about Paul?' The shadow in her eyes became recognizable as fear. 'And Opal?'

His voice was barely audible. 'It's something I've got to see them about.'

She touched one of his cheeks somewhat timidly with bony fingers. 'You're a good boy, Ned,' she said.

He put an arm around her. 'Don't worry, Mom. None of it's bad as it could be. Only – if Opal comes home make her stay – if you can.'

'Is it anything you can tell me, Ned?' she asked.

'Not now and – well – it might be just as well not to let either of them know you think anything's wrong.'

II

Ned Beaumont walked five blocks through the rain to a drugstore. He used a telephone there first to order a taxicab and then to call two numbers and ask for Mr Mathews. He did not get Mr Mathews on the wire.

He called another number and asked for Mr Rumsen. A moment later he was saying: ' 'Lo, Jack, this is Ned Beaumont. Busy? . . . Fine. Here it is. I want to know if the girl we were talking about went to see Mathews of the *Observer* today and what she did afterwards, if she did . . . That's right, Hal Mathews. I tried to get him by phone, there and home, but no luck . . . Well, on the quiet if you can, but get it and get it quick . . . No, I'm out of the hospital. I'll be home waiting. You know my number . . .

Yes, Jack. Fine, thanks, and ring me as often as you can . . . 'By.'

He went out to the waiting taxicab, got into it, and gave the driver his address, but after half a dozen blocks he tapped the front window with his fingers and gave the driver another address.

Presently the taxicab came to rest in front of a squat greyish house set in the center of a steeply sloping smooth lawn. 'Wait,' he told the driver as he got out.

The greyish house's front door was opened to his ring by a red-haired maid.

'Mr Farr in?' he asked her.

'I'll see. Who shall I tell him?'

'Mr Beaumont.'

The District Attorney came into the reception-hall with both hands out. His florid pugnacious face was all smiling. 'Well, well, Beaumont, this is a real pleasure,' he said as he rushed up to his visitor. 'Here, give me your coat and hat.'

Ned Beaumont smiled and shook his head. 'I can't stay,' he said. 'I just dropped in for a second on my way home from the hospital.'

'All shipshape again? Splendid!'

'Feeling pretty good,' Ned Beaumont said. 'Anything new?'

'Nothing very important. The birds who manhandled you are still loose – in hiding somewhere – but we'll get them.'

Ned Beaumont made a depreciatory mouth. 'I didn't die and they weren't trying to kill me: you could only stick them with an assault-charge.' He looked somewhat drowsily at Farr. 'Had any more of those three-question epistles?'

The District Attorney cleared his throat. 'Uh – yes, come to think of it, there were one or two more of them.'

'How many?' Ned Beaumont asked. His voice was politely casual. The ends of his lips were raised a little in an idle smile. Amusement glinted in his eyes, but his eyes held Farr's.

The District Attorney cleared his throat. 'Three,' he said

reluctantly. Then his eyes brightened. 'Did you hear about the splendid meeting we had at—?'

Ned Beaumont interrupted him. 'All along the same line?' he asked.

'Uh – more or less.' The District Attorney licked his lips and a pleading expression began to enter his eyes.

'How much more – or less?'

Farr's eyes slid their gaze down from Ned Beaumont's eyes to his necktie and sidewise to his left shoulder. He moved his lips vaguely, but did not utter a sound.

Ned Beaumont's smile was openly malicious now. 'All saying Paul killed Taylor Henry?' he asked in a sugary voice.

Farr jumped, his face faded to a light orange, and in his excitement he let his startled eyes focus on Ned Beaumont's eyes again. 'Christ, Ned!' he gasped.

Ned Beaumont laughed. 'You're getting nerves, Farr,' he said, still sugary of voice. 'Better watch yourself or you'll be going to pieces.' He made his face grave. 'Has Paul said anything to you about it? About your nerves, I mean.'

'N-no.'

Ned Beaumont smiled again. 'Maybe he hasn't noticed it – yet.' He raised an arm, glanced at his wrist-watch, then at Farr. 'Found out who wrote them yet?' he asked sharply.

The District Attorney stammered: 'Look here, Ned, I don't – you know – it's not—' floundered and stopped.

Ned Beaumont asked: 'Well?'

The District Attorney gulped and said desperately: 'We've got something, Ned, but it's too soon to say. Maybe there's nothing to it. You know how these things are.'

Ned Beaumont nodded. There was nothing but friendliness in his face now. His voice was level and cool without chilliness saying: 'You've learned where they were written and you've found the machine they were written on, but that's all you've got so far. You haven't got enough to even guess who wrote them.'

'That's right, Ned,' Farr blurted out with a great air of relief.

Ned Beaumont took Farr's hand and shook it cordially. 'That's the stuff,' he said. 'Well, I've got to run along. You can't go wrong taking things slowly, being sure you're right before you go ahead. You can take my word for that.'

The District Attorney's face and voice were warm with emotion. 'Thanks, Ned, thanks!'

III

At ten minutes past nine o'clock that evening the telephone-bell in Ned Beaumont's living-room rang. He went quickly to the telephone. 'Hello . . . Yes, Jack . . . Yes . . . Yes . . . Where? . . . Yes, that's fine . . . That'll be all tonight. Thanks a lot.'

When he rose from the telephone he was smiling with pale lips. His eyes were shiny and reckless. His hands shook a little.

The telephone-bell rang again before he had taken his third step. He hesitated, went back to the telephone. 'Hello . . . Oh, hello, Paul . . . Yes, I got tired of playing invalid . . . Nothing special – just thought I'd drop in and see you . . . No, I'm afraid I can't. I'm not feeling as strong as I thought I was, so I think I'd better go to bed . . . Yes, tomorrow, sure . . . 'By.'

He put on rain-coat and hat going downstairs. Wind drove rain in at him when he opened the street-door, drove it into his face as he walked half a block to the garage on the corner.

In the garage's glass-walled office a lanky, brown-haired man in once-white overalls was tilted back on a wooden chair, his feet on a shelf above an electric heater, reading a newspaper. He lowered the newspaper when Ned Beaumont said: ' 'Lo, Tommy.'

The dirtiness of Tommy's face made his teeth seem whiter than they were. He showed many of them in a grin and said: 'Kind of weatherish tonight.'

'Yes. Got an iron I can have? One that'll carry me over country roads tonight?'

Tommy said: 'Jesus! Lucky for you you could pick your night. You might've had to go on a bad one. Well, I got a Buick that I don't care what happens to.'

'Will it get me there?'

'It's just as likely to as anything else,' Tommy said, 'tonight.'

'All right. Fill it up for me. What's the best road up Lazy Creek way on a night like this?'

'How far up?'

Ned Beaumont looked thoughtfully at the garageman then said: 'Along about where it runs into the river.'

Tommy nodded. 'The Mathews place?' he asked.

Ned Beaumont did not say anything.

Tommy said: 'It makes a difference which place you're going to.'

'Yes? The Mathews place.' Ned Beaumont frowned. 'This is under the hat, Tommy.'

'Did you come to me because you thought I'd talk or because you knew I wouldn't?' Tommy demanded argumentatively.

Ned Beaumont said: 'I'm in a hurry.'

'Then you take the New River Road as far as Barton's, take the dirt road over the bridge there – if you can make it at all – and then the first cross-road back east. That'll bring you in behind Mathews's place along about the top of the hill. If you can't make the dirt road in this weather you'll have to go on up the New River Road to where it crosses and then cut back along the old one.'

'Thanks.'

When Ned Beaumont was getting into the Buick Tommy said to him in a markedly casual tone: 'There's an extra gun in the side-pocket.'

Ned Beaumont stared at the lanky man. 'Extra?' he asked blankly.

'Pleasant trip,' Tommy said.

Ned Beaumont shut the door and drove away.

The clock in the dashboard said ten thirty-two. Ned Beaumont switched off the lights and got somewhat stiffly out of the Buick. Wind-driven rain hammered tree, bush, ground, man, car with incessant wet blows. Downhill, through rain and foliage, irregular small patches of yellow light glowed faintly. Ned Beaumont shivered, tried to draw his rain-coat closer around him, and began to stumble downhill through drenched underbrush towards the patches of light.

Wind and rain on his back pushed him downhill towards the patches. As he went downhill stiffness gradually left him so that, though he stumbled often and staggered, and was tripped by obstacles underfoot, he kept his feet under him and moved nimbly enough, if erratically, towards his goal.

Presently a path came under his feet. He turned into it, holding it partly by its sliminess under his feet, partly by the feel of the bushes whipping his face on either side, and not at all by sight. The path led him off to the left for a little distance, but then, swinging in a broad curve, brought him to the brink of a small gorge through which water rushed noisily and from there, in another curve, to the front door of the building where the yellow light glowed.

Ned Beaumont went straight up to the door and knocked.

The door was opened by a grey-haired bespectacled man. His face was mild and greyish and the eyes that peered anxiously through the pale-tortoise-shell-encircled lenses of his spectacles were grey. His brown suit was neat and of good quality, but not fashionably cut. One side of his rather high stiff white collar had been blistered in four places by drops of water. He stood aside holding the door open and said, 'Come in, sir, come in out of the rain,' in a friendly if not hearty voice. 'A wretched night to be out in.'

Ned Beaumont lowered his head no more than two inches in

the beginning of a bow and stepped indoors. He was in a large room that occupied all the building's ground-floor. The sparseness and simplicity of the room's furnishings gave it a primitive air that was pleasantly devoid of ostentation. It was a kitchen, a dining-room, and a living-room.

Opal Madvig rose from the footstool on which she had been sitting at one end of the fireplace and, holding herself tall and straight, stared with hostile bleak eyes at Ned Beaumont.

He took off his hat and began to unbutton his rain-coat. The others recognized him then.

The man who had opened the door said, 'Why, it's Beaumont!' in an incredulous voice and looked wide-eyed at Shad O'Rory.

Shad O'Rory was sitting in a wooden chair in the center of the room facing the fireplace. He smiled dreamily at Ned Beaumont, saying, in his musical faintly Irish baritone, 'And so it is,' and, 'How are you, Ned?'

Jeff Gardner's apish face broadened in a grin that showed his beautiful false teeth and almost completely hid his little red eyes. 'By Jesus, Rusty!' he said to the sullen rosy-cheeked boy who lounged on the bench beside him, 'little Rubber Ball has come back to us. I told you he liked the way we bounced him around.'

Rusty lowered at Ned Beaumont and growled something that did not carry across the room.

The thin girl in red sitting not far from Opal Madvig looked at Ned Beaumont with bright interested dark eyes.

Ned Beaumont took off his coat. His lean face, still bearing the marks of Jeff's and Rusty's fists, was tranquil except for the recklessness aglitter in his eyes. He put his coat and hat on a long unpainted chest that was against one wall near the door. He smiled politely at the man who had admitted him and said: 'My car broke down as I was passing. It's very kind of you to give me shelter, Mr Mathews.'

Mathews said, 'Not at all – glad to,' somewhat vaguely. Then his frightened eyes looked pleadingly at O'Rory again.

O'Rory stroked his smooth white hair with a slender pale hand and smiled pleasantly at Ned Beaumont, but did not say anything.

Ned Beaumont advanced to the fireplace. ''Lo, snip,' he said to Opal Madvig.

She did not respond to his greeting. She stood there and looked at him with hostile bleak eyes.

He directed his smile at the thin girl in red. 'This is Mrs Mathews, isn't it?'

She said, 'It is,' in a soft, almost cooing, voice and held out her hand.

'Opal told me you were a schoolmate of hers,' he said as he took her hand. He turned from her to face Rusty and Jeff. ''Lo, boys,' he said carelessly. 'I was hoping I'd see you some time soon.'

Rusty said nothing.

Jeff's face became an ugly mask of grinning delight. 'Me and you both,' he said heartily, 'now that my knuckles are all healed up again. What do you guess it is that makes me get such a hell of a big kick out of slugging you?'

Shad O'Rory gently addressed the apish man without turning to look at him: 'You talk too much with your mouth, Jeff. Maybe if you didn't you'd still have your own teeth.'

Mrs Mathews spoke to Opal in an undertone. Opal shook her head and sat down on the stool by the fire again.

Mathews, indicating a wooden chair at the other end of the fireplace, said nervously: 'Sit down, Mr Beaumont, and dry your feet and – and get warm.'

'Thanks.' Ned Beaumont pulled the chair out more directly in the fire's glow and sat down.

Shad O'Rory was lighting a cigarette. When he had finished he took it from between his lips and asked: 'How are you feeling, Ned?'

'Pretty good, Shad.'

'That's fine.' O'Rory turned his head a little to speak to the two men on the bench: 'You boys can go back to town tomorrow.'

He turned back to Ned Beaumont, explaining blandly: 'We were playing safe as long as we didn't know for sure you weren't going to die, but we don't mind standing an assault-rap.'

Ned Beaumont nodded. 'The chances are I won't go to the trouble of appearing against you, anyhow, on that, but don't forget our friend Jeff's wanted for West's murder.' His voice was light, but into his eyes, fixed on the log burning in the fireplace, came a brief evil glint. There was nothing in his eyes but mockery when he moved them to the left to focus on Mathews. 'Though of course I might so I could make trouble for Mathews for helping you hide out.'

Mathews said hastily: 'I didn't, Mr Beaumont. I didn't even know they were here until we came up today and I was as surprised as—' He broke off, his face panicky, and addressed Shad O'Rory, whining: 'You know you are welcome. You know that, but the point I'm trying to make' – his face was illuminated by a sudden glad smile – 'is that by helping you without knowing it I didn't do anything I could be held legally responsible for.'

O'Rory said softly: 'Yes, you helped me without knowing it.' His notable clear blue-grey eyes looked without interest at the newspaper-publisher.

Mathews's smile lost its gladness, flickered out entirely. He fidgeted with fingers at his necktie and presently evaded O'Rory's gaze.

Mrs Mathews spoke to Ned Beaumont, sweetly: 'Everybody's been so dull this evening. It was simply ghastly until you came.'

He looked at her curiously. Her dark eyes were bright, soft, inviting. Under his appraising look she lowered her head a little and pursed her lips a little, coquettishly. Her lips were thin, too dark with rouge, but beautiful in form. He smiled at her and, rising, went over to her.

Opal Madvig stared at the floor before her. Mathews, O'Rory, and the two men on the bench watched Ned Beaumont and Mathews's wife.

He asked, 'What makes them so dull?' and sat down on the

floor in front of her, cross-legged, not facing her directly, his back to the fire, leaning on a hand on the floor behind him, his face turned up to one side towards her.

'I'm sure I don't know,' she said, pouting. 'I thought it was going to be fun when Hal asked me if I wanted to come up here with him and Opal. And then, when we got here, we found these—' she paused a moment – said, 'friends of Hal's,' with poorly concealed dubiety – and went on: 'here and everybody's been sitting around hinting at some secret they've all got between them that I don't know anything about and it's been unbearably stupid. Opal's been as bad as the rest. She—'

Her husband said, 'Now, Eloise,' in an ineffectually authoritative tone and, when she raised her eyes to meet his, got more embarrassment than authority in his gaze.

'I don't care,' she told him petulantly. 'It's true and Opal is as bad as the rest of you. Why, you and she haven't even talked about whatever business it was you were coming up here to discuss in the first place. Don't think I'd've stayed here this long if it hadn't been for the storm. I wouldn't.'

Opal Madvig's face had flushed, but she did not raise her eyes.

Eloise Mathews bent her head down towards Ned Beaumont again and the petulance in her face became playful. 'That's what you've got to make up for,' she assured him, 'and that and not because you're beautiful is why I was so glad to see you.'

He frowned at her in mock indignation.

She frowned at him. Her frown was genuine. 'Did your car really break down?' she demanded, 'or did you come here to see them on the same dull business that's making them so stupidly mysterious? You did. You're another one of them.'

He laughed. He asked: 'It wouldn't make any difference why I came if I changed my mind after seeing you, would it?'

'No-o-o' – she was suspicious – 'but I'd have to be awfully sure you had changed it.'

'And anyway,' he promised lightly, 'I won't be mysterious

about anything. Haven't you really got an idea of what they're all eating their hearts out about?'

'Not the least,' she replied spitefully, 'except that I'm pretty sure it must be something very stupid and probably political.'

He put his free hand up and patted one of hers. 'Smart girl, right on both counts.' He turned his head to look at O'Rory and Mathews. When his eyes came back to hers they were shiny with merriment. 'Want me to tell you about it?'

'No.'

'First,' he said, 'Opal thinks her father murdered Taylor Henry.'

Opal Madvig made a horrible strangling noise in her throat and sprang up from the footstool. She put the back of one hand over her mouth. Her eyes were open so wide the whites showed all around the irises and they were glassy and dreadful.

Rusty lurched to his feet, his face florid with anger, but Jeff, leering, caught the boy's arm. 'Let him alone,' he rasped good-naturedly. 'He's all right.' The boy stood straining against the apish man's grip on his arm, but did not try to free himself.

Eloise Mathews sat frozen in her chair, staring without comprehension at Opal.

Mathews was trembling, a shrunken grey-faced sick man whose lower lip and lower eyelids sagged.

Shad O'Rory was sitting forward in his chair, finely modeled long face pale and hard, eyes like blue-grey ice, hands gripping chair-arms, feet flat on the floor.

'Second,' Ned Beaumont said, his poise nowise disturbed by the agitation of the others, 'she—'

'Ned, don't!' Opal Madvig cried.

He screwed himself around on the floor then to look up at her.

She had taken her hand from her mouth. Her hands were knotted together against her chest. Her stricken eyes, her whole haggard face, begged mercy of him.

He studied her gravely awhile. Through window and wall came the sound of rain dashing against the building in wild gusts and between gusts the bustling of the near-by river. His eyes, studying her, were cool, deliberate. Presently he spoke to her in a voice kind enough but aloof: 'Isn't that why you're here?'

'Please don't,' she said hoarsely.

He moved his lips in a thin smile that his eyes had nothing to do with and asked: 'Nobody's supposed to go around talking about it except you and your father's other enemies?'

She put her hands – fists – down at her sides, raised her face angrily, and said in a hard ringing voice: 'He did murder Taylor.'

Ned Beaumont leaned back against his hand again and looked up at Eloise Mathews. 'That's what I was telling you,' he drawled. 'Thinking that, she went to your husband after she saw the junk he printed this morning. Of course he didn't think Paul had done any killing: he's just in a tough spot – with his mortgages held by the State Central, which is owned by Shad's candidate for the Senate – and he has to do what he's told. What she—'

Mathews interrupted him. The publisher's voice was thin and desperate. 'Now you stop that, Beaumont. You—'

O'Rory interrupted Mathews. O'Rory's voice was quiet, musical. 'Let him talk, Mathews,' he said. 'Let him say his say.'

'Thanks, Shad,' Ned Beaumont said carelessly, not looking around, and went on: 'She went to your husband to have him confirm her suspicion, but he couldn't give her anything that would do that unless he lied to her. He doesn't know anything. He's simply throwing mud wherever Shad tells him to throw it. But here's what he can do and does. He can print in tomorrow's paper the story about her coming in and telling him she believes her father killed her lover. That'll be a lovely wallop. "Opal Madvig Accuses Father of Murder; Boss's Daughter Says He Killed Senator's Son!" Can't you see that in black ink all across the front of the *Observer*?'

Eloise Mathews, her eyes large, her face white, was listening breathlessly, bending forward, her face above his. Wind-flung rain beat walls and windows. Rusty filled and emptied his lungs with a long sighing breath.

Ned Beaumont put the tip of his tongue between smiling lips, withdrew it, and said: 'That's why he brought her up here, to keep her under cover till the story breaks. Maybe he knew Shad and the boys were here, maybe not. It doesn't make any difference. He's getting her off where nobody can find out what she's done till the papers are out. I don't mean that he'd've brought her here, or would hold her here, against her will — that wouldn't be very bright of him the way things stack up now — but none of that's necessary. She's willing to go to any lengths to ruin her father.'

Opal Madvig said, in a whisper, but distinctly: 'He did kill him.'

Ned Beaumont sat up straight and looked at her. He looked solemnly at her for a moment, then smiled, shook his head in a gesture of amused resignation, and leaned back on his elbows.

Eloise Mathews was staring with dark eyes wherein wonder was predominant at her husband. He had sat down. His head was bowed. His hands hid his face.

Shad O'Rory recrossed his legs and took out a cigarette. 'Through?' he asked mildly.

Ned Beaumont's back was to O'Rory. He did not turn to reply: 'You'd hardly believe how through I am.' His voice was level, but his face was suddenly tired, spent.

O'Rory lit his cigarette. 'Well,' he said when he had done that, 'what the hell does it all amount to? It's our turn to hang a big one on you and we're doing it. The girl came in with the story on her own hook. She came here because she wanted to. So did you. She and you and anybody else can go wherever they want to go whenever they want to.' He stood up. 'Personally, I'm wanting to go to bed. Where do I sleep, Mathews?'

Eloise Mathews spoke, to her husband: 'This is not true, Hal.' It was not a question.

He was slow taking his hands from his face. He achieved dignity saying: 'Darling, there is a dozen times enough evidence against Madvig to justify us in insisting that the police at least question him. That is all we have done.'

'I did not mean that,' his wife said.

'Well, darling, when Miss Madvig came—' He faltered, stopped, a grey-faced man who shivered before the look in his wife's eyes and put his hands over his face again.

V

Eloise Mathews and Ned Beaumont were alone in the large ground-floor room, sitting, in chairs a few feet apart, with the fireplace in front of them. She was bent forward, looking with tragic eyes at the last burning log. His legs were crossed. One of his arms was hooked over the back of his chair. He smoked a cigar and watched her surreptitiously.

The stairs creaked and her husband came half-way down them. He was fully clothed except that he had taken off his collar. His necktie, partially loosened, hung outside his vest. He said: 'Darling, won't you come to bed? It's midnight.'

She did not move.

He said: 'Mr Beaumont, will you—?'

Ned Beaumont, when his name was spoken, turned his face towards the man on the stairs, a face cruelly placid. When Mathews's voice broke, Ned Beaumont returned his attention to his cigar and Mathews's wife.

After a little while Mathews went upstairs again.

Eloise Mathews spoke without taking her gaze from the fire. 'There is some whisky in the chest. Will you get it?'

'Surely.' He found the whisky and brought it to her, then found some glasses. 'Straight?' he asked.

She nodded. Her round breasts were moving the red silk of her dress irregularly with her breathing.

He poured two large drinks.

She did not look up from the fire until he had put one glass in her hand. When she looked up she smiled, crookedly, twisting her heavily rouged exquisite thin lips sidewise. Her eyes, reflecting red light from the fire, were too bright.

He smiled down at her.

She lifted her glass and said, cooing: 'To my husband!'

Ned Beaumont said, 'No,' casually and tossed the contents of his glass into the fireplace, where it sputtered and threw dancing flames up.

She laughed in delight and jumped to her feet. 'Pour another,' she ordered.

He picked the bottle up from the floor and refilled his glass.

She lifted hers high over her head. 'To you!'

They drank. She shuddered.

'Better take something with it or after it,' he suggested.

She shook her head. 'I want it that way.' She put a hand on his arm and turned her back to the fire, standing close beside him. 'Let's bring that bench over here.'

'That's an idea,' he agreed.

They moved the chairs from in front of the fireplace and brought the bench there, he carrying one end, she the other. The bench was broad, low, backless.

'Now turn off the lights,' she said.

He did so. When he returned to the bench she was sitting on it pouring whisky into their glasses.

'To you, this time,' he said and they drank and she shuddered.

He sat beside her. They were rosy in the glow from the fireplace.

The stairs creaked and her husband came down them. He halted on the bottom step and said: 'Please, darling!'

She whispered in Ned Beaumont's ear, savagely: 'Throw something at him.'

Ned Beaumont chuckled.

She picked up the whisky-bottle and said: 'Where's your glass?'

While she was filling their glasses Mathews went upstairs.

She gave Ned Beaumont his glass and touched it with her own. Her eyes were wild in the red glow. A lock of dark hair had come loose and was down across her brow. She breathed through her mouth, panting softly. 'To us!' she said.

They drank. She let her empty glass fall and came into his arms. Her mouth was to his when she shuddered. The fallen glass broken noisily on the wooden floor. Ned Beaumont's eyes were narrow, crafty. Hers were shut tight.

They had not moved when the stairs creaked. Ned Beaumont did not move then. She tightened her thin arms around him. He could not see the stairs. Both of them were breathing heavily now.

Then the stairs creaked again and, shortly afterwards, they drew their heads apart, though they kept their arms about one another. Ned Beaumont looked at the stairs. Nobody was there.

Eloise Mathews slid her hand up the back of his head, running her fingers through his hair, digging her nails into his scalp. Her eyes were not now altogether closed. They were laughing dark slits. 'Life's like that,' she said in a small bitter mocking voice, leaning back on the bench, drawing him with her, drawing his mouth to hers.

They were in that position when they heard the shot.

Ned Beaumont was out of her arms and on his feet immediately. 'His room?' he asked sharply.

She blinked at him in dumb terror.

'His room?' he repeated.

She moved a feeble hand. 'In front,' she said thickly.

He ran to the stairs and went up in long leaps. At the head of the stairs he came face to face with the apish Jeff, dressed except for his shoes, blinking sleep out of his swollen eyes. Jeff put a hand to his hip, put the other hand out to stop Ned Beaumont, and growled: 'Now what's all this?'

Ned avoided the outstretched hand, slid past it, and drove his left fist into the apish muzzle. Jeff staggered back snarling. Ned Beaumont sprang past him and ran towards the front of the building. O'Rory came out of another room and ran behind him.

From downstairs came Mrs Mathews's scream.

Ned Beaumont flung a door open and stopped. Mathews lay on his back on the bedroom-floor under a lamp. His mouth was open and a little blood had trickled from it. One of his arms was thrown out across the floor. The other lay on his chest. Over against the wall, where the outstretched arm seemed to be pointing at it, was a dark revolver. On a table by the window was a bottle of ink – its stopper upside down beside it – a pen, and a sheet of paper. A chair stood close to the table, facing it.

Shad O'Rory pushed past Ned Beaumont and knelt beside the man on the floor. While he was there Ned Beaumont, behind him, swiftly glanced at the paper on the table, then thrust it into his pocket.

Jeff came in, followed by Rusty, naked.

O'Rory stood up and spread his hands apart in a little gesture of finality. 'Shot himself through the roof of the mouth,' he said. 'Finis.'

Ned Beaumont turned and went out of the room. In the hall he met Opal Madvig.

'What, Ned?' she asked in a frightened voice.

'Mathews has shot himself. I'll go down and stay with her till you get some clothes on. Don't go in there. There's nothing to see.' He went downstairs.

Eloise Mathews was a dim shape lying on the floor beside the bench.

He took two quick steps towards her, halted, and looked around the room with shrewd cold eyes. Then he walked over to the woman, went down on one knee beside her, and felt her pulse. He looked at her as closely as he could in the dull light of the dying fire. She gave no sign of consciousness. He pulled the paper he had taken from her husband's table out of his pocket and moved on his knees to the fireplace, where, in the red embers' glow, he read:

I, Howard Keith Mathews, being of sound mind and memory, declare this to be my last will and testament:

I give and bequeath to my beloved wife, Eloise Braden Mathews, her heirs and assigns, all my real and personal property, of whatever nature or kind.

I hereby appoint the State Central Trust Company the sole executor of this will.

In witness whereof I have hereunto subscribed my name this . . .

Ned Beaumont, smiling grimly, stopped reading and tore the will three times across. He stood up, reached over the fire-screen, and dropped the torn pieces of paper into the glowing embers. The fragments blazed brightly a moment and were gone. With the wrought-iron shovel that stood beside the fire he mashed the paper-ash into the wood-coals.

Then he returned to Mrs Mathews's side, poured a little whisky into the glass he had drunk from, raised her head, and forced some of the liquor between her lips. She was partly awake, coughing, when Opal Madvig came downstairs.

VI

Shad O'Rory came down the stairs. Jeff and Rusty were behind him. All of them were dressed. Ned Beaumont was standing by the door, in rain-coat and hat.

'Where are you going, Ned?' Shad asked.

'To find a phone.'

O'Rory nodded. 'That's a good enough idea,' he said, 'but there's something I want to ask you about.' He came the rest of the way down the stairs, his followers close behind him.

Ned Beaumont said: 'Yes?' He took his hand out of his pocket. The hand was visible to O'Rory and the men behind him, but Ned Beaumont's body concealed it from the bench where Opal sat with arms around Eloise Mathews. A square pistol was in the hand. 'Just so there won't be any foolishness. I'm in a hurry.'

O'Rory did not seem to see the pistol, though he came no nearer. He said, reflectively: 'I was thinking that with an open ink-bottle and a pen on the table and a chair up to it it's kind of funny we didn't find any writing up there.'

Ned Beaumont smiled in mock astonishment. 'What, no writing?' He took a step backwards, towards the door. 'That's a funny one, all right. I'll discuss it with you for hours when I come back from phoning.'

'Now would be better,' O'Rory said.

'Sorry.' Ned Beaumont backed swiftly to the door, felt behind him for the knob, found it, and had the door open. 'I won't be gone long.' He jumped out and slammed the door.

The rain had stopped. He left the path and ran through tall grass around the other side of the house. From the house came the sound of another door slamming in the rear. The river was audible not far to Ned Beaumont's left. He worked his way through underbrush towards it.

A high-pitched sharp whistle, not loud, sounded somewhere behind him. He floundered through an area of soft mud to a clump of trees and turned away from the river among them. The whistle came again, on his right. Beyond the trees were shoulder-high bushes. He went among them, bending forward from the waist for concealment, though the night's blackness was all but complete.

His way was uphill, up a hill frequently slippery, always uneven, through brush that tore his face and hands, caught his clothing. Three times he fell. He stumbled many times. The whistle did not come again. He did not find the Buick. He did not find the road along which he had come.

He dragged his feet now and stumbled when there were no obstructions and when presently he had topped the hill and was going down its other slope he began to fall more often. At the bottom of the hill he found a road and turned to the right on it. Its clay stuck to his feet in increasing bulk so that he had to stop time after time to scrape it off. He used his pistol to scrape it off.

When he heard a dog bark behind him he stopped and turned drunkenly to look back. Close to the road, fifty feet behind him, was the vague outline of a house he had passed. He retraced his steps and came to a tall gate. The dog – a shapeless monster in the night – hurled itself at the other side of the gate and barked terrifically.

Ned Beaumont fumbled along an end of the gate, found the catch, unfastened it, and staggered in. The dog backed away, circling, feinting attacks it never made, filling the night with clamor.

A window screeched up and a heavy voice called: 'What the hell are you doing to that dog?'

Ned Beaumont laughed weakly. Then he shook himself and replied in not too thin a voice: 'This is Beaumont of the District Attorney's office. I want to use your phone. There's a dead man down there.'

The heavy voice roared: 'I don't know what you're talking about. Shut up, Jeanie!' The dog barked three times with increased energy and became silent. 'Now what is it?'

'I want to phone. District Attorney's office. There's a dead man down there.'

The heavy voice exclaimed: 'The hell you say!' The window screeched shut.

The dog began its barking and circling and feinting again. Ned Beaumont threw his muddy pistol at it. It turned and ran out of sight behind the house.

The front door was opened by a red-faced barrel-bodied short man in a long blue night-shirt. 'Holy Maria, you're a mess!' he gasped when Ned Beaumont came into the light from the doorway.

'Phone,' Ned Beaumont said.

The red-faced man caught him as he swayed. 'Here,' he said gruffly, 'tell me who to call and what to say. You can't do anything.'

'Phone,' Ned Beaumont said.

The red-faced man steadied him along a hallway, opened a door, said: 'There she is and it's a damned good thing for you the old woman ain't home or you'd never get in with all that mud on you.'

Ned Beaumont fell into the chair in front of the telephone, but he did not immediately reach for the telephone. He scowled at the man in the blue night-shirt and said thickly: 'Go out and shut the door.'

The red-faced man had not come into the room. He shut the door.

Ned Beaumont picked up the receiver, leaned forward so that he was propped against the table by his elbows on it, and called Paul Madvig's number. Half a dozen times while he waited his eyelids closed, but each time he forced them open again and when, at last, he spoke into the telephone it was clearly.

''Lo, Paul – Ned . . . Never mind that. Listen to me. Mathews's committed suicide at his place on the river and didn't leave a will . . . Listen to me. This is important. With a lot of debts and no will naming an executor it'll be up to the courts to appoint somebody to administer the estate. Get that? . . . Yes. See that it comes up before the right judge – Phelps, say – and we can keep the *Observer* out of the fight – except on our side – till after the election. Got that? . . . All right, all right, now listen. That's only part of it. This is what's got to be done now. The *Observer* is loaded with dynamite for the morning. You've got to stop it. I'd say get Phelps out of bed and get an injunction out of him – anything to stop it till you can show the *Observer*'s hired men where they stand now that the paper's going to be bossed for a month or so by our friends . . . I can't tell you now, Paul, but it's dynamite and you've got to keep it from going on sale. Get Phelps out of bed and go down and look at it yourselves. You've got maybe three hours before it's out on the streets . . . That's right . . . What? . . . Opal? Oh, she's all right. She's with me . . . Yes, I'll bring her home . . . And will you phone the county people about Mathews? I'm going back there now. Right.'

He laid the receiver on the table and stood up, staggered to the door, got it open after the second attempt, and fell out into the hallway, where the wall kept him from tumbling down on the floor.

The red-faced man came hurrying to him. 'Just lean on me, brother, and I'll make you comfortable. I got a blanket spread over the davenport so we won't have to worry about the mud and—'

Ned Beaumont said: 'I want to borrow a car. I've got to go back to Mathews's.'

'Is it him that's dead?'

'Yes.'

The red-faced man raised his eyebrows and made a squeaky whistling sound.

'Will you lend me the car?' Ned Beaumont demanded.

'My God, brother, be reasonable! How could you drive a car?'

Ned Beaumont backed away from the other, unsteadily. 'I'll walk,' he said.

The red-faced men glared at him. 'You won't neither. If you'll keep your hair on till I get my pants I'll drive you back, though likely enough you'll die on me on the way.'

Opal Madvig and Eloise Mathews were together in the large ground-floor room when Ned Beaumont was carried rather than led into it by the red-faced man. The men had come in without knocking. The two girls were standing close together, wide-eyed, startled.

Ned Beaumont pulled himself out of his companion's arms and looked dully around the room. 'Where's Shad?' he mumbled.

Opal answered him: 'He's gone. All of them have gone.'

'All right,' he said, speaking difficultly. 'I want to talk to you alone.'

Eloise Mathews ran over to him. 'You killed him!' she cried.

He giggled idiotically and tried to put his arms around her.

She screamed, struck him in the face with an open hand.

He fell straight back without bending. The red-faced man tried to catch him, but could not. He did not move at all after he struck the floor.

7 The Henchmen

I

Senator Henry put his napkin on the table and stood up. Rising, he seemed taller than he was and younger. His somewhat small head, under its thin covering of grey hair, was remarkably symmetrical. Aging muscles sagged in his patrician face, accentuating its vertical lines, but slackness had not yet reached his lips, nor was it apparent that the years had in any way touched his eyes: they were a greenish grey, deep-set, not large but brilliant, and their lids were firm. He spoke with studied grave courtesy: 'You'll forgive me if I carry Paul off upstairs for a little while?'

His daughter replied: 'Yes, if you'll leave me Mr Beaumont and if you'll promise not to stay up there all evening.'

Ned Beaumont smiled politely, inclining his head.

He and Janet Henry went into a white-walled room where coal burned sluggishly in a grate under a white mantelpiece and put somber red gleams on the mahogany furniture.

She turned on a lamp beside the piano and sat down there with her back to the keyboard, her head between Ned Beaumont and the lamp. Her blond hair caught lamplight and held it in a nimbus around her head. Her black gown was of some suede-like material that reflected no light and she wore no jewelry.

Ned Beaumont leaned over to knock ash from his cigar down on the burning coal. A dark pearl in his shirt-bosom, twinkling in the fire's glow as he moved, was like a red eye winking. When he straightened, he asked: 'You'll play something?'

'Yes, if you wish – though I don't play exceptionally well – but later. I'd like to talk to you now while I've an opportunity.' Her hands were together in her lap. Her arms, held straight, forced her shoulders up and in towards her neck.

Ned Beaumont nodded politely, but did not say anything. He left the fireplace and sat not far from her on a sofa with lyre ends. Though he was attentive, there was no curiosity in his mien.

Turning on the piano-bench to face him directly, she asked: 'How is Opal?' Her voice was low, intimate.

His voice was casual: 'Perfectly all right as far as I know, though I haven't seen her since last week.' He lifted his cigar half a foot towards his mouth, lowered it, and as if the question had just come to his mind asked: 'Why?'

She opened her brown eyes wide. 'Isn't she in bed with a nervous break-down?'

'Oh, that!' he said carelessly, smiling. 'Didn't Paul tell you?'

'Yes, he told me she was in bed with a nervous break-down.' She stared at him, perplexed. 'He told me that.'

Ned Beaumont's smile became gentle. 'I suppose he's sensitive about it,' he said slowly, looking at his cigar. Then he looked up at her and moved his shoulders a little. 'There's nothing the matter with her that way. It's simply that she got the foolish idea that he had killed your brother and – still more foolishly – was going around talking about it. Well, Paul couldn't have his daughter running around accusing him of murder, so he had to keep her home till she gets the notion out of her head.'

'You mean she's—' she hesitated: her eyes were bright '—she's – well – a prisoner?'

'You make it sound melodramatic,' he protested carelessly.

'She's only a child. Isn't making children stay in their rooms one of the usual ways of disciplining them?'

Janet Henry replied hastily: 'Oh, yes! Only—' She looked at her hands in her lap, up at his face again. 'But why did she think that?'

Ned Beaumont's voice was tepid as his smile. 'Who doesn't?' he asked.

She put her hands on the edge of the piano-bench beside her and leaned forward. Her white face was earnestly set. 'That's what I wanted to ask you, Mr Beaumont. Do people think that?'

He nodded. His face was placid.

Her knuckles were white over the bench-edge. Her voice was parched asking: 'Why?'

He rose from the sofa and crossed to the fireplace to drop the remainder of his cigar into the fire. When he returned to his seat he crossed his long legs and leaned back at ease. 'The other side thinks it's good politics to make people think that,' he said. There was nothing in his voice, his face, his manner to show that he had any personal interest in what he was talking about.

She frowned. 'But, Mr Beaumont, why should people think it unless there's some sort of evidence, or something that can be made to look like evidence?'

He looked curiously and amusedly at her. 'There is, of course,' he said. 'I thought you knew that.' He combed a side of his mustache with a thumb-nail. 'Didn't you get any of the anonymous letters that've been going around?'

She stood up quickly. Excitement distorted her face. 'Yes, today!' she exclaimed. 'I wanted to show it to you, to—'

He laughed softly and raised a hand, palm out in an arresting gesture. 'Don't bother. They all seem to be pretty much alike and I've seen plenty of them.'

She sat down again, slowly, reluctantly.

He said: 'Well, those letters, the stuff the *Observer* was printing till we pulled it out of the fight, the talk the others have been circulating' – he shrugged his thin shoulders – 'they've taken what facts there are and made a pretty swell case against Paul.'

She took her lower lip from between her teeth to ask: 'Is – is he actually in danger?'

Ned Beaumont nodded and spoke with calm certainty: 'If he loses the election, loses his hold on the city and state government, they'll electrocute him.'

She shivered and asked in a voice that shook: 'But he's safe if he wins?'

Ned Beaumont nodded again. 'Sure.'

She caught her breath. Her lips trembled so that her words came out jerkily. 'Will he win?'

'I think so.'

'And it won't make any difference then no matter how much evidence there is against him, he'll—' her voice broke '—he'll not be in danger?'

'He won't be tried,' Ned Beaumont told her. Abruptly he sat up straight. He shut his eyes tight, opened them, and stared at her tense pale face. A glad light came into his eyes, gladness spread over his face. He laughed – not loud but in complete delight – and stood up exclaiming: 'Judith herself!'

Janet Henry sat breathlessly still, looking at him with uncomprehending brown eyes in a blank white face.

He began to walk around the room in an irregular route, talking happily – not to her – though now and then he turned his head over his shoulder to smile at her. 'That's the game, of course,' he said. 'She could put up with Paul – be polite to him – for the sake of the political backing her father needed, but that would have its limits. Or that's all that would be necessary, Paul being so much in love with her. But when she decided Paul had killed her brother and was going to escape punishment unless she— That's splendid! Paul's daughter and his sweetheart both trying to steer him to the electric chair. He certainly has a lot of luck with women.' He had a slender pale-green-spotted cigar in one hand now. He halted in front of Janet Henry, clipped the end of the cigar, and said, not accusingly, but as if sharing a discovery with her: 'You sent those anonymous letters around. Certainly you did. They were written on the typewriter in the room where your brother and Opal used to meet. He had a key and she had a key. She didn't write them because she was stirred up by them. You did. You took his key when it was turned over to you and your father with the rest of his stuff by the police, sneaked into the room, and wrote them. That's fine.' He began to walk again. He said: 'Well, we'll have to make the Senator get in a squad of good able-bodied nurses and lock you in your room with a nervous break-down. It's getting to be epidemic among our politicians' daughters, but we've got to make sure of the election even if every house in town has to have its patient.' He turned his head over his shoulder to smile amiably at her.

She put a hand to her throat. Otherwise she did not move. She did not speak.

He said: 'The Senator won't give us much trouble, luckily. He doesn't care about anything – not you or his dead son – as much as he does about being re-elected and he knows he can't do that without Paul.' He laughed. 'That's what drove you into the Judith rôle, huh? You knew your father wouldn't split with Paul – even if he thought him guilty – till the election was won. Well, that's a comforting thing to know – for us.'

When he stopped talking to light his cigar she spoke. She had taken her hand down from her throat. Her hands were in her lap. She sat erect without stiffness. Her voice was cool and composed. She said: 'I am not good at lying. I know Paul killed Taylor. I wrote the letters.'

Ned Beaumont took the burning cigar from his mouth, came back to the lyre-end sofa, and sat down facing her. His face was grave, but without hostility. He said: 'You hate Paul, don't you? Even if I proved to you that he didn't kill Taylor you'd still hate him, wouldn't you?'

'Yes,' she replied, her light brown eyes steady on his darker ones, 'I think I should.'

'That's it,' he said. 'You don't hate him because you think he killed your brother. You think he killed your brother because you hate him.'

She moved her head slowly from side to side. 'No,' she said.

He smiled skeptically. Then he asked: 'Have you talked it over with your father?'

She bit her lip and her face flushed a little.

Ned Beaumont smiled again. 'And he told you it was ridiculous,' he said.

Pink deepened in her cheeks. She started to say something, but did not.

He said: 'If Paul killed your brother your father knows it.'

She looked down at her hands in her lap and said dully, miserably: 'My father should know it, but he will not believe it.'

Ned Beaumont said: 'He ought to know.' His eyes became narrower. 'Did Paul say anything at all to him that night about Taylor and Opal?'

She raised her head, astonished. 'Don't you know what happened that night?' she asked.

'No.'

'It hadn't anything to do with Taylor and Opal,' she said, word tumbling over word in her eagerness to get them spoken. 'It—' She jerked her face towards the door and shut her mouth with a click. Deep-chested rumbling laughter had come through the door, and the sound of approaching steps. She faced Ned Beaumont again, hastily, lifting her hands in an appealing gesture. 'I've got to tell you,' she whispered, desperately earnest. 'Can I see you tomorrow?'

'Yes.'

'Where?'

'My place?' he suggested.

She nodded quickly. He had time to mutter his address, she to whisper, 'After ten?' and he to nod before Senator Henry and Paul Madvig came into the room.

II

Paul Madvig and Ned Beaumont said good-night to the Henrys at half past ten o'clock and got into a brown sedan which Madvig drove down Charles Street. When they had ridden a block and a half Madvig blew his teeth out in a satisfied gust and said: 'Jesus, Ned, you don't know how tickled I am that you and Janet are hitting it off so nice.'

Ned Beaumont, looking obliquely at the blond man's profile, said: 'I can get along with anybody.'

Madvig chuckled. 'Yes you can,' he said indulgently, 'like hell.'

Ned Beaumont's lips curved in a thin secretive smile. He said: 'I've got something I want to talk to you about tomorrow. Where'll you be, say, in the middle of the afternoon?'

Madvig turned the sedan into China Street. 'At the office,' he said. 'It's the first of the month. Why don't you do your talking now? There's a lot of night left yet.'

'I don't know it all now. How's Opal?'

'She's all right,' Madvig said gloomily, then exclaimed: 'Christ! I wish I could be sore at the kid. It'd make it a lot easier.' They passed a street-light. He blurted out: 'She's not pregnant.'

Ned Beaumont did not say anything. His face was expressionless.

Madvig reduced the sedan's speed as they approached the Log Cabin Club. His face was red. He asked huskily: 'What do you think, Ned? Was she' – he cleared his throat noisily – 'his mistress? Or was it just boy and girl stuff?'

Ned Beaumont said: 'I don't know. I don't care. Don't ask her, Paul.'

Madvig stopped the sedan and sat for a moment at the wheel staring straight ahead. Then he cleared his throat again and spoke in a low hoarse voice: 'You're not the worst guy in the world, Ned.'

'Uh-uh,' Ned Beaumont agreed as they got out of the sedan.

They entered the Club, separating casually under the Governor's portrait at the head of the stairs on the second floor.

Ned Beaumont went into a rather small room in the rear where five men were playing stud poker and three were watching them play. The players made a place for him at the table and by three o'clock, when the game broke up, he had won some four hundred dollars.

III

It was nearly noon when Janet Henry arrived at Ned Beaumont's rooms. He had been pacing the floor, alternately biting his finger-nails and puffing at cigars, for more than an hour. He went without haste to the door when she rang, opened it, and, smiling with an air of slight but pleasant surprise, said: 'Good morning.'

'I'm awfully sorry to be late,' she began, 'but—'

'But you're not,' he assured her. 'It was to have been any time after ten.'

He ushered her into his living-room.

'I like this,' she said, turning around slowly, examining the old-fashioned room, the height of its ceiling, the width of its windows, the tremendous mirror over the fireplace, the red plush of the furniture. 'It's delightful.' She turned her brown eyes towards a half-open door. 'Is that your bedroom?'

'Yes. Would you like to see it?'

'I'd love to.'

He showed her the bedroom, then the kitchen and bathroom.

'It's perfect,' she said as they returned to the living-room. 'I didn't know there could be any more of these left in a city as horribly up to date as ours has become.'

He made a little bow to acknowledge her approval. 'I think it's rather nice and, as you can see, there's no one here to eavesdrop on us unless they're stowed away in a closet, which isn't likely.'

She drew herself up and looked straight into his eyes. 'I did not think of that. We may not agree, may even become – or now be – enemies, but I know you're a gentleman, or I shouldn't be here.'

He asked in an amused tone: 'You mean I've learned not to wear tan shoes with blue suits? Things like that?'

'I don't mean things like that.'

He smiled. 'Then you're wrong. I'm a gambler and a politician's hanger-on.'

'I'm not wrong.' A pleading expression came into her eyes. 'Please don't let us quarrel, at least not until we must.'

'I'm sorry.' His smile was apologetic now. 'Won't you sit down?'

She sat down. He sat in another wide chair facing her. He said: 'Now you were going to tell me what happened at your house the night your brother was killed.'

'Yes,' issuing from her mouth, was barely audible. Her face became pink and she transferred he gaze to the floor. When she raised her eyes again they were shy. Embarrassment clogged her voice: 'I wanted you to know. You are Paul's friend and that – that may make you my enemy, but – I think when you know what happened – when you know the truth – you'll not be – at least not be my enemy. I don't know. Perhaps you'll— But you ought to know. Then you can decide. And he hasn't told you.' She looked intently at him so that shyness went out of her eyes. 'Has he?'

'I don't know what happened at your house that night,' he said. 'He didn't tell me.'

She leaned towards him quickly to ask: 'Doesn't that show it's something he wants to conceal, something he has to conceal?'

He moved his shoulders. 'Suppose it does?' His voice was unexcited, uneager.

She frowned. 'But you must see— Never mind that now. I'll tell you what happened and you can see it for yourself.' She continued to lean far forward, staring at his face with intent brown eyes. 'He came to dinner, the first time we'd had him to dinner.'

'I knew that,' Ned Beaumont said, 'and your brother wasn't there.'

'Taylor wasn't at the dinner-table,' she corrected him earnestly, 'but he was up in his room. Only Father, Paul, and I were at the table. Taylor was going out to dinner. He – he wouldn't eat with Paul because of the trouble they'd had about Opal.'

Ned Beaumont nodded attentively without warmth.

'After dinner Paul and I were alone for a little while in – in the room where you and I talked last night and he suddenly put his arms around me and kissed me.'

Ned Beaumont laughed, not loudly, but with abrupt irrepressible merriment.

Janet Henry looked at him in surprise.

He modified his laugh to a smile and said: 'I'm sorry. Go on. I'll tell you later why I laughed.' But when she would have gone on he said: 'Wait. Did he say anything when he kissed you?'

'No. That is, he may have, but nothing I understood.' Perplexity was deepening in her face. 'Why?'

Ned Beaumont laughed again. 'He ought to've said something about his pound of flesh. It was probably my fault. I had been trying to persuade him not to support your father in the election, had told him that your father was using you as bait to catch his support, and had advised him that if he was willing to be bought that way he ought to be sure and collect his pound of flesh ahead of the election or he'd never get it.'

She opened her eyes wide and there was less perplexity in them.

He said: 'That was that afternoon, though I didn't think I'd had much luck putting it over.' He wrinkled his forehead. 'What did you do to him? He was meaning to marry you and was chockfull of respect and what not for you and you must have rubbed him pretty thoroughly the wrong way to make him jump at you like that.'

'I didn't do anything to him,' she replied slowly, 'though it had been a difficult evening. None of us was comfortable. I thought –

I tried not to show that — well — that I resented having to entertain him. He wasn't at ease, I know, and I suppose that — his embarrassment — and perhaps a suspicion that you had been right made him—' She finished the sentence with a brief quick outward motion of both hands.

Ned Beaumont nodded. 'What happened then?' he asked.

'I was furious, of course, and left him.'

'Didn't you say anything to him?' Ned Beaumont's eyes twinkled with imperfectly hidden mirth.

'No, and he didn't say anything I could hear. I went upstairs and met Father coming down. While I was telling him what had happened — I was angry with Father as with Paul, because it was Father's fault that Paul was there — we heard Paul going out the front door. And then Taylor came down from his room.' Her face became white and tense, her voice husky with emotion. 'He had heard me talking to Father and he asked me what had happened, but I left him there with Father and went on to my room, too angry to talk any more about it. And I didn't see either of them again until Father came to my room and told me Taylor had — had been killed.' She stopped talking and looked white-faced at Ned Beaumont, twisting her fingers together, awaiting his response to her story.

His response was a cool question: 'Well, what of it?'

'What of it?' she repeated in amazement. 'Don't you see? How could I help knowing then that Taylor had run out after Paul and had caught up with him and had been killed by him? He was furious and—' Her face brightened. 'You know his hat wasn't found. He was too much in a hurry — too angry — to stop for his hat. He—'

Ned Beaumont shook his head slowly from side to side and interrupted her. His voice held nothing but certainty. 'No,' he said. 'That won't do. Paul wouldn't've had to kill Taylor and he wouldn't've done it. He could have managed him with one hand and he doesn't lose his head in a fight. I know that. I've seen Paul fight and I've fought with him. That won't do.' He drew eyelids closer together around eyes that had become stony. 'But suppose he did? I mean accidentally, though I can't believe even that. But could you make anything out of it except self-defense?'

She raised her head scornfully. 'If it were self-defense, why should he hide it?'

Ned Beaumont seemed unimpressed. 'He wants to marry you,' he explained. 'It wouldn't help him much to admit he'd killed your brother even—' He chuckled. 'I'm getting as bad as you are. Paul didn't kill him, Miss Henry.'

Her eyes were stony as his had been. She looked at him and did not speak.

His expression became thoughtful. He asked: 'You've only' – he wriggled the fingers of one hand – 'the two and two you think you've put together to tell you that your brother ran out after Paul that night?'

'That is enough,' she insisted. 'He did. He must've. Otherwise – why, otherwise what would he have been doing down there in China Street bare-headed?'

'Your father didn't see him go out?'

'No. He didn't know it either until we heard—'

He interrupted her. 'Does he agree with you?'

'He must,' she cried. 'It's unmistakable. He must, no matter what he says, just as you must.' Tears were in her eyes now. 'You can't expect me to believe that you don't, Mr Beaumont. I don't know what you knew before. You found Taylor dead. I don't know what else you found, but now you must know the truth.'

Ned Beaumont's hands began to tremble. He slumped farther down in his chair so he could thrust his hands into his trousers-pockets. His face was tranquil except for hard lines of strain around his mouth. He said: 'I found him dead. There was nobody else there. I didn't find anything else.'

'You have now,' she said.

His mouth twitched under his dark mustache. His eyes became hot with anger. He spoke in a low, harsh, deliberately bitter voice: 'I know whoever killed your brother did the world a favor.'

She shrank back in her chair with a hand thrown up to her throat, at first, but almost immediately the horror went out of her face and she sat upright and looked compassionately at him. She said softly: 'I know. You're Paul's friend. It hurts.'

He lowered his head a little and muttered: 'It was a rotten thing to say. It was silly.' He smiled wryly. 'You see I was right about not being a gentleman.' He stopped smiling and shame went out of his eyes leaving them clear and steady. He said in a quiet voice: 'You're right about my being Paul's friend. I'm that no matter who he killed.'

After a long moment of earnest staring at him she spoke in a small flat voice: 'Then this is useless? I thought if I could show you the truth—' She broke off with a hopeless gesture in which hands, shoulders, and head took part.

He moved his head slowly from side to side.

She sighed and stood up holding out her hand. 'I'm sorry and disappointed, but we needn't be enemies, need we?'

He rose facing her, but did not take her hand. He said: 'The part of you that's tricked Paul and is trying to trick him is my enemy.'

She held her hand there while asking: 'And the other part of me, the part that hasn't anything to do with that?'

He took her hand and bowed over it.

IV

When Janet Henry had gone Ned Beaumont went to his telephone, called a number, and said: 'Hello, this is Mr Beaumont. Has Mr Madvig come in yet? . . . When he comes will you tell him I called and will be in to see him? . . . Yes, thanks.'

He looked at his wrist-watch. It was a little after one o'clock. He lit a cigar and sat down at a window, smoking and staring at the grey church across the street. Out-blown cigar-smoke recoiled from the window-panes in grey clouds over his head. His teeth crushed the end of his cigar. He sat there for ten minutes, until his telephone-bell rang.

He went to the telephone. 'Hello . . . Yes, Harry . . . Sure. Where are you? . . . I'm coming downtown. Wait there for me . . . Half an hour . . . Right.'

He threw his cigar into the fireplace, put on his hat and overcoat, and went out. He walked six blocks to a restaurant, ate a salad and rolls, drank a cup of coffee, walked four blocks to a small hotel named Majestic, and rode to the fourth floor in an elevator operated by an undersized youth who called him Ned and asked what he thought of the third race.

Ned Beaumont thought and said: 'Lord Byron ought to do it.'

The elevator-operator said: 'I hope you're wrong. I got Pipe-organ.'

Ned Beaumont shrugged. 'Maybe, but he's carrying a lot of weight.' He went to room 417 and knocked on the door.

Harry Sloss, in his shirt-sleeves, opened the door. He was a thickset pale man of thirty-five, broad-faced and partially bald. He said: 'On the dot. Come on in.'

When Sloss had shut the door Ned Beaumont asked: 'What's the diffugalty?'

The thickset man went over to the bed and sat down. He scowled anxiously at Ned Beaumont. 'It don't look so damned good to me, Ned.'

'What don't?'

'This thing of Ben going to the Hall with it.'

Ned Beaumont said irritably: 'All right. Any time you're ready to tell me what you're talking about's soon enough for me.'

Sloss raised a pale broad hand. 'Wait, Ned, I'll tell you what it's about. Just listen.' He felt in his pocket for cigarettes, bringing out a package mashed limp. 'You remember the night the Henry kid was pooped?'

Ned Beaumont's 'Uh-huh' was carelessly uttered.

'Remember me and Ben had just come in when you got there, at the Club?'

'Yes.'

'Well, listen: we saw Paul and the kid arguing up there under the trees.'

Ned Beaumont brushed a side of his mustache with a thumbnail, once, and spoke slowly, looking puzzled: 'But I saw you get out of the car in front of the Club – that was just after I found him – and you came up the other way.' He moved a forefinger. 'And Paul was already in the Club ahead of you.'

Sloss nodded his broad head vigorously. 'That's all right,' he said, 'but we'd drove on down China Street to Pinky Klein's place and he wasn't there and we turned around and drove back to the Club.'

Ned Beaumont nodded. 'Just what did you see?'

'We saw Paul and the kid standing there under the trees arguing.'

'You could see that as you rode past?'

Sloss nodded vigorously again.

'It was a dark spot,' Ned Beaumont reminded him. 'I don't see how you could've made out their faces riding past like that, unless you slowed up or stopped.'

'No, we didn't, but I'd know Paul anywhere,' Sloss insisted.

'Maybe, but how'd you know it was the kid with him?'

'It was. Sure, it was. We could see enough of him to know that.'

'And you could see they were arguing? What do you mean by that? Fighting?'

'No, but standing like they were having an argument. You know how you can tell when people are arguing sometimes by the way they stand.'

Ned Beaumont smiled mirthlessly. 'Yes, if one of them's standing on the other's face.' His smile vanished. 'And that's what Ben went to the Hall with?'

'Yes. I don't know whether he went in with it on his own

account or whether Farr got hold of it somehow and sent for him, but anyhow he spilled it to Farr. That was yesterday.'

'How'd you hear about it, Harry?'

'Farr's hunting for me,' Sloss said. 'That's the way I heard about it. Ben'd told him I was with him and Farr sent word for me to drop in and see him, but I don't want any part of it.'

'I hope you don't, Harry,' Ned Beaumont said. 'What are you going to say if Farr catches you?'

'I'm not going to let him catch me if I can help it. That's what I wanted to see you about.' He cleared his throat and moistened his lips. 'I thought maybe I ought to get out of town for a week or two, till it kind of blows over, and that'd take a little money.'

Ned Beaumont smiled and shook his head. 'That's not the thing to do,' he told the thickset man. 'If you want to help Paul go tell Farr you couldn't recognize the two men under the trees and that you don't think anybody in your car could.'

'All right, that's what I'll do,' Sloss said readily, 'but, listen, Ned, I ought to get something out of it. I'm taking a chance and — well — you know how it is.'

Ned Beaumont nodded. 'We'll pick you out a soft job after election, one you'll have to show up on maybe an hour a day.'

'That'll be——' Sloss stood up. His green-flecked palish eyes were urgent. 'I'll tell you, Ned, I'm broke as hell. Couldn't you make it a little dough now instead? It'd come in damned handy.'

'Maybe. I'll talk it over with Paul.'

'Do that, Ned, and give me a ring.'

'Sure. So long.'

V

From the Majestic Hotel Ned Beaumont went to the City Hall, to the District Attorney's office, and said he wanted to see Mr Farr.

The round-faced youth to whom he said it left the outer office, returning a minute later apologetic of mien. 'I'm sorry, Mr Beaumont, but Mr Farr is not in.'

'When will he be back?'

'I don't know. His secretary says he didn't leave word.'

'I'll take a chance. I'll wait awhile in his office.'

The round-faced youth stood in his way. 'Oh, you can't do—'

Ned Beaumont smiled his nicest smile at the youth and asked softly: 'Don't you like this job, son?'

The youth hesitated, fidgeted, and stepped out of Ned Beaumont's way. Ned Beaumont walked down the inner corridor to the District Attorney's door and opened it.

Farr looked up from his desk, sprang to his feet. 'Was that you?' he cried. 'Damn that boy! He never gets anything right. A Mr Bauman, he said.'

'No harm done,' Ned Beaumont said mildly. 'I got in.'

He let the District Attorney shake his hand up and down and lead him to a chair. When they were seated he asked idly: 'Anything new?'

'Nothing.' Farr rocked back in his chair, thumbs hooked in lower vest-pockets. 'Just the same old grind, though God knows there's enough of that.'

'How's the electioneering going?'

'It could be better' – a shadow passed over the District Attorney's pugnacious red face – 'but I guess we'll manage all right.'

Ned Beaumont kept idleness in his voice. 'What's the matter?'

'This and that. Things always come up. That's politics, I guess.'

'Anything I can do – or Paul – to help?' Ned Beaumont asked and then, when Farr had shaken his red-stubble-covered head: 'This talk that Paul's got something to do with the Henry killing the worst thing you're up against?'

A frightened gleam came into Farr's eyes, disappeared as he blinked. He sat up straight in his chair. 'Well,' he said cautiously, 'there's a lot of feeling that we ought to've cleared the murder up before this. That is one of the things – maybe one of the biggest.'

'Made any progress since I saw you last? Turned up anything new on it?'

Farr shook his head. His eyes were wary.

Ned Beaumont smiled without warmth. 'Still taking it slow on some of the angles?'

The District Attorney squirmed in his chair. 'Well, yes, of course, Ned.'

Ned Beaumont nodded approvingly. His eyes were shiny with malice. His voice was a taunt: 'Is the Ben Ferriss angle one of them that you're taking it slow on?'

Farr's blunt undershot mouth opened and shut. He rubbed his lips together. His eyes, after their first startled widening, became devoid of expression. He said: 'I don't know whether there's anything at all in Ferriss's story or not, Ned. I don't guess there is. I didn't even think enough of it to tell you about it.'

Ned Beaumont laughed derisively.

Farr said: 'You know I wouldn't hold out anything on you and Paul, anything that was important. You know me well enough for that.'

'We knew you before you got nerves,' Ned Beaumont replied. 'But that's all right. If you want the fellow that was in the car with Ferriss you can pick him up right now in room 417 at the Majestic.'

Farr was staring at his green desk-set, at the dancing nude figure holding an airplane aloft between two slanting pens. His face was lumpy. He said nothing.

Ned Beaumont rose from his chair smiling with thin lips. He said: 'Paul's always glad to help the boys out of holes. Do you think it would help if he'd let himself be arrested and tried for the Henry murder?'

Farr did not move his eyes from the green desk-set. He said doggedly: 'It's not for me to tell Paul what to do.'

'There's a thought!' Ned Beaumont exclaimed. He leaned over the side of the desk until his face was near the District Attorney's ear and lowered his voice to a confidential key. 'And here's another one that goes with it. It's not for you to do much Paul wouldn't tell you to do.'

He went out grinning, but stopped grinning when he was outside.

8 The Kiss-off

Ned Beaumont opened a door marked *East State Construction & Contracting Company* and exchanged good-afternoons with the two young ladies at desks inside, then he passed through a larger room in which there were half a dozen men to whom he spoke and opened a door marked *Private.* He went into a square room where Paul Madvig sat at a battered desk looking at papers placed in front of him by a small man who hovered respectfully over his shoulder.

Madvig raised his head and said: 'Hello, Ned.' He pushed the papers aside and told the small man: 'Bring this junk back after awhile.'

The small man gathered up his papers and, saying, 'Certainly, sir,' and, 'How do you do, Mr Beaumont?' left the room.

Madvig said: 'You look like you'd had a tough night, Ned. What'd you do? Sit down.'

Ned Beaumont had taken off his overcoat. He put it on a chair, put his hat on it, and took out a cigar. 'No, I'm all right. What's new in your life?' He sat on a corner of the battered desk.

'I wish you'd go see M'Laughlin,' the blond man said. 'You can handle him if anybody can.'

'All right. What's the matter with him?'

Madvig grimaced. 'Christ knows! I thought I had him lined up, but he's going shifty on us.'

A somber gleam came into Ned Beaumont's dark eyes. He looked down at the blond man and said: 'Him too, huh?'

Madvig asked slowly, after a moment's deliberation: 'What do you mean by that, Ned?'

Ned Beaumont's reply was another question: 'Is everything going along to suit you?'

Madvig moved his big shoulders impatiently, but his eyes did not lose their surveying stare. 'Nor so damned bad either,' he said. 'We can get along without M'Laughlin's batch of votes if we have to.'

'Maybe,' Ned Beaumont's lips had become thin, 'but we can't keep on losing them and come out all right.' He put his cigar in a corner of his mouth and said around it: 'You know we're not as well off as we were two weeks ago.'

Madvig grinned indulgently at the man on his desk. 'Jesus, you like to sing them, Ned! Don't anything ever look right to you?' He did not wait for a reply, but went on placidly: 'I've never been through a campaign yet that didn't look like it was going to hell at some time or other. They don't, though.'

Ned Beaumont was lighting his cigar. He blew smoke out and said: 'That doesn't mean they never will.' He pointed the cigar at Madvig's chest. 'If Taylor Henry's killing isn't cleared up pronto you won't have to worry about the campaign. You'll be sunk whoever wins.'

Madvig's blue eyes became opaque. There was no other change in his face. His voice was unchanged. 'Just what do you mean by that, Ned?'

'Everybody in town thinks you killed him.'

'Yes?' Madvig put a hand up to his chin, rubbed it thoughtfully. 'Don't let that worry you. I've had things said about me before.'

Ned Beaumont smiled tepidly and asked with mock admiration: 'Is there anything you haven't been through before? Ever been given the electric cure?'

The blond man laughed. 'And don't think I ever will,' he said.

'You're not very far from it right now, Paul,' Ned Beaumont said softly.

Madvig laughed again. 'Jesus Christ!' he scoffed.

Ned Beaumont shrugged. 'You're not busy?' he asked. 'I'm not taking up your time with my nonsense?'

'I'm listening to you,' Madvig told him quietly. 'I never lost anything listening to you.'

'Thank you, sir. Why do you suppose M'Laughlin's wiggling out from under?'

Madvig shook his head.

'He figures you're licked,' Ned Beaumont said. 'Everybody knows the police haven't tried to find Taylor's murderer and everybody think it's because you killed him. M'Laughlin figures that's enough to lick you at the polls this time.'

'Yes? He figures they'd rather have Shad running the city than me? He figures being suspected of one murder makes my rep worse than Shad's?'

Ned Beaumont scowled at the blond man. 'You're either kidding yourself or trying to kid me. What's Shad's reputation got to do with it? He's not out in the open behind his candidates. You are and it's your candidates who're responsible for nothing being done about the murder.'

Madvig put his hand to his chin again and leaned his elbow on the desk. His handsome ruddy face was unlined. He said: 'We've been talking a lot about what other people figure, Ned. Let's talk about what you figure. Figure I'm licked?'

'You probably are,' Ned Beaumont said in a low sure voice. 'It's a cinch you are if you sit still.' He smiled. 'But your candidates ought to come out all right.'

'That,' Madvig said phlegmatically, 'ought to be explained.'

Ned Beaumont leaned over and carefully knocked cigar-ash

into the brass spittoon beside the desk. Then he said, unemotionally: 'They're going to cross you up.'

'Yes?'

'Why not? You've let Shad take most of the riffraff from behind you. You're counting on the respectable people, the better element, to carry the election. They're getting leery. Well, your candidates make a grandstand-play, arrest you for murder, and the respectable citizens – delighted with these noble officials who are brave enough to jail their own acknowledged boss when he breaks the law – trample each other to death in their hurry to get to the polls and elect the heroes to four more years of city-administering. You can't blame the boys much. They know they're sitting pretty if they do it and out of work if they don't.'

Madvig took his hand from his chin to ask: 'You don't count much on their loyalty, do you, Ned?'

Ned Beaumont smiled. 'Just as much as you do,' he replied. His smile went away. 'I'm not guessing, Paul. I went in to see Farr this afternoon. I had to walk in, crash the gate – he tried to dodge me. He pretended he hadn't been digging into the killing. He tried to stall me on what he'd found out. In the end he dummied up on me.' He made a disdainful mouth. 'Farr, the guy I could always make jump through hoops.'

'Well, that's only Farr,' Madvig began.

Ned Beaumont cut him short. 'Only Farr, and that's the tip-off. Rutlege or Brody or even Rainey might clip you on their own, but if Farr's doing anything it's a pipe he knows the others are with him.' He frowned at the blond man's stolid face. 'You can stop believing me any time you want to, Paul.'

Madvig made a careless gesture with the hand he had held to his chin. 'I'll let you know when I stop,' he said. 'How'd you happen to drop in on Farr?'

'Harry Sloss called me up today. It seems he and Ben Ferriss saw you arguing with Taylor in China Street the night of the murder, or claim they did.' Ned Beaumont was looking with eyes that held no particular expression at the blond man and his voice was matter-of-fact. 'Ben had gone to Farr with it. Harry wanted to be paid for not going. There's a couple of your Club-members reading the signs. I've been watching Farr lose his nerve for some time, so I went in to check him up.'

Madvig nodded. 'And you're sure he's knifing me?'

'Yes.'

Madvig got up from his chair and went to the window. He stood there, hands in trousers-pockets, looking through the glass for perhaps three minutes while Ned Beaumont, sitting on the desk, smoked and looked at the blond man's wide back. Then, not turning his head, Madvig asked: 'What'd you say to Harry?'

'Stalled him.'

Madvig left the window and came back to the desk, but he did not sit down. His ruddiness had deepened. Otherwise no change had come into his face. His voice was level. 'What do you think we ought to do?'

'About Sloss? Nothing. The other monkey's already gone to Farr. It doesn't make much difference what Sloss does.'

'I didn't mean that. I meant about the whole thing.'

Ned Beaumont dropped his cigar into the spittoon. 'I've told you. If Taylor Henry's murder isn't cleared up pronto you're sunk. That's the whole thing. That's the only thing worth doing anything about.'

Madvig stopped looking at Ned Beaumont. He looked at a wide vacant space on the wall. He pressed his full lips together. Moisture appeared on his temples. He said from deep in his chest: 'That won't do. Think up something else.'

Ned Beaumont's nostrils moved with his breathing and the brown of his eyes seemed dark as the pupils. He said: 'There isn't anything else, Paul. Any other way plays into the hands of either Shad or Farr and his crew and either of them will ruin you.'

Madvig said somewhat hoarsely: 'There must be an out, Ned. Think.'

Ned Beaumont left the desk and stood close in front of the

blond man. 'There isn't. That's the only way. You're going to take it whether you like it or not, or I'm going to take it for you.'

Madvig shook his head violently. 'No. Lay off.'

Ned Beaumont said: 'That's one thing I won't do for you, Paul.'

Then Madvig looked Ned Beaumont in the eyes and said in a harsh whisper: 'I killed him, Ned.'

Ned Beaumont drew a breath in and let it out in a long sigh.

. Madvig put his hands on Ned Beaumont's shoulders and his words came out thick and blurred: 'It was an accident, Ned. He ran down the street after me when I left, with a cane he'd picked up on the way out. We'd had – there'd been some trouble there and he caught up with me and tried to hit me with the stick. I don't know how it happened, but pulling it away from him I hit him on the head with it – not hard – it couldn't've been very hard – but he fell back and smashed his head on the kerb.'

Ned Beaumont nodded. His face had suddenly become empty of all expression except hard concentration on Madvig's words. He asked in a crisp voice that matched his face: 'What happened to the cane?'

'I took it away under my overcoat and burned it. After I knew he was dead I found it in my hand, when I was walking down to the Club, so I put it under my overcoat and then burned it.'

'What kind of cane was it?'

'A rough brown one, heavy.'

'And his hat?'

'I don't know, Ned. I guess it was knocked off and somebody picked it up.'

'He had one on?'

'Yes, sure.'

Ned Beaumont brushed a side of his mustache with a thumb-nail. 'You remember Sloss's and Ferriss's car passing you?'

Madvig shook his head. 'No, though they may have.'

Ned Beaumont frowned at the blond man. 'You gummed things up plenty by running off with the stick and burning it and keeping quiet all this time,' he grumbled. 'You had a clear self-defense plea.'

'I know, but I didn't want that, Ned,' Madvig said hoarsely. 'I want Janet Henry more than I ever wanted anything in my life and what chance would I have then, even if it was an accident?' Ned Beaumont laughed in Madvig's face. It was a low laugh and bitter. He said: 'You'd have more chance than you've got now.'

Madvig, staring at him, said nothing.

Ned Beaumont said: 'She's always thought you killed her brother. She hates you. She's been trying to play you into the electric chair. She's responsible for first throwing suspicion on you with anonymous letters sent around to everybody that might be interested. She's the one that turned Opal against you. She was in my rooms this morning telling me this, trying to turn me. She—'

Madvig said: 'That's enough.' He stood erect, a big blond man whose eyes were cold blue disks. 'What is it, Ned? Do you want her yourself or is it—' He broke off contemptuously. 'It doesn't make any difference.' He jerked a thumb carelessly at the door. 'Get out, you heel, this is the kiss-off.'

Ned Beaumont said: 'I'll get out when I've finished talking.'

Madvig said: 'You'll get out when you're told to. You can't say anything I'll believe. You haven't said anything I believe. You never will now.'

Ned Beaumont said: 'Oke.' He picked up his hat and overcoat and went out.

II

Ned Beaumont went home. His face was pale and sullen. He slouched down in one of the big red chairs with a bottle of Bourbon whisky and a glass on the table beside him, but he did not drink. He stared gloomily at his black-shod feet and bit a

164

finger-nail. His telephone-bell rang. He did not answer it. Twilight began to displace day in the room. The room was dusky when he rose and went to the telephone.

He called a number. Then: 'Hello, I'd like to speak to Miss Henry, please.' After a pause that he spent whistling tunelessly under his breath, he said: 'Hello, Miss Henry? . . . Yes . . . I've just come from telling Paul all about it, about you . . . Yes, and you were right. He did what you counted on his doing . . .' He laughed. 'You did. You knew he'd call me a liar, refuse to listen to me, and throw me out, and he did all of it . . . No, no, that's all right. It had to happen . . . No, really . . . Oh, it's probably permanent enough. Things were said that can't easily be unsaid . . . Yes, all evening, I think . . . That'll be fine . . . All right. 'By.'

He poured out a glass of whisky then and drank it. After that he went into his darkening bedroom, set his alarm-clock for eight o'clock, and lay down fully clothed on his back on the bed. For a while he looked at the ceiling. Then he slept, breathing irregularly, until the alarm rang.

He got up sluggishly from his bed and, switching on lights, went into the bathroom, washed his face and hands, put on a fresh collar, and started a fire in the living-room fireplace. He read a newspaper until Janet Henry arrived.

She was excited. Though she at once began to assure Ned Beaumont that she had not foreseen the result of his telling Paul about her visit, had not counted on it, elation danced frankly in her eyes and she could not keep smiles from curving her lips while they shaped the apologetic words.

He said: 'It doesn't matter. I'd've had to do it if I'd known how it was going to turn out. I suppose I did know down underneath. It's one of those things. And if you'd told me it would happen I'd only've taken that for a challenge and would've jumped to it.'

She held her hands out to him. 'I'm glad,' she said. 'I won't pretend I'm not.'

'I'm sorry,' he told her as he took her hands, 'but I wouldn't have gone a step out of my way to avoid it.'

She said: 'And now you know I'm right. He did kill Taylor.' Her eyes were inquisitive.

He nodded. 'He told me he did.'

'And you'll help me now?' Her hands pressed his. She came closer to him.

He hesitated, frowning down at her eager face. 'It was self-defense, or an accident,' he said slowly. 'I can't—'

'It was murder!' she cried. 'Of course he'd say it was self-defense!' She shook her head impatiently. 'And even if it was self-defense or an accident, shouldn't he be made to go into court and prove it like anybody else?'

'He's waited too long. This month he's kept quiet would be against him.'

'Well, whose fault was that?' she demanded. 'And do you think he would have kept quiet so long if it had been self-defense?'

He nodded with slow emphasis. 'That was on your account. He's in love with you. He didn't want you to know he'd killed your brother.'

'I do know it!' she cried fiercely. 'And everybody's going to know it!'

He moved his shoulders a little. His face was gloomy.

'You won't help me?' she asked.

'No.'

'Why? You've quarreled with him.'

'I believe his story. I know it's too late for him to put it across in court. We're through, but I won't do that to him.' He moistened his lips. 'Let him alone. It's likely they'll do it to him without your help or mine.'

'I won't,' she said. 'I won't let him alone until he's been punished as he deserves.' She caught her breath and her eyes darkened. 'Do you believe him enough to risk finding proof that he lied to you?'

'What do you mean?' he asked cautiously.

'Will you help me find proof of the truth, whether he's lying or not? There must be positive proof somewhere, some proof that we can find. If you really believe him you won't be afraid to help me find it.'

He studied her face awhile before asking: 'If I do and we find your positive proof, will you promise to accept it whichever way it stacks up?'

'Yes,' she said readily, 'if you will too.'

'And you'll keep what we find to yourself till we've finished the job – found our proof positive – won't use what we find against him till we've got it all?'

'Yes.'

'It's a bargain,' he said.

She sobbed happily and tears came to her eyes.

He said: 'Sit down.' His face was lean and hard, his voice curt. 'We've got to get schemes rigged. Have you heard from him this afternoon or evening, since he and I had our row?'

'No.'

'Then we can't be sure how you stand with him. There's a chance he may have decided later that I was right. That won't make any difference between him and me now – we're done – but we've got to find out as soon as we can.' He scowled at her feet and brushed his mustache with a thumb-nail. 'You'll have to wait till he comes to you. You can't afford to call him up. If he's shaky about you that might decide him. How sure of him are you?'

She was sitting in the chair by the table. She said: 'I'm as sure of him as a woman can be of a man.' She uttered a little embarrassed laugh. 'I know that sounds— But I am, Ned Beaumont.'

He nodded. 'Then that's probably all right, but you ought to know definitely by tomorrow. Have you ever tried to pump him?'

'Not yet, not really. I was waiting—'

'Well, that's out for the time being. No matter how sure you are of him you'll have to be careful now. Have you picked up anything you haven't told me about?'

'No,' she said, shaking her head. 'I haven't known very well how to go about it. That's why I so wanted you to—'

He interrupted her again: 'Didn't it occur to you to hire a private detective?'

'Yes, but I was afraid, afraid I'd go to one who'd tell Paul. I didn't know who to go to, who I could trust.'

'I've got one we can use.' He ran fingers through his dark hair. 'Now there are two things I want you to find out, if you don't know them now. Are any of your brother's hats missing? Paul says he had a hat on. There was none there when I found him. See if you can find out how many he had and if they're all accounted for' – he smiled obliquely – 'except the one I borrowed.'

She paid no attention to his smile. She shook her head and raised her hands a little, dispiritedly. 'I can't,' she said. 'We got rid of all his things some time ago and I doubt if anybody knew exactly what he had anyway.'

Ned Beaumont shrugged. 'I didn't think we'd get anywhere on that,' he told her. 'The other thing's a walking-stick, whether any of them – his or your father's – are missing, particularly a rough heavy brown one.'

'It would be Father's,' she said eagerly, 'and I think it's there.'

'Check it up.' He bit his thumb-nail. 'That'll be enough for you to do between now and tomorrow, that and maybe find out how you stand with Paul.'

'What is it?' she asked. 'I mean about the stick.' She stood up, excited.

'Paul says your brother attacked him with it and was struck by it while Paul was taking it away from him. He says he carried the stick away and burned it.'

'Oh, I'm sure Father's sticks are all there,' she cried. Her face was white, her eyes wide.

'Didn't Taylor have any?'

'Only a silver-headed black one.' She put a hand on his wrist. 'If they're all there it will mean that—'

'It might mean something,' he said and put a hand on her hand. 'But no tricks,' he warned her.

'I won't,' she promised. 'If you only knew how happy I am to have your help, how much I've wanted it, you'd know you could trust me.'

'I hope so.' He took his hand from hers.

III

Alone in his rooms Ned Beaumont walked the floor awhile, his face pinched, his eyes shiny. At twenty minutes to ten he looked at his wrist-watch. Then he put on his overcoat and went down to the Majestic Hotel, where he was told that Harry Sloss was not in. He left the hotel, found a taxicab, got into it, and said: 'West Road Inn.'

The West Road Inn was a square white building – grey in the night – set among trees back from the road some three miles beyond the city limits. Its ground-floor was brightly lighted and half a dozen automobiles stood in front of it. Others were in a long dark shed off to the left.

Ned Beaumont, nodding familiarly at the doorman, went into a large dining-room where a three-man orchestra was playing extravagantly and eight or ten people were dancing. He passed down an aisle between tables, skirted the dance-floor, and stopped in front of the bar that occupied one corner of the room. He was alone on the customers' side of the bar.

The bar-tender, a fat man with a spongy nose, said: 'Evening, Ned. We ain't been seeing you much lately.'

' 'Lo, Jimmy. Been behaving. Manhattan.'

The bar-tender began to mix the cocktail. The orchestra finished its piece. A woman's voice rose thin and shrill: 'I won't stay in the same place with that Beaumont bastard.'

Ned Beaumont turned around, leaning back against the edge

of the bar. The bar-tender became motionless with the cocktail-shaker in his hand.

Lee Wilshire was standing in the center of the dance-floor glaring at Ned Beaumont. One of her hands was on the forearm of a bulky youth in a blue suit a bit too tight for him. He too was looking at Ned Beaumont, rather stupidly. She said: 'He's a no-good bastard and if you don't throw him out I'm going out.'

Everyone else in the place was attentively silent.

The youth's face reddened. His attempt at a scowl increased his appearance of embarrassment.

The girl said: 'I'll go over and slap him myself if you don't.'

Ned Beaumont, smiling, said: ''Lo, Lee. Seen Bernie since he got out?'

Lee cursed him and took an angry step forward.

The bulky youth put out a hand and stopped her. 'I'll fix him,' he said, 'the bastard.' He adjusted his coat-collar to his neck, pulled the front of his coat down, and stalked off the dance-floor to face Ned Beaumont. 'What's the idea?' he demanded. 'What's the idea of talking to the little lady like that?'

Ned Beaumont, staring soberly at the youth, stretched his right arm out to the side and laid his hand palm-up on the bar. 'Give me something to tap him with, Jimmy,' he said. 'I don't feel like fist-fighting.'

One of the bar-tender's hands was already out of sight beneath the bar. He brought it up holding a small bludgeon and put the bludgeon in Ned Beaumont's hand. Ned Beaumont let it lie there while he said: 'She gets called a lot of things. The last guy I saw her with was calling her a dumb cluck.'

The youth drew himself up straight, his eyes shifting from side to side. He said: 'I won't forget you and some day me and you will meet when there's nobody around.' He turned on his heel and addressed Lee Wilshire. 'Come on, let's blow out of this dump.'

'Go ahead and blow,' she said spitefully. 'I'll be God-damned if I'm going with you. I'm sick of you.'

A thick-bodied man with nearly all gold teeth came up and said: 'Yes you will, the both of you. Get.'

Ned Beaumont laughed and said: 'The – uh – little lady's with me, Corky.'

Corky said, 'Fair enough,' and then to the youth: 'Outside, bum.'

The youth went out.

Lee Wilshire had returned to her table. She sat there with her cheeks between her fists, staring at the cloth.

Ned Beaumont sat down facing her. He said to the waiter: 'Jimmy's got a Manhattan that belongs to me. And I want some food. Eaten yet, Lee?'

'Yes,' she said without looking up. 'I want a silver fizz.'

Ned Beaumont said: 'Fine. I want a minute steak with mushrooms, whatever vegetable Tony's got that didn't come out of a can, some lettuce and tomatoes with Roquefort dressing, and coffee.'

When the waiter had gone Lee said bitterly: 'Men are no good, none of them. That big false alarm!' She began to cry silently.

'Maybe you pick the wrong kind,' Ned Beaumont suggested.

'You should tell me that,' she said, looking up angrily at him, 'after the lousy trick you played me.'

'I didn't play you any lousy trick,' he protested. 'If Bernie had to hock your pretties to pay back the money he'd gypped me out of it wasn't my fault.'

The orchestra began to play.

'Nothing's ever a man's fault,' she complained. 'Come on and dance.'

'Oh, all right,' he said reluctantly.

When they returned to the table his cocktail and her fizz were there.

'What's Bernie doing these days?' he asked as they drank.

'I don't know. I haven't seen him since he got out and I don't want to see him. Another swell guy! What breaks I've been getting this year! Him and Taylor and this bastard!'

'Taylor Henry?' he asked.

'Yes, but I didn't have much to do with him,' she explained quickly, 'because that's while I was living with Bernie.'

Ned Beaumont finished his cocktail before he said: 'You were just one of the girls who used to meet him in his Charter Street place now and then.'

'Yes,' she said, looking warily at him.

He said: 'I think we ought to have a drink.'

She powdered her face while he caught their waiter's attention and ordered their drinks.

IV

The door-bell awakened Ned Beaumont. He got drowsily out of bed, coughing a little, and put on kimono and slippers. It was a few minutes after nine by his alarm-clock. He went to the door.

Janet Henry came in apologizing. 'I know it's horribly early, but I simply couldn't wait another minute. I tried and tried to get you on the phone last night and hardly slept a wink because I couldn't. All of Father's sticks are there. So, you see, he lied.'

'Has he got a heavy rough brown one?'

'Yes, that's the one Major Sawbridge brought him from Scotland. He never uses it, but it's there.' She smiled triumphantly at Ned Beaumont.

He blinked sleepily and ran fingers through his tousled hair. 'Then he lied, right enough,' he said.

'And,' she said gaily, 'he was there when I got home last night.'

'Paul?'

'Yes. And he asked me to marry him.'

Sleepiness went out of Ned Beaumont's eyes. 'Did he say anything about our battle?'

'Not a word.'

'What did you say?'

'I said it was too soon after Taylor's death for me even to engage myself to him, but I didn't say I wouldn't a little later, so we've got what I believe is called an understanding.'

He looked curiously at her.

Gaiety went out of her face. She put a hand on his arm. Her voice broke a little. 'Please don't think I'm altogether heartless,' she said, 'but – oh! – I do so want to – to do what we set out to do that everything else seems – well – not important at all.'

He moistened his lips and said in a grave gentle voice: 'What a spot he'd be in if you loved him as much as you hate him.'

She stamped her foot and cried: 'Don't say that! Don't ever say that again!'

Irritable lines appeared in his forehead and his lips tightened together.

She said, 'Please,' contritely, 'but I can't bear that.'

'Sorry,' he said. 'Had breakfast yet?'

'No. I was too anxious to bring my news to you.'

'Fine. You'll eat with me. What do you like?' He went to the telephone.

After he had ordered breakfast he went into the bathroom to wash his teeth, face, and hands and brush his hair. When he returned to the living-room she had removed her hat and coat and was standing by the fireplace smoking a cigarette. She started to say something, but stopped when the telephone-bell rang.

He went to the telephone. 'Hello . . . Yes, Harry, I stopped in, but you were out . . . I wanted to ask you about – you know – the chap you saw with Paul that night. Did he have a hat? . . . He did? Sure? . . . And did he have a stick in his hand? . . . Oke . . . No, I couldn't do anything with Paul on that, Harry. Better see him yourself . . . Yes . . . 'By.'

Janet Henry's eyes questioned him as he got up from the telephone.

He said: 'That was one of a couple of fellows who claim they saw Paul talking to your brother in the street that night. He says he saw the hat, but not the stick. It was dark, though, and this pair were riding past in a car. I wouldn't bet they saw anything very clearly.'

'Why are you so interested in the hat? Is it so important?'

He shrugged. 'I don't know. I'm only an amateur detective, but it looks like a thing that might have some meaning, one way or another.'

'Have you learned anything else since yesterday?'

'No. I spent part of the evening buying drinks for a girl Taylor used to play around with, but there wasn't anything there.'

'Anyone I know?' she asked.

He shook his head, then looked sharply at her and said: 'It wasn't Opal, if that's what you're getting at.'

'Don't you think we might be able to – to get some information from her?'

'Opal? No. She thinks her father killed Taylor, but she thinks it was on her account. It wasn't anything she knew that sent her off – not any inside stuff – it was your letters and the *Observer* and things like that.'

Janet Henry nodded, but seemed unconvinced.

Their breakfast arrived.

The telephone-bell rang while they were eating. Ned Beaumont went to the telephone and said: 'Hello . . . Yes, Mom . . . What?' He listened, frowning, for several seconds, then said: 'There isn't much you can do about it except let them and I don't think it'll do any harm . . . No, I don't know where he is . . . I don't think I will . . . Well, don't worry about it, Mom, it'll be all right . . . Sure, that's right . . . 'By.' He returned to the table smiling. 'Farr's got the same idea you had,' he said as he sat down. 'That was Paul's mother. A man from the District Attorney's office is there to question Opal.' A bright gleam awakened in his eyes. 'She can't help them any, but they're closing in on him.'

'Why did she call you?' Janet Henry asked.

'Paul had gone out and she didn't know where to find him.'

'Doesn't she know that you and Paul have quarreled?'

'Apparently not.' He put down his fork. 'Look here. Are you sure you want to go through with this thing?'

'I want to go through with it more than I ever wanted to do anything in my life,' she told him.

Ned Beaumont laughed bitterly, said: 'They're practically the same words Paul used telling me how much he wanted you.'

She shuddered, her face hardened, and she looked coldly at him.

He said: 'I don't know about you, I'm not sure of you. I had a dream I don't much like.'

She smiled then. 'Surely you don't believe in dreams?'

He did not smile. 'I don't believe in anything, but I'm too much of a gambler not to be affected by a lot of things.'

Her smile became less mocking. She asked: 'What was this dream that makes you mistrust me?' She held up a finger, pretending seriousness. 'And then I'll tell you one I had about you.'

'I was fishing,' he said, 'and I caught an enormous fish – a rainbow trout, but enormous – and you said you wanted to look at it and you picked it up and threw it back in the water before I could stop you.'

She laughed merrily. 'What did you do?'

'That was the end of the dream.'

'It was a lie,' she said. 'I won't throw your trout back. Now I'll tell you mine. I was—' Her eyes widened. 'When was yours? The night you came to dinner?'

'No. Last night.'

'Oh, that's too bad. It would be nicer in an impressive way if we'd done our dreaming on the same night and the same hour and the same minute. Mine was the night you were there. We were – this is in the dream – we were lost in a forest, you and I, tired and starving. We walked and walked till we came to a little house and we knocked on the door, but nobody answered. We tried the door. It was locked. Then we peeped through a window and inside we could see a great big table piled high with all imaginable kinds of food, but we couldn't get in through either of the windows because they had iron bars over them. So we went back to the door and knocked and knocked again and still nobody answered. Then we thought that sometimes people left their keys under door-mats and we looked and there it was. But when we opened the door we saw hundreds and hundreds of snakes on the floor where we hadn't been able to see them through the window and they all came sliding and slithering towards us. We slammed the door shut and locked it and stood there frightened to death listening to them hissing and knocking their heads against the inside of the door. Then you said that perhaps if we opened the door and hid from the snakes they'd come out and go away, so we did. You helped me climb up on the roof – it was low in this part of the dream: I don't remember what it was like before – and you climbed up after me and leaned down and unlocked the door, and all the snakes came slithering out. We lay holding our breath on the roof until the last of the hundreds and hundreds of them had slithered out of sight into the forest. Then we jumped down and ran inside and locked the door and ate and ate and ate and I woke sitting up in bed clapping my hands and laughing.'

'I think you made that up,' Ned Beaumont said after a little pause.

'Why?'

'It starts out to be a nightmare and winds up something else and all the dreams I ever had about food ended before I got a chance to do any actual eating.'

Janet Henry laughed. 'I didn't make all of it up,' she said, 'but you needn't ask which part is true. You've accused me of lying and I'll tell you nothing now.'

'Oh, all right.' He picked up his fork again, but did not eat. He asked, with an air of just having the thought: 'Does your father know anything? Do you think we could get anything out of him if we went to him with what we know?'

'Yes,' she said eagerly, 'I do.'

He scowled thoughtfully. 'The only trouble is he might go up in the air and explode the works before we're ready. He's hot-headed, isn't he?'

Her answer was given reluctantly: 'Yes, but' – her face brightened, pleadingly – 'I'm sure if we showed him why it's important to wait until we've— But we are ready now, aren't we?'

He shook his head. 'Not yet.'

She pouted.

'Maybe tomorrow,' he said.

'Really?'

'That's not a promise,' he cautioned her, 'but I think we will be.'

She put a hand across the table to take one of his hands. 'But you will promise to let me know the very minute we're ready, no matter what time of day or night it is?'

'Sure, I'll promise you that.' He looked obliquely at her. 'You're not very anxious to be in at the death, are you?'

His tone brought a flush to her face, but she did not lower her eyes. 'I know you think I'm a monster,' she said. 'Perhaps I am.'

He looked down at his plate and muttered: 'I hope you like it when you get it.'

9 The Heels

I

After Janet Henry had gone Ned Beaumont went to his telephone, called Jack Rumsen's number, and when he had that one on the wire said: 'Can you drop in to see me, Jack? . . . Fine. 'By.'

He was dressed by the time Jack arrived. They sat in facing chairs, each with a glass of Bourbon whisky and mineral water, Ned Beaumont smoking a cigar, Jack a cigarette.

Ned Beaumont asked: 'Heard anything about the split between Paul and me?'

Jack said, 'Yes,' casually.

'What do you think of it?'

'Nothing. I remember the last time it was supposed to happen it turned out to be a trick on Shad O'Rory.'

Ned Beaumont smiled as if he had expected that reply. 'Is that what everybody thinks it is this time?'

The dapper young man said: 'A lot of them do.'

Ned Beaumont inhaled cigar-smoke slowly, asked: 'Suppose I told you it was on the level this time?'

Jack said nothing. His face told nothing of his thoughts.

Ned Beaumont said: 'It is.' He drank from his glass. 'How much do I owe you?'

'Thirty bucks for that job on the Madvig girl. You settled for the rest.'

Ned Beaumont took a roll of paper money from a trousers-pocket, separated three ten-dollar bills from the roll, and gave them to Jack.

Jack said: 'Thanks.'

Ned Beaumont said: 'Now we're quits.' He inhaled smoke and blew it out while saying: 'I've got another job I want done. I'm after Paul's scalp on the Taylor Henry killing. He told me he did it, but I need a little more proof. Want to work on it for me?'

Jack said: 'No.'

'Why not?'

The dark young man rose to put his empty glass on the table. 'Fred and I are building up a nice little private-detective business here,' he said. 'A couple of years more and we'll be sitting pretty. I like you, Beaumont, but not enough to monkey with the man that runs the city.'

Ned Beaumont said evenly: 'He's on the chutes. The whole crew's getting ready to ditch him. Farr and Rainey are—'

'Let them do it. I don't want in on that racket and I'll believe they can do it when it's done. Maybe they'll give him a bump or two, but making it stick's another thing. You know him better than I do. You know he's got more guts than all the rest of them put together.'

'He has and that's what's licking him. Well, if you won't, you won't.'

Jack said, 'I won't,' and picked up his hat. 'Anything else I'll be glad to do, but—' He moved one hand in a brief gesture of finality.

Ned Beaumont stood up. There was no resentment in his manner, none in his voice when he said: 'I thought you might feel that way about it.' He brushed a side of his mustache with a thumb and stared thoughtfully past Jack. 'Maybe you can tell me this: any idea where I can find Shad?'

Jack shook his head. 'Since the third time they knocked his place over – when the two coppers were killed – he's been laying low, though they don't seem to have a hell of a lot on him personally.' He took his cigarette from his mouth. 'Know Whisky Vassos?'

'Yes.'

'You might find out from him if you know him well enough. He's around town. You can usually find him some time during the night at Tim Walker's place on Smith Street.'

'Thanks, Jack. I'll try that.'

'That's all right,' Jack said. He hesitated. 'I'm sorry as hell you and Madvig split. I wish you—' He broke off and turned towards the door. 'You know what you're doing.'

II

Ned Beaumont went down to the District Attorney's office. This time there was no delay in ushering him into Farr's presence.

Farr did not get up from his desk, did not offer to shake hands. He said: 'How do you do, Beaumont? Sit down.' His voice was coldly polite. His pugnacious face was not so red as usual. His eyes were level and hard.

Ned Beaumont sat down, crossed his legs comfortably, and said: 'I wanted to tell you about what happened when I went to see Paul after I left here yesterday.'

Farr's 'Yes?' was cold and polite.

'I told him how I'd found you – panicky.' Ned Beaumont, smiling his nicest smile, went on in the manner of one telling a fairly amusing but unimportant anecdote: 'I told him I thought you were trying to get up enough nerve to hang the Taylor Henry murder on him. He believed me at first, but when I told him the only way to save himself was by turning up the real murderer, he said that was no good. He said he was the real murderer, though he called it an accident or self-defense or something.'

Farr's face had become paler and was stiff around the mouth, but he did not speak.

Ned Beaumont raised his eyebrows. 'I'm not boring you, am I?' he asked.

'Go on, continue,' the District Attorney said coldly.

Ned Beaumont tilted his chair back. His smile was mocking. 'You think I'm kidding, don't you? You think it's a trick we're playing on you.' He shook his head and murmured: 'You're a timid soul, Farr.'

Farr said: 'I'm glad to listen to any information you can give me, but I'm very busy, so I'll have to ask you—'

Ned Beaumont laughed then and replied: 'Oke. I thought maybe you'd like to have this information in an affidavit or something.'

'Very well.' Farr pressed one of the pearl buttons on his desk.

A grey-haired woman in green came in.

'Mr Beaumont wants to dictate a statement,' Farr told her.

She said, 'Yes, sir,' sat at the other side of Farr's desk, put her notebook on the desk, and, holding a silver pencil over the book, looked at Ned Beaumont with blank brown eyes.

He said: 'Yesterday afternoon in his office in the Nebel Building, Paul Madvig told me that he had been to dinner at Senator Henry's house the night Taylor Henry was killed; that he and Taylor Henry had some sort of trouble there; that after he left the house Taylor Henry ran after him and caught up with him and tried to hit him with a rough heavy brown walking-stick; that in trying to take the stick from Taylor Henry he accidentally struck him on the forehead with it, knocking him down; and that he carried the stick away with him and burned it. He said his only reason for concealing his part in Taylor Henry's death was his desire to keep it from Janet Henry. That's all of it.'

Farr addressed the stenographer: 'Transcribe that right away.'

She left the office.

Ned Beaumont said: 'I thought I was bringing you news that would get you all excited.' He sighed. 'I thought you'd fairly tear your hair over it.'

The District Attorney looked steadily at him.

Ned Beaumont, unabashed, said: 'I thought at least you'd have Paul dragged in and confronted with this' – he waved a hand – '"damaging disclosure" is a good phrase.'

The District Attorney spoke in a restrained tone: 'Please permit me to run my own office.'

Ned Beaumont laughed again and relapsed into silence until the grey-haired stenographer returned with a typed copy of his statement. Then he asked: 'Do I swear to it?'

'No,' Farr said, 'just sign it. That will be sufficient.'

Ned Beaumont signed the paper. 'This isn't nearly so much fun as I thought it was going to be,' he complained cheerfully.

Farr's undershot jaw tightened. 'No,' he said with grim satisfaction, 'I don't suppose it is.'

'You're a timid soul, Farr,' Ned Beaumont repeated. 'Be careful about taxis when you cross streets.' He bowed. 'See you later.'

Outside, he grimaced angrily.

III

That night Ned Beaumont rang the door-bell of a dark three-story house in Smith Street. A short man who had a small head and thick shoulders opened the door half a foot, said, 'All right,' and opened it the rest of the way.

Ned Beaumont, saying, ''Lo,' entered, walked twenty feet down a dim hallway past two closed doors on the right, opened a door on the left, and went down a wooden flight of steps into a basement where there was a bar and where a radio was playing softly.

Beyond the bar was a frosted glass door marked *Toilet*. This door opened and a man came out, a swarthy man with something apish in the slope of his big shoulders, the length of his thick arms, the flatness of his face, and the curve of his bowed legs – Jeff Gardner.

He saw Ned Beaumont and his reddish small eyes glistened. 'Well, blind Christ, if it ain't Sock-me-again Beaumont!' he roared, showing his beautiful teeth in a huge grin.

Ned Beaumont said, '' 'Lo, Jeff,' while everyone in the place looked at them.

Jeff swaggered over to Ned Beaumont, threw his left arm roughly around his shoulders, seized Ned Beaumont's right hand with his right hand, and addressed the company jovially: 'This is the swellest guy I ever skinned a knuckle on and I've skinned them on plenty.' He dragged Ned Beaumont to the bar. 'We're all going to have a little drink and then I'll show you how it's done. By Jesus, I will!' He leered into Ned Beaumont's face. 'What do you say to that, my lad?'

Ned Beaumont, looking stolidly at the ugly dark face so close to, though lower than, his, said: 'Scotch.'

Jeff laughed delightedly and addressed the company again: 'You see, he likes it. He's a—' he hesitated, frowning, wet his lips '—a God-damned massacrist, that's what he is.' He leered at Ned Beaumont. 'You know what a massacrist is?'

'Yes.'

Jeff seemed disappointed. 'Rye,' he told the bartender. When their drinks were set before them he released Ned Beaumont's hand, though he kept his arm across his shoulders. They drank. Jeff set down his glass and put his hand on Ned Beaumont's wrist. 'I got just the place for me and you upstairs,' he said, 'a room that's too little for you to fall down in. I can bounce you around off the walls. That way we won't be wasting a lot of time while you're getting up off the floor.'

Ned Beaumont said: 'I'll buy a drink.'

'That ain't a dumb idea,' Jeff agreed.

They drank again.

When Ned Beaumont had paid for the drinks Jeff turned him towards the stairs. 'Excuse us, gents,' he said to the others at the bar, 'but we got to go up and rehearse our act.' He patted Ned Beaumont's shoulder. 'Me and my sweetheart.'

They climbed two flights of steps and went into a small room in which a sofa, two tables, and half a dozen chairs were crowded. There were some empty glasses and plates holding the remains of sandwiches on one table.

Jeff peered near-sightedly around the room and demanded: 'Now where in hell did she go?' He released Ned Beaumont's wrist, took the arm from around his shoulders, and asked: 'You don't see no broad here, do you?'

'No.'

Jeff wagged his head up and down emphatically. 'She's gone,' he said. He took an uncertain step backwards and jabbed the bell-button beside the door with a dirty finger. Then, flourishing his hand, he made a grotesque bow and said: 'Set down.'

Ned Beaumont sat down at the less disorderly of the two tables.

'Set in any God-damned chair you want to set in,' Jeff said with another large gesture. 'If you don't like that one, take another. I want you to consider yourself my guest and the hell with you if you don't like it.'

'It's a swell chair,' Ned Beaumont said.

'It's a hell of a chair,' Jeff said. 'There ain't a chair in the dump that's worth a damn. Look.' He picked up a chair and tore one of its front legs out. 'You call that a swell chair? Listen, Beaumont, you don't know a damned thing about chairs.' He put the chair down, tossed the leg on the sofa. 'You can't fool me. I know what you're up to. You think I'm drunk, don't you?'

Ned Beaumont grinned. 'No, you're not drunk.'

'The hell I'm not drunk. I'm drunker than you are. I'm drunker than anybody in this dump. I'm drunk as hell and don't think I'm not, but—' He held up a thick unclean forefinger.

A waiter came in the doorway asking: 'What is it gents?'

Jeff turned to confront him. 'Where've you been? Sleeping? I rung for you one hour ago.'

The waiter began to say something.

Jeff said: 'I bring the best friend I got in the world up here for a drink and what the hell happens? We have to sit around a whole God-damned hour waiting for a lousy waiter. No wonder he's sore at me.'

'What do you want?' the waiter asked indifferently.

'I want to know where in hell the girl that was in here went to.'

'Oh, her? She's gone.'

'Gone where?'

'I don't know.'

Jeff scowled. 'Well, you find out, and God-damned quick. What's the idea of not knowing where she went? If this ain't a swell joint where nobody—' A shrewd light came into his red eyes. 'I'll tell you what to do. You go up to the ladies' toilet and see if she's there.'

'She ain't there,' the waiter said. 'She went out.'

'The dirty bastard!' Jeff said and turned to Ned Beaumont. 'What'd you do to a dirty bastard like that? I bring you up here because I want you to meet her because I know you'll like her and she'll like you and she's too God-damned snooty to meet my friends and out she goes.'

Ned Beaumont was lighting a cigar. He did not say anything.

Jeff scratched his head, growled, 'Well, bring us something to drink, then,' sat down across the table from Ned Beaumont, and said savagely: 'Mine's rye.'

Ned Beaumont said: 'Scotch.'

The waiter went away.

Jeff glared at Ned Beaumont. 'Don't get the idea that I don't know what you're up to, either,' he said angrily.

'I'm not up to anything,' Ned Beaumont replied carelessly. 'I'd like to see Shad and I thought maybe I'd find Whisky Vassos here and he'd send me to Shad.'

'Don't you think I know where Shad is?'

'You ought to.'

'Then why didn't you ask me?'

'All right. Where is he?'

Jeff slapped the table mightily with an open hand and bawled: 'You're a liar. You don't give a God-damn where Shad is. It's me you're after.'

Ned Beaumont smiled and shook his head.

'It is,' the apish man insisted. 'You know God-damned well that—'

A young-middle-aged man with plump red lips and round eyes came to the door. He said: 'Cut it out, Jeff. You're making more noise than everybody else in the place.'

Jeff screwed himself around in his chair. 'It's this bastard,' he told the man in the doorway, indicating Ned Beaumont with a jerk of his thumb. 'He thinks I don't know what he's up to. I know what he's up to. He's a heel and that's what he is. And I'm going to beat hell out of him and that's what I'm going to do.'

The man in the doorway said reasonably, 'Well, you don't have to make so much noise about it,' winked at Ned Beaumont, and went away.

Jeff said gloomily: 'Tim's turning into a heel too.' He spit on the floor.

The waiter came in with their drinks.

Ned Beaumont raised his glass, said, 'Looking at you,' and drank.

Jeff said: 'I don't want to look at you. You're a heel.' He stared somberly at Ned Beaumont.

'You're crazy.'

'You're a liar. I'm drunk. But I ain't so drunk that I don't know what you're up to.' He emptied his glass, wiped his mouth with the back of his hand. 'And I say you're a heel.'

Ned Beaumont, smiling amiably, said: 'All right. Have it your way.'

Jeff thrust his apish muzzle forward a little. 'You think you're smart as hell, don't you?'

Ned Beaumont did not say anything.

'You think it's a damned smart trick coming in here and trying to get me plastered so you can turn me up.'

'That's right,' Ned Beaumont said carelessly, 'there is a murder-charge against you for bumping off Francis West, isn't there?'

Jeff said: 'Hell with Francis West.'

Ned Beaumont shrugged. 'I didn't know him.'

Jeff said: 'You're a heel.'

Ned Beaumont said: 'I'll buy you a drink.'

The apish man nodded solemnly and tilted his chair back to reach the bell-button. With his finger on the button he said: 'But you're still a heel.' His chair swayed back under him, turning. He got his feet flat on the floor and brought the chair down on all fours before it could spill him. 'The bastard!' he snarled, pulling it around to the table again. He put his elbows on the table and propped his chin up on one fist. 'What the hell do I care who turns me up? You don't think they'd ever fry me, do you?'

'Why not?'

'Why not? Jesus! I wouldn't have to stand the rap till after election and then it's all Shad's.'

'Maybe.'

'Maybe hell!'

The waiter came in and they ordered their drinks.

'Maybe Shad would let you take the fall anyhow,' Ned Beaumont said idly when they were alone again. 'Things like that have happened.'

'A swell chance,' Jeff scoffed, 'with all I've got on him.'

Ned Beaumont exhaled cigar-smoke. 'What've you got on him?'

The apish man laughed, boisterously, scornfully, and pounded the table with an open hand. 'Christ!' he roared, 'he thinks I'm drunk enough to tell him.'

From the doorway came a quiet voice, a musical slightly Irish baritone: 'Go on, Jeff, tell him.' Shad O'Rory stood in the doorway. His grey-blue eyes looked somewhat sadly at Jeff.

Jeff squinted his eyes merrily at the man in the doorway and said: 'How are you, Shad? Come in and set down to a drink. Meet Mr Beaumont. He's a heel.'

O'Rory said softly: 'I told you to stay under cover.'

'But, Jesus, Shad, I was getting so's I was afraid I'd bite myself! And this joint's under cover, ain't it? It's a speakeasy.'

O'Rory looked a moment longer at Jeff, then at Ned Beaumont. 'Good evening, Beaumont.'

' 'Lo, Shad.'

O'Rory smiled gently and, indicating Jeff with a tiny nod, asked: 'Get much out of him?'

'Not much I didn't already know,' Ned Beaumont replied. 'He makes a lot of noise, but all of it doesn't make sense.'

Jeff said: 'I think you're a pair of heels.'

The waiter arrived with their drinks. O'Rory stopped him. 'Never mind. They've had enough.' The waiter carried their drinks away. Shad O'Rory came into the room and shut the door. He stood with his back against it. He said: 'You talk too much, Jeff. I've told you that before.'

Ned Beaumont deliberately winked at Jeff.

Jeff said angrily to him: 'What the hell's the matter with you?'

Ned Beaumont laughed.

'I'm talking to you, Jeff,' O'Rory said.

'Christ, don't I know it?'

O'Rory said: 'We're coming to the place where I'm going to stop talking to you.'

Jeff stood up. 'Don't be a heel, Shad,' he said. 'What the hell?' He came around the table. 'Me and you've been pals a long time. You always were my pal and I'll always be yours.' He put his arms out to embrace O'Rory, lurching towards him. 'Sure, I'm smoked, but—'

O'Rory put a white hand on the apish man's chest and thrust him back. 'Sit down.' He did not raise his voice.

Jeff's left fist whipped out at O'Rory's face.

O'Rory's head moved to the right, barely enough to let the fist whip past his cheek. O'Rory's long finely sculptured face was gravely composed. His right hand dropped down behind his hip.

Ned Beaumont flung from his chair at O'Rory's right arm, caught it with both hands, going down on his knees.

Jeff, thrown against the wall by the impetus behind his left fist, now turned and took Shad O'Rory's throat in both hands. The apish face was yellow, distorted, hideous. There was no longer any drunkenness in it.

'Got the roscoe?' Jeff panted.

'Yes.' Ned Beaumont stood up, stepped back holding a black pistol leveled at O'Rory.

O'Rory's eyes were glassy, protuberant, his face mottled, turgid. He did not struggle against the man holding his throat.

Jeff turned his head over his shoulder to grin at Ned Beaumont. The grin was wide, genuine, idiotically bestial. Jeff's little red eyes glinted merrily. He said in a hoarse good-natured voice: 'Now you see what we got to do. We got to give him the works.'

Ned Beaumont said: 'I don't want anything to do with it.' His voice was steady. His nostrils quivered.

'No?' Jeff leered at him. 'I expect you think Shad's a guy that'll forget what we done.' He ran his tongue over his lips. 'He'll forget. I'll fix that.'

Grinning from ear to ear at Ned Beaumont, not looking at the man whose throat he held in his hands, Jeff began to take in and let out long slow breaths. His coat became lumpy over his shoulders and back and along his arms. Sweat appeared on his ugly dark face.

Ned Beaumont was pale. He too was breathing heavily and moisture filmed his temples. He looked over Jeff's lumpy shoulder at O'Rory's face.

O'Rory's face was liver-colored. His eyes stood far out, blind. His tongue came out blue between bluish lips. His slender body writhed. One of his hands began to beat the wall behind him, mechanically, without force.

Grinning at Ned Beaumont, not looking at the man whose throat he held, Jeff spread his legs a little wider and arched his back. O'Rory's hand stopped beating the wall. There was a muffled crack, then, almost immediately, a sharper one. O'Rory did not writhe now. He sagged in Jeff's hands.

Jeff laughed in his throat. 'That's keno,' he said. He kicked a chair out of the way and dropped O'Rory's body on the sofa. O'Rory's body fell there face down, one hand and his feet hanging down to the floor. Jeff rubbed his hands on his hips and faced Ned Beaumont. 'I'm just a big good-natured slob,' he said. 'Anybody can kick me around all they want to and I never do nothing about it.'

Ned Beaumont said: 'You were afraid of him.'

Jeff laughed. 'I hope to tell you I was. So was anybody that was in their right mind. I suppose you wasn't?' He laughed again, looked around the room, said: 'Let's screw before anybody pops in.' He held out his hand. 'Give me the roscoe. I'll ditch it.'

Ned Beaumont said: 'No.' He moved his hand sideways until the pistol was pointed at Jeff's belly. 'We can say this was self-defense. I'm with you. We can beat it at the inquest.'

'Jesus, that's a bright idea!' Jeff exclaimed. 'Me with a murder-rap hanging over me for that West guy!' His small red eyes kept shifting their focus from Ned Beaumont's face to the pistol in his hand.

Ned Beaumont smiled with thin pale lips. 'That's what I was thinking about,' he said softly.

'Don't be a God-damned sap,' Jeff blustered, taking a step forward. 'You—'

Ned Beaumont backed away, around one of the tables. 'I don't mind plugging you, Jeff,' he said. 'Remember I owe you some-thing.'

Jeff stood still and scratched the back of his head. 'What kind of a heel are you?' he asked perplexedly.

'Just a pal.' Ned Beaumont moved the pistol forward suddenly. 'Sit down.'

Jeff, after a moment's glowering hesitation, sat down.

Ned Beaumont put out his left hand and pressed the bell-button.

Jeff stood up.

Ned Beaumont said: 'Sit down.'

Jeff sat down.

Ned Beaumont said: 'Keep your hands on the table.'

Jeff shook his head lugubriously. 'What a half-smart bastard you turned out to be,' he said. 'You don't think they're going to let you drag me out of here, do you?'

Ned Beaumont went around the table again and sat on a chair facing Jeff and facing the door.

Jeff said: 'The best thing for you to do is give me that gun and hope I'll forget you made the break. Jesus, Ned, this is one of my hang-outs! You ain't got a chance in the world of pulling a fast one here.'

Ned Beaumont said: 'Keep your hand away from the catchup-bottle.'

The waiter opened the door, goggled at them.

'Tell Tim to come up,' Ned Beaumont said, and then, to the apish man when he would have spoken: 'Shut up.'

The waiter shut the door and hurried away.

Jeff said: 'Don't be a sap, Neddy. This can't get you anything but a rub-out. What good's it going to do you to try to turn me up? None.' He wet his lips with his tongue. 'I know you're kind of sore about the time we were rough with you, but – hell! – that wasn't my fault. I was just doing what Shad told me, and ain't I evened that up now by knocking him off for you?'

Ned Beaumont said: 'If you don't keep your hand away from that catchup-bottle I'm going to shoot a hole in it.'

Jeff said: 'You're a heel.'

The young-middle-aged man with plump lips and round eyes opened the door, came in quickly, and shut it behind him.

Ned Beaumont said: 'Jeff's killed O'Rory. Phone the police. You'll have time to clear the place before they get here. Better get a doctor, too, in case he's not dead.'

Jeff laughed scornfully. 'If he ain't dead I'm the Pope.' He stopped laughing and addressed the plump-mouthed man with careless familiarity: 'What do you think of this guy thinking you're going to let him get away with that? Tell him what a fat chance he has of getting away with it, Tim.'

Tim looked at the dead man on the sofa, at Jeff, and at Ned Beaumont. His round eyes were sober. He spoke to Ned Beaumont, slowly: 'This is a tough break for the house. Can't we drag him out in the street and let him be found there?'

Ned Beaumont shook his head. 'Get your place cleaned up before the coppers get here and you'll be all right. I'll do what I can for you.'

While Tim hesitated Jeff said: 'Listen, Tim, you know me. You know—'

Tim said without especial warmth: 'For Christ's sake pipe down.'

Ned Beaumont smiled. 'Nobody knows you, Jeff, now Shad's dead.'

'No?' The apish man sat back more comfortably in his chair and his face cleared. 'Well, turn me up. Now I know what kind of sons of bitches you are I'd rather take the fall than ask a God-damned thing of either of you.'

Tim, ignoring Jeff, asked: 'Have to play it that way?'

Ned Beaumont nodded.

'I guess I can stand it.' Tim said and put his hand on the door-knob.

'Mind seeing if Jeff's got a gun on him?' Ned Beaumont asked.

Tim shook his head. 'It happened here, but I've got nothing to do with it and I'm going to have nothing to do with it,' he said and went out.

Jeff, slouching back comfortably in his chair, his hands idle on the table before him, talked to Ned Beaumont until the police came. He talked cheerfully, calling Ned Beaumont numerous profane and obscene and merely insulting names, accusing him of a long and varied list of vices.

Ned Beaumont listened with polite interest.

A raw-boned white-haired man in a lieutenant's uniform was the first policeman to come in. Half a dozen police detectives were behind him.

Ned Beaumont said: ' 'Lo, Brett. I think he's got a gun on him.'

'What's it all about?' Brett asked, looking at the body on the sofa while two detectives, squeezing past him, took hold of Jeff Gardner.

Ned Beaumont told Brett what had happened. His story was truthful except in giving the impression that O'Rory had been killed in the heat of their struggle and not after he had been disarmed.

While Ned Beaumont was talking a doctor came in, turned Shad O'Rory's body over on the sofa, examined him briefly, and stood up. The Lieutenant looked at the doctor. The doctor said, 'Gone,' and went out of the small crowded room.

Jeff was jovially cursing the two detectives who held him. Every time he cursed, one of the detectives struck him in the face with his fist. Jeff laughed and kept on cursing them. His false teeth had been knocked out. His mouth bled.

Ned Beaumont gave the dead man's pistol to Brett and stood up. 'Want me to come along to headquarters now? Or will tomorrow do?'

'Better come along now,' Brett replied.

IV

It was long past midnight when Ned Beaumont left police headquarters. He said good-night to the two reporters who had come out with him and got into a taxicab. The address he gave the driver was Paul Madvig's.

Lights were on in the ground-floor of Madvig's house and as Ned Beaumont climbed the front steps the door was opened by Mrs Madvig. She was dressed in black and had a shawl over her shoulders.

He said: ''Lo, Mom. What are you doing up so late?'

She said, 'I thought it was Paul,' though she looked at him without disappointment.

'Isn't he home? I wanted to see him.' He looked sharply at her. 'What's the matter?'

The old woman stepped back, pulling the door back with her. 'Come in, Ned.'

He went in.

She shut the door and said: 'Opal tried to commit suicide.'

He lowered his eyes and mumbled: 'What? What do you mean?'

'She had cut one of her wrists before the nurse could stop her. She didn't lose much blood, though, and she's all right if she doesn't try it again.' There was as little of weakness in her voice as in her mien.

Ned Beaumont's voice was not steady. 'Where's Paul?'

'I don't know. We haven't been able to find him. He ought to be home before this. I don't know where he is.' She put a bony hand on Ned Beaumont's upper arm and now her voice shook a little. 'Are you – are you and Paul—?' She stopped, squeezing his arm.

He shook his head. 'That's done for good.'

'Oh, Ned, boy, isn't there anything you can do to patch it up? You and he—' Again she broke off.

He raised his head and looked at her. His eyes were wet. He said gently: 'No, Mom, that's done for good. Did he tell you about it?'

'He only told me, when I said I'd phoned you about that man from the District Attorney's office being here, that I wasn't ever to do anything like that again, that you – that you were not friends now.'

Ned Beaumont cleared his throat. 'Listen, Mom, tell him I came to see him. Tell him I'm going home and will wait there for him, will be waiting all night.' He cleared his throat again and added lamely: 'Tell him that.'

Mrs Madvig put her bony hands on his shoulders. 'You're a good boy, Ned. I don't want you and Paul to quarrel. You're the best friend he ever had, no matter what's come between you. What is it? Is it that Janet—'

'Ask Paul,' he said in a low bitter voice. He moved his head impatiently. 'I'm going to run along, Mom, unless there's something I can do for you or Opal. Is there?'

'Not unless you'd go up to see her. She's not sleeping yet and maybe it would do some good to talk to her. She used to listen to you.'

He shook his head. 'No,' he said, 'she wouldn't want to see me' – he swallowed – 'either.'

10 The Shattered Key

I

Ned Beaumont went home. He drank coffee, smoked, read a newspaper, a magazine, and half a book. Now and then he stopped reading to walk, fidgeting, around his rooms. His door-bell did not ring. His telephone-bell did not ring.

At eight o'clock in the morning he bathed, shaved, and put on fresh clothes. Then he had breakfast sent in and ate it.

At nine o'clock he went to the telephone, called Janet Henry's number, asked for her, and said: 'Good morning . . . Yes, fine, thanks . . . Well, we're ready for the fireworks . . . Yes . . . If your father's there suppose we let him in on the whole thing first . . . Fine, but not a word till I get there . . . As soon as I can make it. I'm leaving now . . . Right. See you in minutes.'

He got up from the telephone staring into space, clapped his hands together noisily, and rubbed their palms together. His mouth was a sullen line under his mustache, his eyes hot brown points. He went to the closet and briskly put on his overcoat and hat. He left his room whistling *Little Lost Lady* between his teeth and took long steps through the streets.

'Miss Henry's expecting me,' he said to the maid who opened the Henrys' door.

She said, 'Yes, sir,' and guided him to a sunny bright-papered room where the Senator and his daughter were at breakfast.

Janet Henry jumped up immediately and came to him with both hands out, crying excitedly: 'Good morning!'

The Senator rose in more leisurely manner, looking with polite surprise at his daughter, then holding his hand out to Ned Beaumont, saying: 'Good morning, Mr Beaumont. I'm very glad to see you. Won't you—?'

'Thanks, no, I've had breakfast.'

Janet Henry was trembling. Excitement had drained her skin of color, had darkened her eyes, giving her the appearance of one drugged. 'We have something to tell you, Father,' she said in a strained uneven voice, 'something that—' She turned abruptly to Ned Beaumont. 'Tell him! Tell him!'

Ned Beaumont glanced obliquely at her, drawing his brows together, then looked directly at her father. The Senator had remained standing by his place at the table. Ned Beaumont said: 'What we've got is pretty strong evidence – including a confession – that Paul Madvig killed your son.'

The Senator's eyes became narrower and he put a hand flat on the table in front of him. 'What is this pretty strong evidence?' he asked.

'Well, sir, the chief thing is the confession, of course. He says your son ran out after him that night and tried to hit him with a rough brown walking-stick and that in taking the stick away from your son he accidentally struck him with it. He says he took the stick away and burned it, but your daughter' – he made a little bow at Janet Henry – 'says it's still here.'

'It is,' she said. 'It's the one Major Sawbridge brought you.'

The Senator's face was pale as marble and as firm. 'Proceed,' he said.

Ned Beaumont made a small gesture with one hand. 'Well, sir, that would blow up his story about its being an accident or self-defense – you son's not having the stick.' He moved his shoulders a little. 'I told Farr this yesterday. He's apparently afraid to take many chances – you know what he is – but I don't see how he can keep from picking Paul up today.'

Janet Henry frowned at Ned Beaumont, obviously perplexed by something, started to speak, but pressed her lips together instead.

Senator Henry touched his lips with the napkin he held in his left hand, dropped the napkin on the table, and asked: 'Is there – ah – any other evidence?'

Ned Beaumont's reply was another question carelessly uttered: 'Isn't that enough?'

'But there is still more, isn't there?' Janet demanded.

'Stuff to back this up,' Ned Beaumont said depreciatively. He addressed the Senator: 'I can give you more details, but you've got the main story now. That's enough, isn't it?'

'Quite enough,' the Senator said. He put a hand to his forehead. 'I cannot believe it, yet it is so. If you'll excuse me for a moment and' – to his daughter – 'you too, my dear, I should like to be alone, to think, to adjust myself to— No, no, stay here. I should like to go to my room.' He bowed gracefully. 'Please remain, Mr Beaumont. I shall not be long – merely a moment to – to adjust myself to the knowledge that this man with whom I've worked shoulder to shoulder is my son's murderer.'

He bowed again and went out, carrying himself rigidly erect.

Ned Beaumont put a hand on Janet Henry's wrist and asked in a low tense voice: 'Look here, is he likely to fly off the handle?'

She looked at him, startled.

'Is he likely to go dashing off hunting for Paul?' he explained. 'We don't want that. There's no telling what would happen.'

'I don't know,' she said.

He grimaced impatiently. 'We can't let him do it. Can't we go somewhere near the front door so we can stop him if he tries it?'

'Yes.' She was frightened.

She led him to the front of the house, into a small room that was dim behind heavily curtained windows. Its door was within a few feet of the street-door. They stood close together in the dim room, close to the door that stood some six inches ajar. Both of them were trembling. Janet Henry tried to whisper to Ned Beaumont, but he sh-h-hed her into silence.

They were not there long before soft footfalls sounded on the hall-carpet and Senator Henry, wearing hat and overcoat, hurried towards the street-door.

Ned Beaumont stepped out and said: 'Wait, Senator Henry.'

The Senator turned. His face was hard and cold, his eyes imperious. 'You will please excuse me,' he said. 'I must go out.'

'That's no good.' Ned Beaumont said. He went up close to the Senator. 'Just more trouble.'

Janet Henry went to her father's side. 'Don't go, Father,' she begged. 'Listen to Mr Beaumont.'

'I have listened to Mr Beaumont,' the Senator said. 'I'm perfectly willing to listen to him again if he has any more information to give me. Otherwise I must ask you to excuse me.' He smiled at Ned Beaumont. 'It is on what you told me that I'm acting now.'

Ned Beaumont regarded him with level eyes. 'I don't think you ought to go to see him,' he said.

The Senator looked haughtily at Ned Beaumont.

Janet said, 'But, Father,' before the look in his eyes stopped her.

Ned Beaumont cleared his throat. Spots of color were in his cheeks. He put his left hand out quickly and touched Senator Henry's right-hand overcoat-pocket.

Senator Henry stepped back indignantly.

Ned Beaumont nodded as if to himself. 'That's no good at all,' he said earnestly. He looked at Janet Henry. 'He's got a gun in his pocket.'

'Father!' she cried and put a hand to her mouth.

Ned Beaumont pursed his lips. 'Well,' he told the Senator,

'it's a cinch we can't let you go out of here with a gun in your pocket.'

Janet Henry said: 'Don't let him, Ned.'

The Senator's eyes burned scornfully at them. 'I think both of you have quite forgotten yourselves,' he said. 'Janet, you will please go to your room.'

She took two reluctant steps away, then halted and cried: 'I won't! I won't let you do it. Don't let him, Ned.'

Ned Beaumont moistened his lips. 'I won't,' he promised.

The Senator, staring coldly at him, put his right hand on the street-door's knob.

Ned Beaumont leaned forward and put a hand over the Senator's. 'Look here, sir,' he said respectfully, 'I can't let you do this. I'm not just interfering.' He took his hand off the Senator's, felt in the inside pocket of his coat, and brought out a torn, creased, and soiled piece of folded paper. 'Here's my appointment as special investigator for the District Attorney's office last month.' He held it out to the Senator. 'It's never been cancelled as far as I know, so' – he shrugged – 'I can't let you go off to shoot somebody.'

The Senator did not look at the paper. He said contemptuously: 'You are trying to save your murderous friend's life.'

'You know that isn't so.'

The Senator drew himself up. 'Enough of this,' he said and turned the door-knob.

Ned Beaumont said: 'Step on the sidewalk with that gun in your pocket and I'll arrest you.'

Janet Henry wailed: 'Oh, Father!'

The Senator and Ned Beaumont stood staring into each other's eyes, both breathing audibly.

The Senator was the first to speak. He addressed his daughter: 'Will you leave us for a few minutes, my dear? There are things I should like to say to Mr Beaumont.'

She looked questioningly at Ned Beaumont. He nodded. 'Yes,' she told her father, 'if you won't go out before I've seen you again.'

He smiled and said: 'You shall see me.'

The two men watched her walk away down the hall, turn to the left with a glance thrown back at them, and vanish through a doorway.

The Senator said ruefully: 'I'm afraid you've not had so good an influence on my daughter as you should. She isn't usually so – ah – headstrong.'

Ned Beaumont smiled apologetically, but did not speak.

The Senator asked: 'How long has this been going on?'

'You mean our digging into the murder? Only a day or two for me. Your daughter's been at it from the beginning. She's always thought Paul did it.'

'What?' The Senator's mouth remained open.

'She's always thought he did it. Didn't you know? She hates him like poison – always has.'

'Hates him?' the Senator gasped. 'My God, no!'

Ned Beaumont nodded and smiled curiously at the man against the door. 'Didn't you know that?'

The Senator blew his breath out sharply. 'Come in here,' he said and led the way into the dim room where Ned Beaumont and Janet Henry had hidden. The Senator switched on the lights while Ned Beaumont was shutting the door. Then they faced one another, both standing.

'I want to talk to you as man to man, Mr Beaumont,' the Senator began. 'We can forget your' – he smiled – 'official connections, can't we?'

Ned Beaumont nodded. 'Yes. Farr's probably forgotten them too.'

'Exactly. Now, Mr Beaumont, I am not a blood-thirsty man, but I'm damned if I can bear the thought of my son's murderer walking around free and unpunished when—'

'I told you they'll have to pick him up. They can't get out of it. The evidence is too strong and everybody knows it.'

The Senator smiled again, icily. 'You are surely not trying to tell me, as one practicing politician to another, that Paul Madvig is in any danger of being punished for anything he might do in this city?'

'I am. Paul's sunk. They're double-crossing him. The only thing that's holding them up is that they're used to jumping when he cracks the whip and they need a little time to gather courage.'

Senator Henry smiled and shook his head. 'You'll allow me to disagree with you? And to point out the fact that I've been in politics more years than you've lived?'

'Sure.'

'Then I can assure you that they never will get the necessary amount of courage, no matter how much time they're given. Paul is their boss and, despite possible temporary rebellions, he will remain their boss.'

'It doesn't look like we'll agree on that,' Ned Beaumont said. 'Paul's sunk.' He frowned. 'Now about this gun business. That's no good. You'd better give it to me.' He held out his hand.

The Senator put his right hand in his overcoat-pocket.

Ned Beaumont stepped close to the Senator and put his left hand on the Senator's wrist. 'Give me it.'

The Senator glared angrily at him.

'All right,' Ned Beaumont said, 'if I've got to do that,' and, after a brief struggle in which a chair was upset, took the weapon – an old-fashioned nickeled revolver – away from the Senator. He was just thrusting the revolver into one of his hip-pockets when Janet Henry, wild of eye, white of face, came in.

'What is it?' she cried.

'He won't listen to reason,' Ned Beaumont grumbled. 'I had to take the gun away from him.'

The Senator's face was twitching and he panted hoarsely. He took a step towards Ned Beaumont. 'Get out of my house,' he ordered.

'I won't,' Ned Beaumont said. The ends of his lips jerked. Anger began to burn in his eyes. He put a hand out and touched Janet Henry's arm roughly. 'Sit down and listen to this. You asked for it and you're going to get it.' He spoke to the Senator: 'I've got a lot to say, so maybe you'd better sit down too.'

Neither Janet Henry nor her father sat down. She looked at Ned Beaumont with wide panic-stricken eyes, he with hard wary ones. Their faces were similarly white.

Ned Beaumont said to the Senator: 'You killed your son.'

Nothing changed in the Senator's face. He did not move.

For a long moment Janet Henry was still as her father. Then a look of utter horror came into her face and she sat down slowly on the floor. She did not fall. She slowly bent her knees and sank down on the floor in a sitting position, leaning to the right, her right hand on the floor for support, her horrified face turned up to her father and Ned Beaumont.

Neither of the men looked at her.

Ned Beaumont said to the Senator: 'You want to kill Paul now so he can't say you killed your son. You know you can kill him and get away with it – dashing gentleman of the old school stuff – if you can put over on the world the attitude you tried to put over on us.' He stopped.

The Senator said nothing.

Ned Beaumont went on: 'You know he's going to stop covering you up if he's arrested, because he's not going to have Janet thinking he killed her brother if he can help it.' He laughed bitterly. 'And what a swell joke on him that is!' He ran fingers through his hair. 'What happened is something like this: when Taylor heard about Paul kissing Janet he ran after him, taking the stick with him and wearing a hat, though that's not as important. When you thought of what might happen to your chances of being re-elected—'

The Senator interrupted him in a hoarse angry tone: 'This is nonsense! I will not have my daughter subjected—'

Ned Beaumont laughed brutally. 'Sure it's nonsense,' he said. 'And your bringing the stick you killed him with back home, and wearing his hat because you'd run out bare-headed after him, is nonsense too, but it's nonsense that'll nail you to the cross.'

Senator Henry said in a low scornful voice: 'And what of Paul's confession?'

Ned Beaumont grinned. 'Plenty of it,' he said. 'I tell you what let's do. Janet, you phone him and ask him to come over right away. Then we'll tell him about your father starting after him with a gun and see what he says.'

Janet stirred, but did not rise from the floor. Her face was blank.

Her father said: 'This is ridiculous. We will do nothing of the sort.'

Ned Beaumont said peremptorily: 'Phone him, Janet.'

She got up on her feet, still blank of face, and paying no attention to the Senator's sharp 'Janet!' went to the door.

The Senator changed his tone then and said: 'Wait, dear,' to her and, 'I should like to speak to you alone again,' to Ned Beaumont.

'All right,' Ned Beaumont said, turning to the girl hesitating in the doorway.

Before he could speak to her she was saying stubbornly: 'I want to hear it. I've a right to hear it.'

He nodded, looked at her father again, and said: 'She has.'

'Janet, dear,' the Senator said, 'I'm trying to spare you. I—'

'I don't want to be spared,' she said in a small flat voice. 'I want to know.'

The Senator turned his palms out in a defeated gesture. 'Then I shall say nothing.'

Ned Beaumont said: 'Phone Paul, Janet.'

Before she could move the Senator spoke: 'No. This is more difficult than it should be made for me, but—' He took out a handkerchief and wiped his hands. 'I am going to tell you exactly what happened and then I am going to ask a favor of you, one I think you cannot refuse. However—' He broke off to look at his daughter. 'Come in, my dear, and close the door, if you must hear it.'

She shut the door and sat on a chair near it, leaning forward, her body stiff, her face tense.

The Senator put his hands behind him, the handkerchief still in them, and, looking without enmity at Ned Beaumont, said: 'I ran out after Taylor that night because I did not care to lose Paul's friendship through my son's hot-headedness. I caught up with them in China Street. Paul had taken the stick from him. They were, or at least Taylor was, quarreling hotly. I asked Paul to leave us, to leave me to deal with my son, and he did so, giving me the stick. Taylor spoke to me as no son should speak to a father and tried to thrust me out of his way so he could pursue Paul again. I don't know exactly how it happened – the blow – but it happened and he fell and struck his head on the kerb. Paul came back then – he hadn't gone far – and we found that Taylor had died instantly. Paul insisted that we leave him there and not admit our part in his death. He said no matter how unavoidable it was a nasty scandal could be made of it in the coming campaign and – well – I let him persuade me. It was he who picked up Taylor's hat and gave it to me to wear home – I had run out bareheaded. He assured me that the police investigation would be stopped if it threatened to come too near us. Later – last week, in fact – when I had become alarmed by the rumors that he had killed Taylor, I went to him and asked him if we hadn't better make a clean breast of it. He laughed at my fears and assured me he was quite able to take care of himself.' He brought his hands from behind him, wiped his face with the handkerchief, and said: 'That is what happened.'

His daughter cried out in a choking voice: 'You let him lie there, like that, in the street!'

He winced, but did not say anything.

Ned Beaumont, after a moment's frowning silence, said: 'A campaign-speech – some truth gaudied up.' He grimaced. 'You had a favor to ask.'

The Senator looked down at the floor, then up at Ned Beaumont again. 'But that is for your ear alone.'

Ned Beaumont said: 'No.'

'Forgive me, dear,' the Senator said to his daughter, then to

Ned Beaumont: 'I have told you the truth, but I realize fully the position I have put myself in. The favor I ask is the return of my revolver and five minutes – a minute – alone in this room.'

Ned Beaumont said: 'No.'

The Senator swayed with a hand to his breast, the handkerchief hanging down from his hand.

Ned Beaumont said: 'You'll take what's coming to you.'

II

Ned Beaumont went to the street-door with Farr, his grey-haired stenographer, two police-detectives, and the Senator.

'Not going along?' Farr asked.

'No, but I'll be seeing you.'

Farr pumped his hand up and down with enthusiasm. 'Make it sooner and oftener, Ned,' he said. 'You play tricks on me, but I don't hold that against you when I see what comes of them.'

Ned Beaumont grinned at him, exchanged nods with the detectives, bowed to the stenographer, and shut the door. He walked upstairs to the white-walled room where the piano was. Janet Henry rose from the lyre-end sofa when he came in.

'They've gone,' he said in a consciously matter-of-fact voice.

'Did – did they—?'

'They got a pretty complete statement out of him – more details than he told us.'

'Will you tell me the truth about it?'

'Yes,' he promised.

'What—' She broke off. 'What will they do to him, Ned?'

'Probably not a great deal. His age and prominence and so on will help him. The chances are they'll convict him of manslaughter and then set the sentence aside or suspend it.'

'Do you think it was an accident?'

Ned Beaumont shook his head. His eyes were cold. He said

bluntly: 'I think he got mad at the thought of his son interfering with his chances of being re-elected and hit him.'

She did not protest. She was twining her fingers together. When she asked her next question it was with difficulty. 'Was – was he going to – to shoot Paul?'

'He was. He could get away with the grand-old-man-avenging-the-death-the-law-couldn't-avenge line. He knew Paul wasn't going to stay dummied up if he was arrested. Paul was doing it, just as he was supporting your father for re-election, because he wanted you. He couldn't get you by pretending he'd killed your brother. He didn't care what anybody else thought, but he didn't know you thought he had and he would have cleared himself in a second if he had.'

She nodded miserably. 'I hated him,' she said, 'and I wronged him and I still hate him.' She sobbed. 'Why is that, Ned?'

He made an impatient gesture with one hand. 'Don't ask me riddles.'

'And you,' she said, 'tricked me and made a fool of me and brought this on me and I don't hate you.'

'More riddles,' he said.

'How long, Ned,' she asked, 'how long have you known – known about Father?'

'I don't know. It's been in the back of my head for a long time. That was about the only thing that'd fit in with Paul's foolishness. If he'd killed Taylor he'd've let me know before this. There was no reason why he should hide that from me. There was a reason why he'd hide you father's crimes from me. He knew I didn't like you father. I'd made that plain enough. He didn't think he could trust me not to knife your father. He knew I wouldn't knife *him*. So, when I'd told him I was going to clear up the killing regardless of what he said, he gave me that phony confession to stop me.'

She asked: 'Why didn't you like Father?'

'Because,' he said hotly, 'I don't like pimps.'

Her face became red, her eyes abashed. She asked in a dry constricted voice: 'And you don't like me because—?'

He did not say anything.

She bit her lip and cried: 'Answer me!'

'You're all right,' he said, 'only you're not all right for Paul, not the way you've been playing him. Neither of you were anything but poison for him. I tried to tell him that. I tried to tell him you both considered him a lower form of animal life and fair game for any kind of treatment. I tried to tell him your father was a man all his life used to winning without much trouble and that in a hole he'd either lose his head or turn wolf. Well, he was in love with you, so——' He snapped his teeth together and walked over to the piano.

'You despise me,' she said in a low hard voice. 'You think I'm a whore.'

'I don't despise you,' he said irritably, not turning to face her. 'Whatever you've done you've paid for and been paid for and that goes for all of us.'

There was a silence between them then until she said: 'Now you and Paul will be friends again.'

He turned from the piano with a movement as if he were about to shake himself and looked at the watch on his wrist: 'I'll have to say good-by now.'

A startled light came into her eyes. 'You're not going away?'

He nodded. 'I can catch the four-thirty.'

'You're not going away for good?'

'If I can dodge being brought back for some of these trials and I don't think that'll be so hard.'

She held her hands out impulsively. 'Take me with you.'

He blinked at her. 'Do you really want to go or are you just being hysterical?' he asked. Her face was crimson by then. Before she could speak he said: 'It doesn't make any difference. I'll take you if you want to go.' He frowned. 'But all this' – he waved a hand to indicate the house – 'who'll take care of that?'

She said bitterly: 'I don't care – our creditors.'

'There's another thing you ought to think about,' he said slowly. 'Everybody's going to say you deserted your father as soon as he got in trouble.'

'I am deserting him,' she said, 'and I want people to say that. I don't care what they say – if you'll take me away.' She sobbed. 'If – I wouldn't if only he hadn't gone away and left him lying there alone in that dark street.'

Ned Beaumont said brusquely: 'Never mind that now. If you're going get packed. Only what you can get in a couple of bags. We can send for the other stuff later, maybe.'

She uttered a high-pitched unnatural laugh and ran out of the room. He lit a cigar, sat down at the piano, and played softly until she returned. She had put on a black hat and black coat and was carrying two traveling-bags.

III

They rode in a taxicab to his rooms. For most of the ride they were silent. Once she said suddenly: 'In that dream – I didn't tell you – the key was glass and shattered in our hands just as we got the door open, because the lock was stiff and we had to force it.'

He looked sidewise at her and asked: 'Well?'

She shivered. 'We couldn't lock the snakes in and they came out all over us and I woke up screaming.'

'That was only a dream,' he said. 'Forget it.' He smiled without merriment. 'You threw my trout back – in the dream.'

The taxicab stopped in front of his house. They went up to his rooms. She offered to help him pack, but he said: 'No, I can do it. Sit down and rest. We've got an hour before the train leaves.'

She sat in one of the red chairs. 'Where are you – we going?' she asked timidly.

'New York, first anyhow.'

He had one bag packed when the door-bell rang. 'You'd better go into the bedroom,' he told her and carried her bags in there. He shut the connecting door when he came out.

He went to the outer door and opened it.

Paul Madvig said: 'I came to tell you you were right and I know it now.'

'You didn't come last night.'

'No, I didn't know it then. I got home right after you left.'

Ned Beaumont nodded. 'Come in,' he said, stepping out of the doorway.

Madvig went into the living-room. He looked immediately at the bags, but let his glance roam around the room for a while before asking: 'Going away?'

'Yes.'

Madvig sat in the chair Janet Henry had occupied. His age showed in his face and he sat down wearily.

'How's Opal?' Ned Beaumont asked.

'She's all right, poor kid. She'll be all right now.'

'You did it to her.'

'I know, Ned. Jesus, I know it!' Madvig stretched his legs out and looked at his shoes. 'I hope you don't think I'm feeling proud of myself.' After a pause Madvig added: 'I think – I know Opal'd like to see you before you go.'

'You'll have to say good-by to her for me and to Mom too. I'm leaving on the four-thirty.'

Madvig raised blue eyes clouded by anguish. 'You're right, of course, Ned,' he said huskily, 'but – well – Christ knows you're right!' He looked down at his shoes again.

Ned Beaumont asked: 'What are you going to do with your not quite faithful henchmen? Kick them back in line? Or have they kicked themselves back?'

'Farr and the rest of those rats?'

'Uh-huh.'

'I'm going to teach them something.' Madvig spoke with determination, but there was no enthusiasm in his voice and he did not look up from his shoes. 'It'll cost me four years, but I can use those four years cleaning house and putting together an organization that will stay put.'

Ned Beaumont raised his eyebrows. 'Going to knife them at the polls?'

'Knife them, hell, dynamite them! Shad's dead. I'm going to let his crew run things for the next four years. There's none of them that can build anything solid enough for me to worry about. I'll get the city back next time and by then I'll have done my housecleaning.'

'You could win now,' Ned Beaumont said.

'Sure, but I don't want to win with those bastards.'

Ned Beaumont nodded. 'It takes patience and guts, but it's the best way to play it, I reckon.'

'They're all I've got,' Madvig said miserably. 'I'll never have any brains.' He shifted the focus of his eyes from his feet to the fireplace. 'Have you got to go, Ned?' he asked almost inaudibly.

'Got to.'

Madvig cleared his throat violently. 'I don't want to be a God-damned fool,' he said, 'but I'd like to think that whether you went or stayed you weren't holding against against me, Ned.'

'I'm not holding anything against you, Paul.'

Madvig raised his head quickly. 'Shake hands with me?'

'Certainly.'

Madvig jumped up. His hand caught Ned Beaumont's, crushed it. 'Don't go, Ned. Stick it out with me. Christ knows I need you now. Even if I didn't – I'll do my damndest to make up for all that.'

Ned Beaumont shook his head. 'You haven't got anything to make up for with me.'

'And you'll—?'

Ned Beaumont shook his head again. 'I can't. I've got to go.'

Madvig released the other's hand and sat down again, morosely, saying: 'Well, it serves me right.'

Ned Beaumont made an impatient gesture. 'That's got nothing to do with it.' He stopped and bit his lip. Then he said bluntly: 'Janet's here.'

Madvig stared at him.

Janet Henry opened the bedroom-door and came into the living-room. Her face was pale and drawn, but she held it high. She went straight up to Paul Madvig and said: 'I've done you a lot of harm, Paul. I've—'

His face had become pale as hers. Now blood rushed into it. 'Don't, Janet,' he said hoarsely. 'Nothing you could do.' The rest of his speech was unintelligibly mumbled.

She stepped back, flinching.

Ned Beaumont said: 'Janet is going away with me.'

Madvig's lips parted. He looked dumbly at Ned Beaumont and as he looked the blood went out of his face again. When his face was quite bloodless he mumbled something of which only the word 'luck' could be understood, turned clumsily around, went to the door, opened it, and went out, leaving it open behind him.

Janet Henry looked at Ned Beaumont. He stared fixedly at the door.